ALSO BY CATHRYN GRANT

THE FORMER OCCUPANT

A PSYCHOLOGICAL THRILLER

CATHRYN GRANT

ISBN: 978-1-943142-80-4

This book is a work of fiction. References to real people, events, establishments, organizations, or locales are intended only to provide a sense of authenticity, and are used fictitiously. All other characters, and incidents and dialogue, are drawn from the author's imagination and are not to be construed as real.

Visit Cathryn online at CathrynGrant.com

Cover design by Lydia Mullins Copyright © 2024

PROLOGUE

NOW: CHARLOTTE

hen Sara's house sold, I felt as if I'd finally buried my best friend. At the same time, I felt as if I were helping her live on, giving new life to the home she'd always seen as a creative extension of herself.

Until that moment, the responsibilities I had as both the executor of her trust and her real estate agent had weighed heavily on me.

Not that I viewed carrying out her wishes as a burden, I was honored. My heart had broken into a hundred pieces as I watched her body grow frail, then fade into a pale shadow—her dark hair losing its luster, her eyes growing dim, and her breath becoming weaker each time she spoke. Every facet of her but her spirit. That remained vibrant until it slipped out of her body, utterly intact.

She left behind that beautiful Craftsman house, built in 1923. Sara adored that house and she'd poured her life and her heart into refurbishing it. To me, it felt as if the powerful force who was Sara Janine Linden-Price lived on in the wood and plaster, the paint and varnish of that house. Her spirit was embodied in the very atmosphere of her charming home.

In recent years, I'd asked myself how a house could start out with such love and hope, shaped into something so beautiful and welcoming, turning, almost overnight, into a place filled with animosity, and finally death?

Selling it to that couple filled me with hope again.

David and Trinity.

All the sadness would be washed away by this couple.

They had recently become guardians of her sister's one-year-old son. Trinity had fallen in love with the house and had dreams of their newly formed family spending summers there. They would plant a vegetable garden and hang a swing from one of the three heritage oak trees on the half-acre property. She wanted to refill the pond with water and populate it with fluffy yellow ducklings. An arborist would be called in to look at the struggling peach tree.

This was a couple who knew what they wanted, two people who shared a singular vision, not the constantly shifting alliances and betrayals that Sara's life had turned into as the years passed. Trinity and David and their adopted son would make it into the beautiful, love-filled home that Sara had envisioned, but sadly, never turned into reality.

It was touching to watch how that man cared for his wife. When Trinity left to care for her sister, David had taken over. He made all the arrangements to complete the sale. It melted my heart to see how eager he was to supervise the inspections and ensure all the paperwork was completed without Trinity having to worry about anything.

I was a little concerned when I found out Trinity couldn't be there because her sister was dying of cancer. Just like Sara had. But David said Trinity didn't need to know about that. Not right away. She would find out eventually, of course, but not for a while, not until after she'd had some time to heal from the loss of her sister.

I agreed. She didn't need to know. I wouldn't say a word.

I disclosed everything I knew about the history of the house. The abandoned well on the property, the beam in the living room ceiling that needed replacing. The age of the gas cooktop and oven. I'm required by law to disclose every little thing, down to the smallest detail—including information about the neighbors, natural pests, wildlife, traffic, and plans for future road expansion. I even had to mention noise disturbances. There were none in this quiet, rural neighborhood thirty miles inland from the Central California Coast.

But you can't disclose what you don't know. I might have suspected, but I didn't *know*. I might have had a very strong suspicion. But because I didn't *know* for certain, I had plausible deniability. That's probably a legal term I shouldn't have been tossing around, even in my mind, but I thought it applied to me. It sounded comforting on my tongue when I whispered it to myself—plausible deniability.

1 NOW: TRINITY

*C*harlotte was waiting for me on the front porch of the house when I pulled into the driveway. The house was even more charming than I'd remembered. The certainty that it was meant to be ours overcame me with such force I had to rest my forehead on the steering wheel for a moment to catch my breath.

I hadn't seen it for five months. During those horrible five months, I'd barely had time to look at pictures to remind me of how I'd fallen in love at first sight. Over the course of those five months, my entire life had turned inside out. David was the only one who had kept my head above water. My rock.

Five months earlier, my sister had been a vibrant, laughing, thirty-year-old woman. Now, my little sister's ashes were scattered in the Pacific Ocean and I was about to become the caretaker of her one-year-old orphaned son. Her little boy—giving me hope that life did indeed go on, the promise that I would be able to find joy again, even without my sister in the world.

For now, Ryan was living in the only home he'd ever known, cared for by my brother and my pregnant sister-in-law. They would provide him with continuity in his familiar surroundings. Once I'd finished fixing up our new summer home, Ryan would come to live with David and me—a part of my sister whom I would love and nurture into adulthood.

I'd spent most of the horrible five months living with Jennifer. First, just being her friend—cooking for her and playing with Ryan. Reliving our childhood, talking about what was coming, although not too much of that. Then I'd stayed beside her as hospice took over, right up to the end.

It came so fast. Some people say that's a good thing, but I don't know. Is there anything good when a person you love, a person who has been at the center of your heart, is ripped out of your life?

I was learning to live with the constant, pressing ache. Thinking about Ryan and preparing for his future helped. A little. And now, this house. Even though David had seemed a little ambivalent about it, he'd done everything necessary to make sure it became ours.

It was a charming house that had been around for a century, sitting on half an acre. David would have preferred something more modern. But he conceded that having a large piece of property was nice. And he thought there was potential for modernizing the interior. I didn't want to do that, but I hadn't made too big a point of it. Once he got used to the house, spent some time there, and saw my ideas for painting and refinishing, he would realize that it just needed a gentle makeover, not violent plastic surgery.

He'd been incredibly sweet about it, though. While I was with my sister, he'd done everything to take care of the purchase—going over all the details of the inspections, the disclosures, and working on the loan. We didn't really need a loan, we could have paid cash, but David thought a loan was better for tax purposes, and because of my sister, I was in no state to debate the issue.

I was beyond lucky that we could afford such a thing. I'd been beyond lucky—working as an executive assistant at a startup company that was acquired for its cutting edge technology, leaving me with more money than I could spend in a lifetime. And David had a good career as a sales training manager for a tech company.

We were so fortunate. Not a day went by that I didn't feel immense gratitude for that.

My dream was that we would spend every summer in our 1920s bungalow. It was a decent-sized, two-story house, a little large to be called a bungalow, but that's how the real estate flyer had described it.

Our soon-to-be adopted son, and his future sibling, or siblings, hopefully, would have the excitement and advantages of growing up in the heart of Silicon Valley, surrounded by the futuristic experience of the tech industry. At the same time, they would enjoy other facets of life—appreciating gardening and climbing trees, spreading their wings as they ran in uncrowded open spaces. They would play board games as well as video games and relish outdoor life before being introduced to virtual reality.

I walked toward the front porch as Charlotte descended the steps. She wore a pale pink dress and flat black shoes. Her short, dark hair was a mass of wild curls. Her smile was warm and sympathetic. She held a key on a thick gold chain with a gold disk hanging from it.

"Trinity! It's so good to see you after all this time." She gave me a gentle hug. "I'm so sorry for your loss."

"Thank you." For the first time, I didn't feel the tears that constantly pricked at my eyes—when I expected them, and when I didn't. They ambushed me at the strangest times, like when I was choosing apples in the grocery store. Maybe they didn't come now because Charlotte was a stranger and I sensed her desire to be finished with her obligatory condolences so she could move on to business.

"You must be so excited," she said.

"I am. I can't wait to see it again." It was the truth. The ache of losing my sister was going to be a permanent part of me. I knew that now. But I was also ready to look toward the future. Ready for something to fill my mind and put a new shape to my life. Something I could talk to Jennifer about in my thoughts.

It might seem foolish that I talked to Jennifer inside my head, but I'd always been a person who believed, or wanted to believe, there's more to our existence than what we experience with our five senses. I did believe there were things we couldn't see or hear or touch. I did not believe in angels or ghosts. I didn't believe in anything supernatural. Not telekinesis or mind reading or fortunetelling. But I think everyone, on some level, knows there's something more. Otherwise, where does love exist?

Jennifer had been so excited about the house. She made me promise to enjoy every minute of fixing it up—for her. For her little boy.

Don't sit around being sad. Please, she'd said. *Don't let your life end too.*

2 NOW: TRINITY

Charlotte inserted the key into the lock and opened the door.

As I followed her around the house, I realized I hadn't forgotten a single thing about it, even though I thought it had faded to an indistinct shadow at the back of my mind. In fact, it was more charming than I remembered—filled with light, quiet and peaceful, waiting for David and me to make it our own.

"How does it feel, now that it's yours?" Charlotte asked.

"Absolutely perfect."

"David said you'll be doing some remodeling."

I nodded. "But nothing drastic, just some touch-ups. We'll probably modernize the kitchen."

Charlotte nodded. "Your husband has been so attentive. Keeping all the appointments for inspections. He even stopped by a few times on his own to check that everything was in order."

I smiled. Maybe David liked the house more than he'd let on.

I touched the painted mural of a group of musicians in a wine bar that covered two of the dining room walls. "I'm sure this meant something, but it's not ..." I paused. "I just realized I know nothing about the previous owner."

Charlotte laughed softly. "That's not important now, is it?" She gave me a gentle smile. "You're the owner."

"Sara … what's her last name?"

"Linden-Price."

"And she—"

Charlotte laughed, her voice unnaturally loud this time. "It's your house, now. You should be thinking about your plans."

"It's good to know its history though, especially with a house this old. The lives of the previous owners still exist within these walls, don't you think? Not just the mural."

Charlotte took a step away from me. "I don't really look at things that way. I'm a very pragmatic person."

I nodded. "So am I. All I mean is that the organic materials of a building absorb the sounds and odors and the skin cells of the people who existed inside that space."

She shrugged, turning her gaze away from mine.

"Why did she sell it?"

"She … well. I mean …"

"It was just her, right? She wasn't married? Kids?"

"She had a partner."

"Had?"

"I mean she … uh … she h—"

"Why did you say *had*? Is she … did she pass away?"

Charlotte gave a stiff nod. "I'm sorry I—"

"Why is that a secret?" I felt cold despite the warm summer day. "Why didn't you just tell me? Was she murdered or something?"

"Oh, no. Nothing like …" She shook her head. "No."

"Then, why?" I felt my stomach tighten. "Did she … oh. Did she die from cancer?"

Charlotte looked like she wanted to cry. "I didn't … I wasn't …"

I felt myself breathing too fast. I tried to take a deeper breath to calm myself, but I couldn't seem to manage. I closed my eyes for a moment, placing my hand on the wall, feeling the glossy finish to the mural. "Does David know?" I opened my eyes, my mind racing.

Would I still have wanted the house? *Did* I still want the house? It meant nothing. Lots of people had cancer. Lots of people died from cancer. It had nothing to do with Jennifer. It had nothing to do with me.

Charlotte folded her hands into a hard knot, holding them in front of her. "Please don't tell David. I told him I wouldn't say anything. He was so worried about you. He didn't want you to be upset. Please, please don't tell him. It's a beautiful home. And her life ended … peacefully. She was ready. She … please don't tell him. He loves you so much and he really wanted you to be happy in this house."

A chill ran through me that was so deep, I wondered if I would ever be able to feel warm and peaceful in this house—the house I'd loved and wanted with all my heart.

I knew David didn't want to upset me. But why did I feel as if I'd been lied to?

3 NOW: TRINITY

*K*nowing that Sara Linden-Price had not only died, but taken her last, soft breath in the sunroom at the back of our new home, made me wonder if that was why David had wanted to do a complete remodel, down to the bones of the house. According to Charlotte, he was simply trying to protect my feelings by keeping the truth from me.

I believed houses kept the essence, the energy, for lack of a better word, of those who had lived there before. How could they not? Paint and wood, plaster and tile are porous materials. They certainly absorb oils and smells from human beings and animals. Who was to say there wasn't a little more to it than that? My thoughts on this, on the dividing line between life and death, had become more fluid since my sister had died. It might have been wishful thinking, it might have been the denial phase of the grief process. But maybe it was true.

The same day I received the key from Charlotte, a truck arrived with some second-hand furniture I'd purchased so the house would be livable while I spent the first part of the summer stripping wallpaper, scraping and painting, and refinishing the rich oak doorframes and beams. I also wanted to put a door between the dining room and the sunroom.

While I pushed my confused questions out of my head, I directed the movers where to place the bed, chest of drawers, the couch and easy chair, and the small kitchen table and chairs. I'd also bought a second double bed and another small chest of drawers in case my lifelong best friend came to stay at some point. She'd been pestering me to see the house, and had offered to come for a week or so to help with my do-it-yourself projects.

After the delivery guys were gone, I unloaded sheets and towels and other supplies from the back of my car. I'd already stocked the kitchen with the groceries I'd bought to last for a few days until I had time to explore the town and figure out where I wanted to shop.

Because all the lots on our street were so large, our neighbors were far enough away that it felt awkward to trek all the way over to ring someone's bell and introduce myself. Especially since I wasn't new in a permanent way. Charlotte had mentioned that not everyone in the neighborhood was thrilled that the house would only be occupied for a few months of the year. Most of the people who lived in the area had been there for decades. They didn't like it that *people with money* were using their quiet neighborhood as a vacation spot.

I didn't think of David and myself as *people with money*. We didn't have a lavish lifestyle, and in fact, although David often wanted to splurge more with nicer cars and vacations, I enjoyed living as I always had. This house was the first thing I'd done, that *we'd* done, which didn't echo the middle class world I'd grown up in.

Despite hanging the towels, pushing open all the windows to let in the warm breeze, and putting sheets on the beds, I still felt cold. I stood in the master bedroom on the second floor and looked out the window toward the back of the property. I couldn't wait to get the trees pruned, the pond filled with water, to repair broken boards in the fence, and start breaking ground for the massive vegetable garden I envisioned. I took a deep breath and let the soft June air fill my lungs. As I let out the air, I heard a crash from somewhere on the ground floor.

I turned quickly and hurried down the stairs. I gripped the railing, which wobbled slightly. Another thing that needed fixing. I realized I should have read the inspection report myself, or at least had David go through it with me over the phone, so I had an idea what I was walking into. When he came for the weekend, he needed to bring it with him.

I stopped at the bottom of the stairs and sent him a text. He didn't respond, but that wasn't unusual. He didn't get a lot of time for personal texts or phone calls when he was traveling.

I hadn't decided whether I would honor Charlotte's request not to tell him she'd slipped and told me about Sara's death from cancer. I would think about that later. Hopefully, he and I would have a chance to catch up tomorrow morning. He was in London, where it was now long after midnight.

Now that I was downstairs, I had no idea from which part of the house the crash had come. Everything in the foyer and the guest room and future playroom at the front of the house looked intact, as did the living room. I walked through the kitchen and peeked into the dining room. None of the open windows had fallen shut.

I checked the pantry, then opened the door to the basement. I flicked on the light and descended the stairs halfway. It was unlikely anything would have made a crashing noise down here. The insulation of the surrounding earth made it feel more like a room sound-proofed for a recording studio, although the odor was the furthest thing imaginable from that. It smelled like slightly damp concrete, which I hoped didn't mean there was water damage to be concerned about.

I returned to the kitchen, turned off the light, and closed the door.

I went back through the living room and opened the door to the sunroom. I saw immediately what had caused the crash. The screen door had fallen onto the back steps. It looked as if the hinges had corroded and the door had chosen that moment to break free.

I returned to the living room, sat on the couch, and called Charlotte.

When she'd handed over the key, she'd acted as if she was relieved to be finished with the house, but it had only been one day. I was here alone, and it was only right that she should at least point me to a handyman who could help me with the door. It would probably be a good idea to have someone like that in my contact list anyway. This was unlikely to be my first repair until David could join me. Even then, David wasn't the kind of man who relished home repairs.

Charlotte sounded slightly pained when she spoke. "What can I do for you, Trinity?"

I told her about the screen door.

"It's an old house. I'm sure by now you've read the inspection reports and the disclosures."

"I haven't had a chance. David—"

"But you're aware the house needs some work."

"Of course. I'm not calling to complain. I wanted to know if you can recommend a handyman."

"Oh. Yes, absolutely." She paused. "The best person, to be honest, is Brian … Price."

"Great, thanks. I'm sure the door won't be the last thing." I laughed. "What's his number?"

"I should explain …"

"Explain what? Wait … Price?"

"He knows the house. All its idiosyncrasies."

"Is he …?"

"Yes. He's Sara's ex-husband."

An uncomfortable sensation, like a soap bubble forming inside my throat, kept me from speaking for a moment. It felt like stepping over a boundary, in several ways. Why would her ex-husband have any interest in—

She cut off my thoughts. "He's a really good guy. And he'll be glad to look at it without charge. He's the one who helped her restore it."

"But ..." I wasn't even sure what my objection was. It just seemed ... strange.

"Trust me. He's the nicest guy you'll ever meet. And he'll be happy to take a look. He's probably the one who installed the door."

"It's corroded. It really has nothing to do with how it was installed."

"Workers around here are booked out for months."

I wasn't surprised. Workers everywhere were booked out for months.

"If you want someone who can take a look right away, someone you can trust, Brian is your man. I'll text you his number. I need to run. Have a terrific day."

With that, she ended the call. A moment later, her text appeared.

I stared at my phone. Inviting the ex-husband of the former owner didn't seem like the best idea. At the same time, I couldn't come up with a specific reason why it was an idea to be avoided at all costs.

4 NOW: TRINITY

To his credit, Brian not only agreed to come by right after work that day, he showed up when he'd said he would. The doorbell rang at five forty-five.

I opened the door to a guy who looked nothing like a handyman. I wondered if he even knew that Charlotte had characterized him as one. If I were to label him, I would have said accountant. But a very cute accountant. He wore stylish glasses with thin black frames that were stark against his light brown hair and brought out his blue eyes. He was slender and only a few inches taller than me, which wasn't an uncommon experience for me, at five-eight.

"Trinity?"

"Yes."

"Brian Price. Charlotte said you need some help with the screen door out back."

Even in a smallish town, I appreciated he identified himself and gave me details. It made me feel comfortable opening the door wider. It's never good when you're the first to blurt out too much identifying information, then realize you've told the other person all they need to know to con their way into your house and your life. Not that I'm so cynical that being conned is always at the top of my mind, but the awareness has to be there. It's the world we live in, unfortunately.

I didn't need to show him the way through to the sunroom, which was a little disconcerting. It shouldn't have been, but knowing the house used to belong to him, and experiencing a man walking through your home as if he's more familiar with the layout than you are, is definitely disconcerting.

"So you're the lucky new owner," Brian said.

"Yes, my husband and I."

"Not a handy guy?"

He said it matter of factly, so I shouldn't have taken it as a dig, but I felt the irrational need to defend David. "He's traveling for work."

He nodded.

"He'll be here this weekend." It was unnecessary information, and David had made no promises about when he would actually be coming to the house. But again, for some reason, I felt the need to polish his image in this stranger's eyes. I was annoyed with myself. What did I care what the ex-husband of the former owner of our new home thought about David's schedule?

I walked quickly across the sunroom and opened the door. "There it is." I ran my fingers over the corroded hinges. "Now that you're here, I feel like I'm wasting your time. It obviously needs replacing, so looking won't accomplish anything."

"It's still good to see what we're dealing with."

He gave me a warm smile as he moved around me to get a closer look at the hinges. "Strange that they deteriorated like this. I've never seen it before."

"It made quite a crash when it fell."

He nodded. "These steel-framed screens are heavy. I can replace the hinges for you."

"How much will that cost?"

"Nothing. They're just hinges."

"I have to pay for your time."

"I'm happy to do it. For Sara."

"For ..." I took a quick, sharp breath. "Oh." He spoke about her as if she were still alive. I had the urge to turn and look into the room behind me, as if I might see her standing there, listening as we discussed the repair of her door, as if she might have an opinion about whether he could be trusted to hang it correctly.

"I didn't mean to scare you." He laughed. "I haven't lost my mind. I know she's gone." He bent over and lifted the door off the steps. He hoisted it up and carried it across the yard. He leaned it against the side of the detached garage beside the garbage and recycling bins. He returned to the back steps and came into the sunroom. We walked through to the front of the house, stopping in the foyer.

"I really want to pay you for your time," I said.

"It's not necessary. I'm happy to do it."

"But—"

"I love this house. It feels great to be inside, and I'm looking forward to seeing what you do with the place."

My chest tightened. Why did he think he would see what we did with the place? Did he assume we would have a housewarming party to show off our touch-ups? Was he expecting we would become friends?

This led me to wondering all sorts of things—How long he and Sara had been married, how many years they'd been divorced, who had ended the marriage, and whether he was grieving. Maybe it was a mistake to let him fix the door. Especially for free. It was starting to feel complicated.

Brian studied my face, waiting for me to say something. Waiting for a thank you, I suppose. Waiting for me to ask when he would return to hang the door, maybe. Or perhaps he was asking himself questions about me—Why was I moving in and starting a remodeling project alone?

"I really appreciate it," I said.

"I can be back with the new hinges tomorrow. What time would be good for you?"

"You're doing me the favor. Whatever fits your schedule."

"Probably early afternoon. I'll text you when I'm on my way."

I moved toward the door, and he followed my lead. "Thanks again."

"No problem," he said. "Good to meet you." He crossed the threshold, then paused. "I loved Sara, and we became close friends in the end. It feels good to be back in the house. A real gift." He gave me a smile that looked like he wanted to rush back and hug me. "Thanks for that." He turned and walked down the steps.

I closed the door and leaned against it. Letting him fix the door seemed like an enormous commitment. It shouldn't have been that way.

5 NOW: TRINITY

For dinner, I broiled a chicken breast and made a salad with sliced avocado and the sweetest grape tomatoes I'd tasted in ages. Lighting the ancient gas stove was tricky, making me realize that even if we didn't do a complete kitchen remodel, we definitely needed to replace the stove. It gave the kitchen character and was a nice contrast to the sleek stainless steel refrigerator and sink, but we needed something safer with a child in the house.

I poured myself a small glass of white wine, but it was lonely sitting at the table for four, eating with no one to talk to. I distracted myself by reading a blog about local history.

After dinner, I walked through the house and made a prioritized list of projects.

I went to bed early, partially due to feeling overwhelmed by all the work facing me. I was excited to get started, but I'd also imagined David and I working on this together, and now, it was just me.

After dozing off three times in front of a movie on my tablet, I gave up and put it away. I snuggled down and was instantly wide awake. I lay there thinking about Brian and how he'd acted as if he missed living in my house. I was glad the screen door repair meant he would be working outside instead of wandering through the rooms, walking down memory lane.

Finally, I drifted into unconsciousness.

I woke suddenly in the dark, unsure what had brought me out of sleep. For a moment, I was disoriented, thinking first that I was back at my sister's home in Southern California. As my head cleared, I wondered if there'd been another loud noise, similar to when the door had crashed onto the back steps.

Sitting up, I reached for my phone. I'd left it on the floor to charge since there was no nightstand. Two-twenty. I pushed the comforter off and got up, made my way to the door, and turned on the overhead light. I was a sound sleeper. I never woke in the middle of the night unless there was heavy rain or an emergency vehicle went down our street.

I stepped into the hallway, listening. I shivered for no reason. Was someone in the house? Did I have a sixth sense telling me something wasn't right? Or was this simply nerves from sleeping alone in an unfamiliar place?

As I stood there, I became aware of a sound coming from downstairs. I couldn't make out what it was. A soft hissing … maybe. But that made no sense.

For half a second, I felt like crying. This was also an unusual experience. I wasn't someone who cried easily, and I didn't enjoy feeling unstable and slightly scared for no real reason. I gripped my phone more tightly and went to the stairs. I whispered to Jen that I was being ridiculous. I imagined her nodding in agreement.

I walked down slowly, wishing I had a weapon in my other hand, annoyed with myself for even thinking in those terms. Before I'd gone to bed, I'd checked that all the doors and windows were locked. This was a quiet community and although the property was good sized, there were neighbors all around. There was no reason to give in to paranoia.

Pushing the fear out of my body, I descended quickly. The hissing sound was immediately louder. I turned the corner into the laundry room and switched on the light. The hose for the washing machine had come loose from the faucet. Water was spraying out. The tops of both machines were wet and there was a sheen of water on the opposite wall, drips running down to the floor where a puddle had formed.

I stepped out of the room and placed my phone on the bottom step. Putting up my arm to shield my face from the spray, I moved toward the washing machine, reached across it, and turned off the faucet. The hissing stopped, and all I heard was the drip of water as it ran down the wall and splashed into the puddle. I didn't have extra towels, and I'd only brought one roll of paper towels.

For a moment, I thought about going out to the garage to look for rags, but when I'd walked through with Charlotte, my impression of the garage was that it had been stripped clean.

I went to the kitchen and used one of my two dish towels to dry my feet, then walked back down the hallway, wiping up my wet footprints. I used the entire roll of paper towels to dry the wall and mop up what I could on the floor.

I went upstairs, dried my face and hands, and climbed into bed.

Staring at my phone, I longed to call David. It was mid-morning in London, so he was probably in meetings. I could text Mia. She probably wouldn't mind. She would say that's what best friends were for.

Even though my logical mind was telling me it was perfectly natural for a hose to come loose at any time, it didn't feel natural. It felt ... I didn't know what it felt ... unsettling.

I couldn't shake the feeling that someone had been inside the house, but it wasn't possible. Everything was locked. There was no way. But why would the hose suddenly slip loose in the middle of the night when no one had touched the washer, no water had passed through that hose in months?

Had the hissing caused me to wake, or something louder? I wasn't even sure I'd heard it until I'd started down the stairs. Now, I couldn't quite remember. Another feeling came over me, the sense of being woken suddenly by a sharper sound, like that of the screen door, not by the slow, steady hiss of leaking water.

Placing my phone beside me on the bed, I laid down and closed my eyes. I couldn't wake Mia at this hour. It wasn't as if I were under threat. I laughed at the thought. What would I tell her? The washing machine hose came loose, and I thought someone was in my house? I could hear her laughing. At the same time, Mia might also make it worse. She was obsessed with her Tarot cards, and I could imagine her seeing some kind of message in this. She might want to do one of her readings over the phone, stirring up my discomfort over the parallel between losing my sister and buying the home of a woman who had lost her life in the same way.

I turned onto my side. I didn't want to think about it. This was why David hadn't wanted me to know about the previous owner.

After a while, I fell into an uncomfortable sleep.

The first thing I did when I woke was text Mia. She called me immediately. I told her about the screen door and Brian, but not about how he'd made me feel. I told her about waking to the broken hose.

She offered to come stay with me. I didn't even have to ask.

6 THEN: CHARLOTTE

*J*n the early days, listening to Sara go on about restoring their 1920s house had driven me insane. You'd think she and Brian were the first people ever to be in love, ever to paint a bedroom wall, ever to find hardwood floors under a layer of tired carpet.

In the beginning, she'd texted me five to ten pictures a day, sent me fifteen questions a week. *You're the expert*, she'd said. As if selling homes had given me some kind of inside knowledge on period houses and interior design. She never seemed to realize that I loved real estate for the thrill of reading people and figuring out what they wanted in a home, then locating the perfect match for them. I loved real estate for the thrill of getting the best deal for my clients, whether they were the buyers or the sellers. I wasn't a historian, and I certainly wasn't a decorator.

But Sara was my best friend, so I tried to offer comments that weren't actual opinions.

More challenging than offering vague advice on everything from light fixtures to flooring, were the other things she asked. Those questions had come later.

When the remodeling project started, she and Brian were so

madly in love, she'd giggled about having sex on the dining room floor in the midst of scraping paint off the window frame. By the time they were twenty-seven months into their project, the finish line finally in sight, the cracks they'd plastered over in the walls of the living room, had run through the house and started to appear as tiny fractures in their marriage.

I don't think she was even aware at that point.

"Men are such clichés," she said.

"What do you mean?" I picked up my chai and took a sip, plucking a cashew out of the bag of nuts I'd bought to share while we drank our tea and talked. We were sitting at an outdoor table. She was shaded by the red canvas umbrella. I was not, but I was enjoying the warmth of the sun on my face.

"They never want to talk about their feelings. You'd think I was trying to get Brian to commit treason, just because I asked him what the house meant to him." She laughed, but it sounded bitter.

"I don't think you can generalize that all men are like that."

"They are. That's why it's a cliché."

"Is it?" I sipped my tea. "Maybe the house doesn't mean as much to him as it does to you. Which is fine. Besides, he's the strong, silent type. Haven't you always loved that about him? He's a good listener."

"Is he?"

"That's what you've always said."

She frowned and looked away from me. She hunched her shoulders slightly.

I'd seen that posture plenty of times before. She thought I didn't get it. "I don't think you realize how painful that is. Wanting the man you love to talk to you, but he refuses, despite repeated requests."

I nodded.

"How can I get him to talk more?"

I shook several cashews out of the bag and put them all in my mouth at once. I suddenly longed for her to ask me about light fixtures or pull some paint chips out of her purse. I had no idea how to get her husband to talk to her. "Ask him questions?"

"I did! I asked what the house means to him."

"Less threatening questions?"

"How is that threatening?"

"Lead up to it more? I don't know."

"I feel like I'm interrogating him!"

"Not if you use the right tone."

"Why are you criticizing me?" Her eyes filled with tears. "I just want him to … I want to feel close to him and I …" She put her hands over her face.

I wanted to comfort her, but she was upset because Brian was simply being himself. He'd always been quiet, and she *had* loved that about him. I didn't know what to say, and I'd ended up saying the wrong thing. "Maybe you're too absorbed by the remodeling. Is it possible he feels like he's been shoved aside?"

She glared at me. She picked up her cup and took a long, rather loud, slurpy sip. "It's not just *my* project. It belongs to both of us. It's our dream home."

I had a feeling the dream was dying, if it wasn't already dead.

7 NOW: TRINITY

*D*avid responded to my text, telling me he couldn't talk—meetings all day—as expected. He said it was good I'd found a handyman who should also be able to fix the washing machine hose. He told me not to let my imagination get *carried away* with the feeling someone had been inside the house. I wished he'd been able to talk. It's hard to explain things in a text.

Mia arrived just before dinner. She was carrying a bouquet of white roses that she handed to me as she kissed my cheek. "For Jen," she whispered.

After I put the roses in a vase she'd brought with her, since she'd guessed I didn't have one at the house yet, she handed me a tiny box wrapped in pink paper with a white bow.

"What's this for?"

"Because."

Inside was a silver, oval-shaped locket that hung from a series of twisted chains.

"I love it." I clipped it around my neck.

"Open it." Instead of waiting for me, she poked her nail into the slot and popped it open. One side held a photo of me, the other a photo of Jen.

Tears filled my eyes, trickling out of the corners. "Oh, Mia. I ..."

"Don't say anything." She hugged me tightly.

Once I was calm, the first thing she wanted to do was to inspect the loose hose. She didn't want a tour, didn't want to admire the oak doorframes, marvel over the size of the lot, or hear about my plans. She wanted me to describe how much water there had been before I'd mopped it up so she could estimate how long it had been spraying into the room.

She leaned over the washing machine, peering into the space behind it. Her long, razor straight blonde hair fell over the machine, but it didn't seem to bother her, even though she normally recoiled from anything that might impact the perfection of her hair, makeup, or clothes.

"These hoses don't look like they've deteriorated," she said.

"Are you a plumbing expert?"

She laughed and straightened, tucking her hair behind her ears, then pulling it around the side of her head so it hung over one shoulder. She ran her fingers through to smooth it. "I just wonder why it came apart."

"I have no idea, but it scared me." I laughed. "It shouldn't have. I feel silly about it now."

She patted my arm. "It's okay. It's scary to sleep alone in an old house in a town where you don't know anyone."

"It's not that."

She cocked her head, looking at me with a doubtful expression.

"Let me give you a tour," I said.

"I should get my stuff out of the car."

"A tour first."

She followed me with a mild lack of enthusiasm. When I'd talked to her on the phone, she'd sounded excited to finally *meet my house in person*, as she'd put it. Now, she seemed overly familiar, as if she'd seen it all in the photographs I'd sent, and there was nothing new. "It needs a lot of work," she said. Not once, but at least three times.

"Mostly cosmetic."

"Not if doors are falling off. I wonder what there is that you can't see."

"Structurally, it's sound," I said.

"How do you know?"

"There were inspections. David was here for all that."

She nodded.

I led her up the stairs. She peeked into each of the rooms but didn't go inside. "I didn't mean to sound negative." She paused outside the master bedroom and gave me a hug. She moved my hair away from the side of my face. "It's adorable. I can hear Ryan's little footsteps running up and down the stairs already." She let go of me and grinned.

"I'm excited to get started."

"It's a lot to take on all by yourself in a short time. How many weeks do you have?"

"Six."

She looked skeptical.

"You know I love doing things with my hands. It's very satisfying."

"But you've never done anything on this scale. This is a lot more than painting a bedroom or refinishing some shelves. Hanging doors, repairing water leaks ..."

"Brian is handling the door."

"Is he doing all your repair work? Maybe it's some kind of scam. He damaged the house before she died, so he'd get hired to make repairs."

I searched her face for a suggestion she was teasing, but her gaze was steady, her eyebrows lifted just a bit.

"That's really cynical. And it's not a scam. He's fixing the door for free."

She laughed. "For free?"

"As a neighborly gesture."

"Is he your neighbor?" She glanced toward the window.

"I don't know where he lives."

"Maybe he wants something else."

I turned away from her and started down the stairs. "Don't say that. He's being nice. Besides, he knows about David."

"But he didn't see any signs of David, did he?"

"I told him—"

"I'm just saying. Be careful."

When we reached the bottom of the stairs, I turned to face her. "It feels like you're trying to spoil something I'm excited about."

"Oh, no. I'm sorry, Trinity. Not at all. I would never do that." She threw her arms around me in yet another enormous hug. "I'm really sorry. I just want you to be careful. You called me because you were scared … alone in a new place where you don't know anyone. You're vulnerable, that's all I'm saying."

"I don't think I am." I pulled away from her.

"I don't always trust people who offer favors too easily," Mia said. "Especially when I don't know them."

"People are nicer in communities like this," I said. "It's not Silicon Valley."

"People are nice there, too."

"They're more open in a place like this."

"At any rate, you're not alone anymore. I came prepared to stay. Two weeks off work. And I can arrange a few more days if you need me." She held up her hands. "I even got my polish stripped off so I can work."

"You didn't have to. We can wear gloves."

"I like to get my hands dirty."

After I made turkey sandwiches and we'd eaten them sitting on the steps to the front porch, we went to the grocery store. When we returned home, Brian's pickup truck was in the driveway. His text that he was on his way had popped up while we were in the checkout line.

I introduced him to Mia and despite her warning and thinly veiled implication that he was either out to scam me or seduce me, she was friendly, without a hint of animosity. In fact, she almost went too far the other way.

"Brian!" She shook his hand, placing her left hand over the back of his right. "It's so sweet of you to help Trinity with her door."

"No problem." He carefully slid his hand out of the enclosure she'd created.

"How alarming to have your door just fall off the house," Mia said.

"It happens. It's an old house."

"But it just fell off. Without any warning?" Mia asked.

"There were probably warnings," he said.

"Oh?"

He shrugged. "I'll get started." He reached into the truck bed and pulled out a toolbox. He turned, lifting his hand in a wave, and walked toward the side of the house.

"Will you need help?" Mia called after him.

"Got it, thanks."

We took our purchases into the house and settled on the couch. I picked up my notebook full of paint chips and wood stains. "I mostly wanted to—"

"He seems like an okay guy," Mia said.

"I told you."

"Did you?"

"I was going to show you my plans. So you can see what part you want to help with. David wants to—"

"He's the ex-husband?"

"Yes."

"When did she die?"

"I'm not sure." The minute I'd blurted out to Mia that Sara had died, I'd regretted it because then I had to swear her to secrecy. It felt icky that David wasn't telling me to avoid upsetting me, and now I wasn't telling him that I knew in order to protect the feelings of our real estate agent. It was a little twisted. I didn't like this knot of secrecy in the middle of our marriage.

"I wonder how long ago they got divorced?" Mia asked.

"I don't know." Suddenly, I didn't want to talk about it. I felt as if it somehow added to the deceit between David and me.

I was extremely grateful for what Brian was doing for me. He was my first acquaintance in our new, part-time home. I wanted to grow roots here. I wanted to form good relationships with our neighbors. I appreciated Mia was looking out for me, and I understood why she was cautious, but it felt like she thought I was naïve. That she didn't trust my judgment.

I went through my notebook with her. "David wants to make more aggressive changes," I said. "He was talking about modernizing more, but I want to keep the character of the original design."

"Well, David's not here, is he?" She patted my leg.

8 NOW: CHARLOTTE

*I*t had been a mistake to stop by Sara's old house to drop off the extra set of keys I'd found. The new owner would probably change the locks anyway. She *should* change the locks. Any cautious person would. But the keys belonged to her, and it was my responsibility to give her all the keys in my possession.

I prided myself on fulfilling my obligations to the letter. Except for that one disclosure … but again, I didn't know for certain, and I wasn't explicitly required to investigate *suspected* issues. I was only required to answer the questions on the form at face value.

Maybe dropping off the extra keys was over-compensation for the whisper of guilt plaguing me, dotting every *i* and crossing every *t* in order to make up for knowingly evading my professional ethics.

Trinity answered the door wearing a long, loose top and leggings. Her feet were bare. Her shoulder-length dark hair was pulled into a ponytail. With all her hair off her face, her perfect complexion was emphasized. Her skin appeared almost flawless, even close up in the bright morning light.

I looked up at her. She was slender and several inches taller than me, even taller as she stood on the threshold. I handed the keys to her. "I suppose these aren't necessary. Maybe you've already had the locks changed."

"I haven't had a chance yet." She stepped back. "Would you like some tea? Or coffee?"

"No thanks. I—"

"A glass of water?"

"No. I only came by to drop—"

"I wanted to tell you about something that happened."

I laughed, knowing I sounded anxious. I didn't want to hear about anything that had *happened*. The fewer conversations she and I had, the fewer opportunities for uncomfortable questions. Our professional interaction was complete. I backed away from the open door.

She stepped down onto the porch.

"I have to meet someone at ten," I said. "So I—"

"This will only take a minute." Her dark eyes bored into mine.

I half-expected her to grab my arm if I tried to take another step away from her. A woman with long blonde hair appeared in the doorway behind her.

"If you have questions about the house, you should hire a contractor," I said, my eyes on the woman behind her, who stood like a protective shadow over Trinity. "The sale is complete, so my role is finished." I smiled, but my lips were so stiff I felt as if my face were made of metal and I was trying to force a resistant material into something resembling a human form.

"But you know the history of the house, and you're the one who—"

"This isn't how things work."

"I just want to ask you about something that happened. I wasn't here for the purchase because my sister was *dying*. Can't you just answer one question?"

I sighed. "Please don't get upset."

"Don't patronize me."

"Your husband was here. He has the inspection reports and the disclosures. The house belongs to you now. I'm simply the person who handled the transaction. You're inflating my role in this."

"I have a question about the washing machine. I could have asked it by now," she snapped.

I smiled, with less effort this time. Clearly, she was still raw with grief. "I doubt I can help, but what's the issue?"

"The hose came unattached and was spraying water all over. I wondered if—"

"I'm really sorry, Trinity. I can't help you. It was an option to have the appliances hauled away. You should go over the inspections and paperwork with your husband." I glanced at my watch, hoping to give the universal signal I was out of time.

She ignored my gesture. "It's not really about the washing machine. I feel silly telling you this …" Her tone of voice changed. It was softer now, friendlier, but filled with uncertainty. "I felt like …" She let out a shrill, uncomfortable laugh. "… someone was in the house. Because it happened so suddenly. I haven't used the machine at all. And I'm not sure—"

"That's not possible. I gave you all the keys. Except this set, which has been locked up at my office." I held up my phone to show her the time. "I really need to go."

"It seems strange that two things like that would happen. The door falling off, and now this. And something woke me. I can't say for sure what it was, but it wasn't the water, and—"

"I don't know why you're fixating on minor issues that happen in all older homes. It has nothing to do with me. I came over to drop off keys. As a favor. It wasn't even really necessary because the locks should be changed. You would be unwise not to do that."

"I will but—"

"And just to assure you, they were already changed once. After Ms. Linden-Price passed away."

"Of course, but—"

"I have nothing else to say. It's an old house. It's going to have creaks and groans. Things are going to break. Brian said the door hinges had corroded."

"You talked to him?"

"Briefly."

"And he thought that was normal?"

"What do you want from me? I'm a real estate agent. I'm not your consultant or your ..." I turned my attention to her friend, still lurking in the doorway. "It looks like you have someone here to help. You really need to look at the paperwork. Sooner rather than later. It's negligent not to."

"I will but—"

"I need to get going."

"Why do you keep interrupting me? It feels like—"

"Because I have another appointment. I told you that. I came by to drop off keys and you're telling me about repair problems that don't concern me. It feels like you're suggesting that S ... well I ..." Without meaning to, as if the things I'd concealed were rising through the floorboards of the porch, like the telltale heart, thumping in my ears, making it impossible for me to think, I felt I couldn't control the words pushing themselves toward the tip of my tongue. If I didn't leave, I might say something I regretted.

What I'd said was absolutely correct—this had nothing at all to do with me. I'd done my job. I'd listed the house at a good price and shown it to buyers, making sure not to take the first offer just because I wanted to be finished. I'd faithfully taken care of Sara's estate according to her wishes. I'd done everything I could to honor our friendship.

I didn't owe anything to Trinity Feld or her husband or this other very chic woman who was now glaring at me for a reason I couldn't begin to imagine.

"What are you not saying?" Trinity asked. "You look like you're almost ... afraid of something."

"I'm not. I'm getting annoyed."

"Do you think it's haunted? Do you think Sara's still here, some-how? That her spirit ... because she died here ... or ...?"

I laughed. "Don't be ridiculous. I don't believe in ghosts. Or anything supernatural."

"Then, what? You started to say something and you stopped. What's going on? Why are these things happening?"

"Because the house was built over one hundred years ago. That's why! And because even though it's been upgraded several times, it's still old. Houses get old, things break, parts deteriorate. Have you ever owned a home?"

"Yes. I know that, but—"

"Then you know they need constant maintenance. Ms. Linden-Price was ill for several years. Some things were neglected. Read the inspection report. Hire a contractor, or a handyman. Brian is more than happy to help. Do whatever feels comfortable or works for you, but it's not my responsibility." I turned and walked down the steps.

"You're not being very professional," Trinity said.

I paused on the bottom step and turned back. "I'm absolutely professional. You're overstepping. I get it that you're fragile because you recently lost your sister, and your husband seems to have handed this off to you without explanation, but I've done my job and I hope you can return to your original enthusiasm and accept this beautiful home for the older beauty it is, but in need of some upkeep."

I walked to my car as fast as I could before she fired another question or accusation at me. I got inside and slammed the door. My heart was pounding. I'd never spoken like that to a client. I couldn't recall ever speaking like that to anyone.

9 NOW: TRINITY

The way Charlotte had turned on me was really upsetting. I was her client, and she'd earned a very nice commission from the sale of this house. I hadn't expected her to treat me as if I were now an annoying and needy shopper seeking a below-market deal.

At the same time, she'd given the distinct impression she was scared out of her mind. She'd acted as if she thought some piece of Sara had remained in the house and was now causing me to feel her presence. The moment I commented on her obvious fear, she'd treated me like I was a loon for even suggesting such a thing. But she was the one who'd looked terrified. I was simply trying to find out why the house seemed to begin breaking apart the moment I stepped inside.

I knew the logical solution was to ask David to go over the inspection reports with me, but every text I sent him came back with the fewest words possible, telling me how buried he was at work, how grueling his schedule was when he was traveling, something I should know by now. Text messages that were so blunt and empty of any feeling, they might as well have been sent by his assistant. Besides, the inspection reports were at our house in

Cupertino. It wasn't as if he'd committed every detail to memory. When I'd returned home from seeing my brother and Ryan, I'd packed so quickly before coming here, the reports hadn't been on my mind.

"You're overreacting," Mia said. "She didn't turn on you."

"She was almost shouting at me."

"You're being too sensitive. She's frustrated. It's not her job to fix things after the house is sold."

"I didn't ask her to fix anything."

"I know, but she seemed to take it that way. Maybe other clients have, and she overreacted, that's all."

For another ten minutes, we argued about Charlotte and how I'd mistaken her tone as well as her words. Finally, I gave up. I pulled an old T-shirt over my clothes and got the metal scraper and solvent I'd bought. I opened the window, put on a mask to protect me from the fumes, and placed a nylon tarp on the dining room floor. I applied solvent and attacked the mural. Underneath, I discovered three more layers of paint—white, a light coffee color, and pale yellow. I had my work cut out for me.

I scraped and peeled layers of paint until two, when Mia insisted I stop to eat something, gently taking the scraper out of my hand.

She'd made barley soup and had run to the store for a baguette and fresh strawberries. I hadn't even heard her leave the house, which made me wonder about the functioning of my senses. When I was in a deep sleep, random creaks in the settling of an old house, or perhaps the slow leak of water, woke me, but when I was fully alert and only forty feet away from where she'd been scraping damaged paint in the laundry room, I hadn't been aware that she'd stopped working, or that she'd left the house entirely, before making the soup.

So much for my sixth sense.

We ate and talked more about what I thought was an overreaction from Charlotte, as well as the obvious look of fear in her eyes.

Mia continued taking her side, insisting I hadn't understood how frustrated Charlotte must be.

"You also have to remember that it sounds like Sara was a close friend. She's probably grieving too."

My throat tightened, and I put down my spoon. Maybe I had been too harsh. Maybe it hadn't been fear I'd seen in Charlotte's eyes, but something else—a kind of futile hope. I knew that feeling. The desire to experience the presence of someone you've lost. The desperate longing for her to let you know she's okay, even though you'll never see her face or hear her voice again. The longing to know she hasn't vanished completely.

That some essential part of her still exists, somewhere, as you wonder with utter futility—What's it like for her? Is she close by? Can she read my thoughts? Is she as fully aware of my life continuing on as I am of hers, having stopped so abruptly?

Maybe those were the things I'd seen in Charlotte's face. Things that couldn't be distilled into something as simplistic as fear. Maybe she wanted to be done with the house because it reminded her of her best friend. And maybe she thought my questions were nothing but complaining. Criticisms of things that had been neglected when Sara could no longer take care of her home.

I blinked back tears. "Thanks for saying that."

Mia gave me a sympathetic smile. She cleared our dishes.

For the rest of the afternoon, we worked in our separate rooms with our separate thoughts. We went out to dinner at a Mexican restaurant where we stuffed ourselves with tortilla chips and guacamole, enchiladas, and the most amazing Spanish rice I'd ever tasted. We each drank an oversized margarita. We didn't take home any leftovers.

We streamed a show on my iPad and went to bed.

When I woke suddenly and fully in the middle of the night, my first thought was that I'd screamed.

Had I been dreaming and something in my dream caused me to

scream, waking me? Was it a physical scream, or something dreamt? If it had been real, Mia would appear in my doorway at any minute.

I waited, gripping the edge of the blankets.

She didn't come.

Once again, I had the distinct feeling there was someone in the house. Not just Mia, but someone downstairs. Did I hear footsteps? Had I heard them while asleep and that caused me to scream? I sat up, my brain twisted into knots. I wasn't sure which thoughts were part of a lingering dream I no longer remembered, which were my imagination stirred by that look on Charlotte's face, and which were my own thoughts, feeding on my uncertainty, growing into a mild case of paranoia.

I strained to hear something, but couldn't make out any sounds. I checked my phone—one twenty-three. The sequential numbers seemed meaningful. I shoved the thought away. This wasn't a time to start becoming superstitious, simply because a real estate agent acted as if a broken water hose and corroded hinges suggested my new house was inhabited by the lingering spirit of its former owner.

Like Charlotte, I did not believe in such things. I might have questions about the nature of reality and the line between life and death. I might long for a sense of my sister's presence, but I certainly didn't believe my new house was inhabited by the spirit of its deceased former owner.

Mia was the one who tended in that direction, demonstrated by her devotion to her Tarot cards. Although I wasn't sure that was the same thing. She might say they were entirely different. I avoided asking her much about them because I didn't like it when she wanted to do so-called *readings* for me. It made me feel awkward and under the spotlight, as if I had to buy in to her belief that mystical drawings on randomly shuffled cards carried a meaningful connection to reality.

I got out of bed and went to the window. The moon was nearly full, and it shone down on the yard, making some areas look bright as day, while others were hid in total darkness. The side of the garage was brightly lit, and the trees near the empty pond stood out. I could see the large, rusted iron disk covering the empty well that had provided water for the house before it was connected to the city water line.

It was one of the things that would have to be taken care of as soon as possible. David and I agreed that even though the iron cover was secured by a bar that latched, it made us uncomfortable to have a hole on our property that was fifty feet deep.

I pressed my face against the glass, trying to figure out what I was looking at. There were no plants growing around the well, no trees in the area. What was that? I strained my eyes. The moonlight that had seemed so bright a moment earlier was now completely inadequate. I pushed my face harder against the glass, as if fusing my bones to the surface would allow my eyes to focus, my vision to sharpen.

It looked like a pile of laundry ... maybe. Some towels and sheets someone had left in the yard, intending to hang them on a clothesline. But we didn't have a clothesline, and I didn't have more than the sheets and towels that were in use in the upstairs bedrooms.

I moved away from the window. It didn't matter. Whatever it was, that wasn't what had woken me. A soft, misshapen pile of rags or possibly some weeds and chunks of overturned earth. The problem was, I couldn't say what had woken me.

I was wide awake and there had to be a reason. I was overcome with a need to know what was lying beside the well. It seemed critical to find out. I grabbed my phone to use as a flashlight, put on my hoodie, picked up my athletic shoes, and went downstairs.

I opened the back door, and the newly installed screen, which glided out silently, perfectly fitted to the hinges. It closed smoothly and softly behind me. I sat on the steps to put on my shoes, then walked quickly across the yard, holding my phone in front of me, showing me the way over the rough surface of the uncared for lawn.

When I was about fifteen feet from the covered well, I raised my phone to let the light shine farther ahead.

I screamed, a sound so loud and unfamiliar it seemed to come from outside me. The phone wobbled and started to slip out of my hand. I tightened my grip and let out a choked sob.

The white pile of fabric was indeed clothing. It covered the body of a woman who was clearly dead, her mouth gaping, her open eyes staring up at the moon.

Charlotte Hughes.

10 NOW: TRINITY

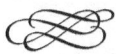

*J*screamed again, backing away from Charlotte's silent, unmoving body. My screams grew louder, seeming to echo across the entire sky. My hands trembled, and I felt my legs growing wobbly. The phone slid out of my hand. I wanted to sit before my legs collapsed under me, but I didn't want to be there at all. I didn't want to be anywhere close to where she lay.

The bright light from my phone shot up like a beacon into the darkness. My screams had faded, but Mia must have heard me. Why wasn't she coming? Even the neighbors, although they were a short distance away on either side and behind my house, must have heard. Why wasn't anyone coming?

The enchilada and margarita from dinner swam in my stomach. Even though I'd moved away, I could see the form of her lying there. Now that I knew it was her, not just a thing … I couldn't stop knowing how empty she looked. I was thankful I could no longer see her eyes.

How had this happened? Had she fallen and smashed her head on the iron bar that secured the cover on the well? But why was she in our yard in the middle of the night?

I turned and bent over. My stomach lurched, and I gagged. I

took a few steps to my phone, picked it up, and straightened. I directed the light toward the ground and stumbled back to the house, screaming Mia's name. Once I was inside, I turned on the lights as I passed through each room, calling her name.

When I reached the stairs, she was halfway down.

"What's wrong?" Her hair glowed in the stairwell light above her, silky and smooth, as unruffled as her face. She hurried to the bottom of the stairs. "What happened? Are you okay?"

I gagged, then put my hand over my mouth. "Charlotte." I pointed toward the back of the house. "She's dead."

She shook her head slightly. "Dead?"

I nodded.

"Are you sure?"

I wanted to slap her. Then I wondered at my reaction. Why would I want to slap her? Because she didn't believe me? Was it shock? Did I feel an irrational need to express my outrage at stumbling across a dead body, a need to be violent? Did that mean I had an instinctive awareness that Charlotte hadn't tripped and fallen, that someone had killed her and I needed to be violent in return?

"Are you okay?" Mia asked.

"No. No, I'm not okay."

She moved toward me, wrapping her arms gently around me. "I'm sorry. What a stupid question. Do you want to ... should we?"

I shook my head. I let her hold me tightly against her for several minutes. Her arms, and the calmness of someone who had not looked upon across a lifeless body in the moonlight. was comforting. She made me feel stronger. After a moment, I pulled away. "I need to call the police."

"Yes."

Within fifteen minutes, a police car arrived. It was soon followed by a dark four-door car and a white van.

Fifteen minutes later, Mia and I were seated on the couch. Two police cars were in the driveway, and I could see the occasional movement of several high-powered flashlights arcing across the backyard.

Things began happening as if we were watching a play. Mia and I remained on the couch, drinking water a detective had offered us from my own kitchen, from glasses he'd taken out of my cabinet.

I'd sent a text to David, but he hadn't responded yet.

So far, Detective Robbins hadn't asked many questions beyond our names, Charlotte's name, and how we knew her. He'd asked how I'd found her and what I was doing walking around the backyard at one thirty in the morning. I'd told him everything, but I hadn't mentioned being woken at one twenty-three. I didn't want him to think I was a nutcase.

I couldn't stop thinking about that: one, two, three. It felt as if it meant something, even though I knew it meant absolutely nothing. I wasn't a superstitious person. It was because Mia was there and I could imagine what she would say about it. Mia with her Tarot cards and her lucky numbers.

"Are you sure you didn't hear something?" Detective Robbins was standing over me. I wished he would sit in the armchair, but he'd said he would stand, for now.

"Not that I was aware of. Like I told you, I woke suddenly, but I wasn't sure why."

"No screaming?"

I shook my head.

"You're sure?"

He was starting to annoy me. It seemed as if he thought that repeating the question would force me to give him a different answer. It seemed as if he couldn't believe that Charlotte had died without screaming.

He tapped a few notes into his phone. Without looking at me, he asked, "What made you walk out to the well?"

"I saw what looked like a pile of rags. I wasn't sure what it was."

"Why did you think you needed to check that out at one thirty in the morning?"

"I'm not sure."

"There must have been a reason. Something that made you go out there. Did you see someone else in the yard when you looked out your window?"

"I already told you, no."

"Calm down."

"I'm calm. But you keep asking me the same questions. I'm really tired."

"I'm trying to jog your memory."

"My memory is clear. And I've told you everything."

"Sometimes shock can—"

"I'm not in shock. There were no screams, unless they happened while I was asleep, and if they did, I can't tell you anything about them because I didn't consciously hear them. I didn't see anyone out there. I went over to the well because I couldn't be sure what I was seeing. I was wide awake and curious. That's all."

"Please calm down, Ms. Feld," Detective Robbins said.

I glared at him.

He tapped a note into his phone.

I could imagine the notes he was making about my state of calm.

After a moment, he looked at me. "The body has been removed. But the area will be cordoned off until we've finished gathering evidence, which we expect to take most of the day. Some work is being done now, but we'll need to wait for daylight to be more thorough."

I nodded.

"Is it safe for us to stay here?" Mia asked.

"I can't answer that," Detective Robbins said.

"Who would kill her?" Mia asked.

"I don't know. That's why every piece of information from witnesses like yourselves is critical," he said.

"We're not witnesses," I said. "We didn't see anything."

He put his phone in his pocket. "Thank you for your time." He handed business cards to both of us. "If you think of anything you've forgotten to tell me, please call me immediately. Once the evidence is collected and we know the approximate time of death, I'll have more questions for you."

He moved toward the doorway. "I'll find my way out."

I wasn't sure what I was supposed to say—*Thanks? See you soon? Nice meeting you?* Even *goodbye* felt somehow inappropriate for the situation.

I said *goodbye.*

When he was gone, Mia and I stared at each other.

"Should we try to sleep?" Mia asked.

"I don't think I can."

She nodded.

"I don't know what to do," I said.

She was quiet for a moment. "First, I'll make us some breakfast."

When she said that, all I could think was—one, two, three.

I wanted my brain to stop playing tricks on me. The detective hadn't helped. Because all that was spinning around inside my head were questions and doubts—*Had* I heard someone scream? *Something* had woken me. Maybe I'd heard a scream, and I'd pushed it aside, fixating on those numbers for no reason. *Did* I see someone in the yard? There were so many shadows. Maybe someone was out there and that was what compelled me to go downstairs for a closer look.

Despite my insistence that I'd told him everything I remembered, I felt as if I couldn't remember anything clearly at all.

11 NOW: TRINITY

Scrambled eggs and toast turned out to be exactly what we needed to calm our nerves, because after we'd eaten, Mia and I found ourselves yawning uncontrollably. We agreed we would try resting even though the sky was growing light. It was possible we might catch thirty minutes of sleep before the sun fully rose.

When I finally woke, I knew it had been hours. The sun was streaming in around the edges of the blinds, sharp as knife blades, slicing across the walls and the comforter that I'd pushed off my upper body as the room had grown warmer while I slept. I looked at my phone. It was almost one o'clock. My stomach growled, acutely aware that the tiny bit of egg and half a slice of toast I'd eaten hours ago were a distant memory.

I sat up and ran my fingers through my hair.

There was a missed call and voicemail, as well as two text messages from David.

The text messages were insistent.

David: *Where are you? I called you hours ago.*

David: *I'm getting worried. Call me!*

I didn't bother listening to the voicemail. I called him as I slid out of bed and grabbed some clothes, headed toward the shower.

"I talked to Mia," he said. "She told me you were sleeping. Are you okay?"

"Yes. I just woke up."

"She was murdered? In our *backyard*? What the *hell*?!?"

"I don't know. They haven't said."

"Well, she didn't just drop dead out there."

"Probably not."

"Couldn't you tell?"

"Tell what? How she died? No. There wasn't any blood, if that's what you mean."

"Are they still there? The cops?"

I hadn't even looked. I returned to the bedroom and twisted the blinds open. The area around the well was surrounded by yellow tape and orange cones. The tired grass had been dug up in some spots, but otherwise, everything was the way I remembered from the previous day.

"It looks like they're finished," I said. "For now."

"Mia said they think you're witnesses."

"It's a little ridiculous. I didn't see anything."

"Are you sure?"

"Yes, I'm sure! You sound like the detective."

"Okay. I'm just asking. It's hard to know when you're woken suddenly."

Was it? Why was everyone saying that?

"How are you feeling?" he asked.

"Right now, I'm starving. And I want a shower."

"I'll let you go. If you're sure you're okay."

"I'm good. Talk to you later?"

"Going to catch up on the email flood and then get to bed. I'll try you around noon my time, but I have a lunch meeting, so …"

"Are you going to make it here this weekend?"

"I'll try. I have some issues that just came up that I have to deal with before the weekend, so I might have to change my flight."

Sometimes, I wasn't sure how I felt about David's long hours. He loved his job, and he'd worked hard to get where he was. It energized him and gave him purpose, like work does for most of us. He was clear from the moment we'd met that the money that had flowed into my life when the startup I worked for was acquired belonged to me.

If we ever wanted to take a step back and figure out a different kind of life, he might give it some thought, but he didn't want to *sponge* off me, which was how he insisted upon putting it. No matter how often I told him to stop using that word, he persisted. We could sell our home and live here, for example. We could explore starting a family business together.

I understood his need to have a career, to not feel as if he depended on me. And he loved traveling all over the world to conduct sales training for his company. I couldn't, I wouldn't, take that away from him. But I hated the hours he put in. Especially now. I wanted him here with me, fixing up our summer home together.

"Love you," I said.

"Love you."

By the time I'd finished my shower, my conversation with David had faded, giving me the eery sensation it had transpired only in my mind. It had been almost two weeks since we'd seen each other. When we were separated for extended periods, he felt less solid with each passing day. I hated being away from him. I hated the sense of unreality that crept over me when we were apart.

Would he ever be here with me? Truly present, creating the kind of low-tech life I wanted in order to keep us centered and grounded, to give Ryan, and any children of our own, a solid foundation? Ryan needed this place. He needed to run outdoors and dig in the earth and play with mud and plant seeds and watch them grow. He needed to pick an apple off the tree and take a bite. He needed to *feel* life.

12 NOW: TRINITY

$\mathcal{D}$ownstairs, I found Mia in the living room, curled on the couch, looking at her phone. "Hi, sleepyhead."

"How long have you been awake?" I asked.

"Hours."

"Were they still here when you got up?"

She nodded. She placed her phone face down on the couch and gave me her full attention. "Even though her body was gone, it was creepy. I wished you were with me." Her lower lip quivered slightly. "But then I thought, you don't need that."

"I can handle it," I said.

"I have no idea what they were doing out there all that time. They were walking around like zombies, staring at the ground, picking up stuff, taking pictures, digging. What would they be digging for?"

"Evidence, I guess."

"It was weird."

"I'm starving." It was crude and disrespectful to be thinking about food, but my body felt so empty, I had to grab the back of the armchair to steady myself.

"Don't eat too much," Mia said. "I was thinking we need something to distract us. So I ran to the store and bought everything for a pasta dinner. Fresh bread ... I'll make meatballs and a huge salad. Does that sound good?"

"I'm hungry now." I turned and started toward the kitchen.

"Just don't overdo it."

After I gobbled down a peanut butter and jelly sandwich, an apple, several carrot sticks, and two oatmeal cookies that Mia had also bought, we went for a walk around the neighborhood.

The couple who lived next door were sitting on their front porch. We waved as we passed. I thought they might call us over to ask about the police, but they didn't. Since they were retired, maybe the police cars had already left before they'd come outside. It was possible, given the size of our yards and the number of trees on both pieces of property, they hadn't been aware of the people poking around our backyard and all the middle of the night activity in our driveway.

Later, while Mia rolled tiny meatballs and chopped veggies for her elaborate salad, I tried to distract myself with a game on my tablet. It was hard not to think about Charlotte. I wanted to know how she'd died, and why she'd been prowling around my yard in the middle of the night. The last time I'd spoken to her, she couldn't wait to get off my property. I'd had the feeling she would be happy never to see me or my house again. And yet, she'd come back in the dark that very night, and been out there ... doing what? And who had been with her? Was it possible she'd simply fallen and hit her head?

I didn't think so. Not the way she was lying there, stretched out in that awkward angle, staring up at the sky.

* * *

Mia's pasta dinner was indeed a welcome distraction. The food was divine. Mia had been a fabulous cook from the time she was a teenager. Her mother was an amazing cook, and Mia had followed her around the kitchen, helping prepare meals while absorbing her mother's skills. They were always in the kitchen together, wearing their matching aprons.

Mia and I met when we were in third grade. We were in the same reading group, and we both devoured every book about horses we could get our hands on. Our friendship grew from there. Nothing could split us apart. Not boys, not mean girls, not my departure for college while she trained to become a hair stylist.

I met David when Mia and I were on a blind double date together. It hadn't worked out for her and the other guy, a casual friend David had since lost touch with.

She didn't have an ounce of jealousy when David and I got engaged and then married. That was one of the things that had held our friendship together. No jealousy, that insidious disease that infects too many female friendships. We cared about and supported each other. We shared our secrets and laughed at the same things. And we still both loved horses.

I wasn't jealous of her stunning good looks, and she wasn't jealous that I'd found the love of my life before she had. We knew we were lucky to have the friendship we did. We knew it was unique. We tolerated and even loved each other's quirks. When she told me I was like a sister, I didn't feel the need to point out that I already had a sister. Because she didn't, I was happy to fill that place in her life. I knew that wouldn't change, even though Jen was gone. My sister was irreplaceable. Still, Mia was a part of my life that felt like family, even if she didn't have a label.

"I remember the first time you made dinner for your mom and me, without her help," I said as I twirled pasta around my fork.

"Do you?"

"It was so cute. She looked so proud. I could see how she wanted to jump up and help you. She almost had to grab the edge of the table to keep herself in the chair."

"You're imagining that," Mia said, her smile telling me she hoped I wasn't.

"I'm not imagining it." I cut a meatball in two and placed half in my mouth. "These are so good."

"Thank you."

"I still think you should consider opening a restaurant," I said.

"That's your dream, not mine," Mia said.

"It's absolutely not my dream. First of all, I don't cook well enough."

"Then stop dreaming about it," she said. "I love cooking and I don't want it to turn into a job."

From there, we dug up other memories, laughing our way through dinner and two glasses of red wine, forgetting about the disturbed area in the backyard, the taped off section around the well, about Charlotte's body lying in a morgue somewhere, waiting for a pathologist to determine why she was dead.

"You know what would be a good idea," Mia said.

"What?" I slotted our plates into the dishwasher.

"I should do a reading for you."

I suppressed a sigh. Long-term friendships are built on being kind to the other person, taking them as they are, not just on keeping jealousy and resentment out of the way. I was pretty good at that. So was Mia. We absolutely tolerated one another's quirks. Except for the Tarot readings. She didn't suggest them often, but when she did, she was relentless.

She performed her *readings* for a lot of her hairdressing clients. She did them for anyone who she thought was headed in the *wrong direction*, anyone she sensed might be confused or uncertain. It was her go-to form of comfort.

But I hadn't said I was confused or upset about finding Charlotte dead in my backyard. I suppose I didn't have to. She knew. She'd been my friend for so long, I couldn't remember my life without her in it.

"I'm a little tired," I said.

"I'll do a short one."

"I—"

"You need this. Finding a dead body in your yard is *not* good. Your new house, all your dreams and plans, bringing your sister's son into your life ... you absolutely need this. I know you think you don't, but I'm not going to let you pretend you're okay."

I closed my eyes for a moment. When I opened them, she was gone. I'd missed any slight chance I had at resisting her offer.

13 NOW: TRINITY

*J*turned off the kitchen light and went into the living room. Mia was already seated cross-legged on the floor in front of the couch. The cards were stacked in front of her.

"I'm going to ask what your future holds in this house," Mia said.

I expected the reading to go pretty much as they always did—I would zone out, half listening to Mia explain what each of the three cards meant based on the order in which it was flipped over. She would ask me questions, growing frustrated with me because nothing *resonated*. She would accuse me of being resistant.

"Remember, you need to open yourself to the process," she said.

"I've told you a hundred times, I don't believe in this."

"Why can't you keep an open mind? I've helped a lot of people."

I placed my hand on her wrist, covering the thick silver bracelet that made me think of a snake, a dark green stone forming the clasp. "I know. And I respect that."

She flipped over the first card and studied it for a moment. The empress.

"These cards have been used to guide people for over two hundred and fifty years," Mia said. "You shouldn't dismiss them so easily. Don't you think you need something more than everyday logic right now? Something very out of the ordinary and upsetting has happened to you. There's a reason Charlotte turned up dead in your yard and—"

"Whatever that reason is, it has nothing to do with me. And randomly placed cards aren't going to give me any peace of mind. Once the detective finds out what happened and starts investigating what was going on in her life, he'll find a logical explanation."

Mia sighed. "You don't think it's significant that the empress came up? She symbolizes motherhood and you're about to become an adoptive mother."

I tried not to laugh. Part of me loved that she loved her cards. It was what made Mia so much fun—she was filled with optimism and hope about every aspect of life, although there was also a dark side to those cards. But for the most part, she liked them because she believed they gave her answers to questions she couldn't find answers to. For some reason I couldn't explain, the cards helped her to see the best in people. But there were plenty of ways to achieve those things without putting your trust in a deck of cards.

"I'm exhausted," I said. "I think we should get a good night's sleep."

Mia turned over another card. The moon card. She stared at it.

I thought about my bed and how tired I was, despite my long nap.

The room was silent as both of us continued looking at the oversized, elaborately decorated card.

The silence was broken by a sound from the kitchen—a soft tap, as if something had been placed on the counter, followed by a slight scuffing noise, like footsteps on the tile floor.

Both of us jerked our heads up, staring at each other. Mia started to get up, placing her hand on the floor to push herself into a standing position, but her hand was on the cards, and they slid, causing her to fall toward me. She caught herself, then sat down hard.

"Ow." Her voice was a faint whisper, as if she were terrified she might be overheard.

"Is someone out there?" I was also whispering.

She put her finger to her lips, then took her wrist in her hand and massaged it for a moment. She got to her feet, and I did the same. We slowly approached the arched opening to the kitchen. Mia reached into the room and pressed the switch for the overhead lights. No one was there. The doors to the dining room were closed, the room dark. There was no exterior door in either room.

We walked toward the pantry and looked inside. The door to the basement was closed. Mia opened it and turned on the light. All that was down there were a few storage cabinets and a workbench. The space was small and we could see the entire area from where we stood at the top of the stairs.

Mia closed the door and looked at me. "What do you think it was?"

"I don't know. I ... maybe it didn't come from inside the house?"

She folded her arms across her ribs, grabbing both her upper arms as if she were cold. "It sounded like it was right here."

I nodded. "But there's nothing."

She turned, carefully studying each corner of the kitchen as if the source of the tapping and scraping might make itself known if she directed her gaze at the right place. When she was facing me again, her eyes were wide. "It sounded like someone was in the room."

"But it's not possible."

She shrugged. "Maybe we're jumpy because of ..." She shivered elaborately. "It must have been outside. We haven't been here long enough to know what the usual sounds are. It could have been a tree or a wild animal. Let's finish your reading." She returned to the living room.

I called after her—"I'm going to make tea." I filled the kettle and turned it on. I dropped two bags of herbal tea into mugs. While I waited for the kettle to boil, I fingered the locket Mia had given me.

60

"I miss you, Jen," I whispered.

When we were settled on the living room floor again, I remembered my earlier desire to go to bed. Now, I felt as if I wanted to stay with Mia all night. Her presence was comforting. I was sure the sound had a natural explanation, but I couldn't come up with a single idea for what that might be.

I wanted to sit close to Mia and drink my tea. I wanted to lose myself in our good memories. I wanted to talk about my plans for the house, if I could manage to do that without thinking about our realtor dying on our property or the house's seeming desire to constantly startle me.

Mia placed her mug on the floor. "Now. Where were we? The moon. So in this position—-"

"I'm not sure I'm in the mood to finish this," I said.

"You have to."

"Do I?"

"Yes. It's important."

"Why?"

"Because it is."

I took a sip of tea.

Mia scooped up the cards. "Let's start over. Take a few deep breaths and give yourself over to the process."

"Mia ..."

"Do you want to go to bed? After hearing those noises?"

I didn't answer. She knew. We knew each other completely. I took another sip of tea and waited.

"I'm going to ask a more specific question," she said. "I have one in mind, unless there's something you'd like to ask?"

I shook my head.

"I think we should ask—What do we need to know about the past, the present, and the future of this house?"

She drew three cards and placed them face down in front of me. She turned over the first one—the empress. Again. She studied it for a moment. "Okay. I think it's really important that she came up again." She gave me a comforting smile. "Along with what I already said, this is ... this suggests there was a lot of nurturing and beauty in the house. Also, abundance." She nodded slowly. "That's really good."

"Does it matter? What matters is what David and I bring—"

"Let's let the cards speak," Mia said.

I picked up my tea and took several sips. I would let her finish. I usually did. It was interesting to hear where her fanciful thoughts took her. She liked giving me reassurance this way, telling me good things were coming into my life. She did the same for herself and at least once a week she texted me a photo of the card she'd drawn that day, excited with what it predicted for her life.

Of course, she always managed to shift the subsequent events of her life to fit what she'd imagined the cards were telling her. She called it her intuitive insight. I called it rewriting history. It wasn't that I didn't believe there was something greater than physical reality at work in the world, something bigger than ourselves. But I certainly didn't think it operated inside a deck of playing cards. I took another sip of tea.

She turned over the second card—the scythe. "Oh." Her mouth was a perfect circle. Then she folded her lips together until they almost disappeared. "This is really helpful. It's telling you to avoid acting in haste." Her voice trembled. "It's good that the message is so clear. But ... I hate telling you this, I really do, but it's also saying we need to be alert to danger."

"It's fine. It has nothing to do with us. With me. Not really." I shrugged. "There's no danger to us. It's awful what happened to Charlotte, but I'm sure they'll figure out it had something to do with an unhappy client of hers, or maybe nothing to do with her profession at all. An abusive relationship, maybe. Who knows?"

"We don't know," Mia said. "It could be anything. Maybe—"

"Let's let the police figure it out," I said. "Do the last card." I swallowed the rest of my tea. "I'm really tired." My anxiety from the sounds we'd heard was fading. I was calmer now, certain they'd been nothing but the sounds of an old house, amplified by frayed nerves after being woken the night before, finding a dead body, and the stress of the detective's repetitious questions. Now, I wanted to sleep.

"Don't rush." She lifted the final card and let out a little shriek. "Oh. This is so scary. I'm …" Without turning over the last card, she swept up the other two and put all three face down on top of the deck. "Maybe I made a mistake. We didn't take enough time to center ourselves before I shuffled them. I shouldn't have …"

Hating myself for being caught up in her game, I blurted out the question before I could stop myself. "What is it?"

"I can't tell you. You're too distrustful. You aren't approaching it with a sense of quiet curiosity." She stood. "Let's go to bed." She bent down and picked up her mug.

Once I was in bed, I found myself unable to sleep after all. I lay staring into the darkness. Images of Charlotte's motionless body in the moonlight, the memory of the inexplicable sounds, and burning curiosity about that final Tarot card circled in my head. The disturbing thoughts turned faster and faster, as if they meant to spin my mind into a state of wakefulness that would remain until daylight.

14 THEN: PETER

The moment I first saw Sara Linden-Price, I think I loved her a bit. Not the stuff of fiction. It wasn't love at first sight—knowing the moment I laid eyes on her she was the woman for me, or we were soul mates from the instant we smiled at each other. But her singular focus on me and my band told me what kind of person she was—fully there in the moment, captivated by our music. I didn't see her even glance at her phone the entire evening, and her table was close enough to the small stage that I would have noticed. That alone set her apart from ninety percent of the others who came to support local musicians in the wine bar where we played.

I also loved that she allowed her body to move with the music. Not wiggling and snapping her fingers, drawing attention to herself, but letting herself gently follow the notes with her entire being.

And then she was gone.

It was another three weeks before I saw her again. *That* night, I knew I had to talk to her.

As soon as I sat at her table and said hello, I noticed she was wearing a wedding band, but by then, it was too late.

She asked how long I'd been playing the guitar. She was stunned and fascinated that I'd written all the music and lyrics myself, so we spent a lot of time talking about that. She was utterly fascinated by my ability to combine chords and notes with words, making them all come together. It's what every songwriting musician does, but she'd never met one before. She listened as if I were explaining the secrets of the universe.

We didn't talk about her art until I was on my second beer and she'd agreed to let me order her another glass of red wine. She was a sculptor, making small figures in clay—mostly dancers without faces, focused on the movement of their bodies and the flow of their hair.

The bar closed, and we said goodnight. She told me she probably wouldn't be back for a few weeks, but she would be back.

It became a regular thing. Every three weeks on Friday night, there she was at the same table. After I finished playing, we talked until the bar closed. One night, after she'd been coming for about three months, I noticed that her wedding ring wasn't on her finger. By then, she'd already told me about her marriage. Before that, we'd talked about all our past loves. She'd mentioned some of the small disappointments in her marriage, then the big ones.

The house of silence, she called it. Her husband was perfectly content to live side by side, sharing meals and a social life, having sex and keeping up their beautiful home, but he wasn't interested in conversation beyond small talk. He didn't have much to say, he'd told her. She already knew everything there was to know about him. What more was there to reveal? His feelings were typical, he said. Sometimes he got angry at petty things, sometimes he felt down, mostly he was content with his life. What was there to share? What feelings was he supposed to be discussing?

"He doesn't get it," Sara said. "I feel as if I'm trying to communicate with a being from another planet." She laughed when she said this, but her eyes glittered with tears.

I let her talk and said little, not wanting to be seen as the guy beating up on someone I now viewed as the competition.

By then, she was coming to my shows every two weeks. On a July evening, after I knew just about everything there was to know about her, we stood in the parking lot outside the darkened bar, and I put my arms around her waist. I pulled her toward me and kissed her. When she kissed me back, I thought my heart might explode across the sky, the pieces of it becoming stars of their own.

By then, I was absolutely in love with her. And I think she was in love with me, although we hadn't said anything about it.

After the night we kissed, we stopped hanging around drinking and talking when I was finished playing. We went to my two-bedroom cottage the minute my guitar case was snapped closed. Thursday, Friday, and Saturday nights until two in the morning. Then she slipped out of bed, dressed, and returned to her husband.

It went on this way for months. For too long, but it took her a while to decide what she wanted to do.

"Brian and I have a history." She was quiet for several minutes. "I'm not sure why I even think that. What is history, even? Our house. We turned it into something amazing together. And trips— we've traveled to so many places. And he's part of my art. It's hard to explain that, but he is. I can point to every piece I've done and tell you how he influenced it. Not directly, not that he told me how to sculpt or what to create or anything controlling like that. But memories, things I was thinking at the time, or what we were going through." She stared into the middle distance, hardly seeming to notice I was there.

I was getting impatient. I wondered what she was waiting for.

15 NOW: TRINITY

When I woke the following morning, I felt rested, although I had the sensation that I'd lain awake for hours, thinking about that final Tarot card, hating myself for wondering what it had been.

I loved Mia, and I completely understood her love for the cards. Her mother had been addicted to them. She bought Mia her first deck for her twelfth birthday. When her mother was diagnosed with Alzheimers and eventually disappeared into a world in which Mia was only the pretty girl who brought fresh flowers every day and homemade cookies once a week, Mia became even more attached to the cards. I got it. And it didn't bother me. Everyone chooses their philosophy with which they approach the mystery of life. I just didn't like it when she shoved them down my throat.

Now, I wasn't sure if she'd been truly frightened, or she was trying to make me beg her for more by stirring up my curiosity. I vowed to put it out of my mind.

Seeing her at the stove making an omelet restored my sense of normality.

"Hi, sleepyhead. Did you have a good rest?" Her voice was cheerful and light.

"I did. How about you?"

"Absolutely. Pleasant dreams and all that." She eased the spatula under the omelet and turned it over. "Have a seat. This is almost ready."

"You're spoiling me."

"You deserve it. Have you heard from David? Is he coming tonight?"

"He's delayed. Some issue I don't really understand."

"Aw. That's too bad. But we can get busy and make lots of progress, so he'll be surprised when he gets here."

"I suppose."

After we ate, washed the dishes, and showered, we went for a walk. We kept our pace brisk, both of us studiously avoiding any mention of Charlotte's death, the secret Tarot card, or anything else related to my new house, which was feeling less tranquil by the day.

When we returned home, Mia went directly to the pantry.

"Hungry already?" I asked.

"No. I was thinking we should check the basement again to see if there's a wild animal trapped down there."

"How would it have gotten in?"

"Those windows. Maybe a broken air vent. Maybe it's a rat. They can get in anywhere."

"But it sounded like it came from the kitchen."

"Kitchen, pantry, basement. They're all on top of each other," Mia said.

"Okay, but—"

"Let's just check."

I followed her down the basement steps. We walked slowly around the concrete enclosure. We opened the storage cabinets, both of which were empty. A few unlabeled moving boxes were stacked neatly under the workbench.

"That's strange they didn't take those out," I said.

Mia agreed.

Neither of us said the obvious—we couldn't call Charlotte about that now. And calling her office at this point in time seemed a little cold-hearted. Maybe I would ask Brian about them. Or simply get rid of them myself after a while. Obviously, no one cared that much about whatever was in them.

We looked up at the three narrow windows that gave a bit of light to the underground space. All were closed and locked. On one wall, underneath the laundry room, was a narrow closet. I felt nervous as I turned the slightly loose, old-fashioned knob to open it. I wasn't sure what I was expecting. The rest of the basement was neat and clean as a basement can be.

I pulled open the door. The closet was empty. I couldn't even see why it was there because it didn't have shelves or a pole to hang clothes. It was possible it had been used to store ski equipment, or supplies for her sculpting work. I closed the door.

"No animals looking for free rent," I said.

"Not even any droppings," Mia said.

We returned to the kitchen. As Mia started into the living room, she stopped and let out a piercing scream. I pressed my fingers against my ears to dull the sound.

"What's wrong?"

Mia stood in the center of the archway as if she were frozen. She stared at the floor in front of the couch. I came up behind her and saw that the Tarot cards from the night before were laid out on the floor. The first two cards were the same ones I'd seen, placed in the same positions—the empress and the scythe. The third, based on the look of terror that consumed Mia's face, must have been the card I hadn't seen. It was an elaborate drawing of a snake draped around the branches of a half-dead tree.

I moved close to her and grabbed her wrist.

Not only was someone in the house right now, or just moments earlier, but someone had been there last night, close enough to have seen the cards she'd laid out. I wanted to cry.

"We should leave," Mia said.

I gripped her wrist more tightly, knowing I was hurting her, but unable to stop my fingers from curling into her flesh and bones, digging deeper, trying to hang on, trying to find strength and some kind of logical explanation for what we were looking at.

"Someone is in the house," she said, her voice half shrieking, half crying. "We need to get out."

"I don't want to leave."

"It could be Charlotte's killer ... or a serial killer. Maybe her killer is a ... they do things like this, lay out clues and hidden messages."

"It's not a hidden message. It's just the cards we were looking at last night."

She peeled my fingers off her arm. "This is absolutely a message."

I was terrified, but I didn't want to leave my house. I was here to fix it up for my sister's son. My son. He would become my son, our son. Would I feel that someday? Would he feel that? I had no way of knowing, but I had to provide everything he needed. And Jen had wanted him to experience a place like this that reminded us of the summers we'd spent at our grandmother's farm.

I didn't want to leave. I *couldn't* leave. I'd dreamed of this house for months. I'd promised Jennifer I would love every minute of creating a home that would build tangible, solid, lifelong memories for Ryan. "There has to be an explanation. Maybe ..." I couldn't think of a single, reasonable explanation.

"What if he was in the house?" Mia asked.

"Who?"

"The ex. He seems to think it's still his house."

"Brian?"

"Yes," Mia said. "He acts like he owns the place."

"No he doesn't."

"Maybe he's being nice, so you'll trust him."

"For what? It's not like he can steal a house."

"He can scare you away." She gave me a look that seemed to say —*You know I'm right.*

But I didn't know that. She was just guessing.

"Charlotte gave you an extra key," she said. "How do you know there weren't more keys? And she gave one to him?"

"Why would she do that?"

"Or maybe he killed her for giving it to you instead of to him, because he wanted that key. And maybe he found a way to get inside without it." She scooped up the cards. "I'm sorry you had to see that."

I ignored her.

She turned to face me. "Do you want to come stay with me? Should you call David first? Or … what? What's wrong?"

"I'm not going to freak out and leave."

"You absolutely should. This is a situation that calls for freaking out."

"Why?"

"Either it was him, or a serial killer, or … maybe this place *is* haunted."

I laughed. "Come on, Mia."

"How else did the cards get out? The person who killed Charlotte—"

"We don't even know yet if she was murdered."

"Someone was in this room! Someone who saw the cards I was holding last night. Doesn't that scare you at all? What's wrong with you?"

"Of course it does. I'm terrified that someone was in the house. But I'm not assuming it was Brian. Or something … else. Are you sure we locked all the doors and windows? Because I will not swear to that a hundred percent. We went into the kitchen when we heard those noises. Someone could have come into the room and looked."

"I laid out new cards after that! Remember?!"

"But did you shuffle them when we went to bed? Those might have been right on top."

She glared at me. She looked almost angry that I had a reasonable explanation, even if it was only partial. She took a deep breath, almost a gasp. "Someone was in your house. The same day you found a dead body in your backyard. How can you stay here?"

I moved closer to her and put my arm loosely around her shoulder. "Of course I'm scared," I whispered. "But I don't want to leave. I just can't. We'll make absolutely sure we lock everything. Both of us will check. In fact, Charlotte said I should have the locks changed. I'll call someone today. But I can't leave. I'm here to fix up this beautiful house for Ryan and David. Once Ryan is with me, I won't have time."

At the mention of the locksmith, she calmed a little.

I made the call and scheduled the locksmith for mid-afternoon, gushing gratitude that she could make room for me that day.

After I called David and told him what had happened, and received his promise he would absolutely try his best to be here in a few days, Mia and I went out for lunch.

We didn't say it, but we needed to escape.

16 NOW: TRINITY

*D*etective Robbins rang the bell at eight thirty the next morning. "May I come in?" He didn't ask if it was a convenient time.

I stepped back and allowed him to step into the foyer. I turned and walked down the hallway to the living room. He gestured for me to take a seat on the couch. It didn't seem worth the effort to offer him a glass of water. He was all business, so we might as well get right to it.

"Where's your friend?" He glanced at his phone. "Ms. Theriault?"

"She's upstairs."

"Will you ask her to join us?"

I was halfway up the stairs when Mia came out of the front bedroom.

"The detective is here," I said.

She followed me down without speaking. When we were seated, Detective Robbins was blunt. "Ms. Hughes was strangled."

I gasped softly. Mia grabbed my hand.

"She died between eleven and one in the morning. So it's possible you heard her scream, or the sounds of a struggle. Arguing …"

"I told you, I didn't hear anything."

"And you?" He looked at Mia.

She shook her head.

"Nothing?"

"The room I'm sleeping in faces the front of the house," Mia said.

"It's likely she would have come from that direction. As would her killer …" His voice hesitated in a way I didn't like.

"I didn't wake up until I heard Trinity calling me," Mia said.

"As far as we've been able to discover so far, you may have been the last people Ms. Hughes spoke with. In person."

I didn't say anything.

"Why was she at your house Wednesday?"

"She came by to give me an extra key she'd forgotten."

"What did you talk about, besides the key?"

"A broken water hose on the washing machine," I said.

"That's it?"

"Yes.

"I understand she was here for more than half an hour."

"How do you—"

"That's a long time to discuss a hose."

"We talked about other things, but it wasn't anything important. Just chit chat."

"Everything is important." He gave me a stern look, as if he believed I'd told him an outright lie. He took a seat in the armchair, suggesting he'd decided this was going to take longer than he'd expected. "What else did you talk about?"

"It was … well, she … she was acting like maybe she thought the house was haunted." I laughed softly. "So I asked her if that's what she believed. It was just a silly conversation about nothing."

He looked at me as if I were unbalanced.

"Your neighbors said they heard raised voices."

"I don't think so."

"They did."

"I guess she was a little upset. I'm not really sure why. I don't think she liked it that I asked her about the hose. She thought her job was finished because the house had been sold."

He nodded. "Did you raise your voice?"

"No."

"Your neighbors said your voices were quite loud."

"What neighbors? I haven't even met my neighbors. I've only been here a few days."

"Did you and Ms. Hughes argue?"

"No. I told you, she was upset that I mentioned some repairs, and she seemed to imply that the house might be haunted." I laughed again, hating how I sounded saying those words. "I think she was upset because the previous owner was a close friend. And she died here." I shrugged. "I don't know what else to tell you."

"There was a text message from Ms. Hughes to a friend of hers saying you were being difficult."

I laughed. "I don't think asking my real estate agent, who made a very nice commission on this house, a few questions about repairs, should be considered difficult."

"Having a shouted argument and talking to a grieving woman about ghosts could be considered ... upsetting."

I felt as if my breath was frozen inside my lungs. I tried to let it out slowly but instead, I coughed, feeling tears prick the backs of my eyes. "You're making more out of this than is there. She brought an extra key. I asked about a broken hose. She acted like she was afraid of something, or that there was something she wasn't telling me. When I pushed her on it, she danced around the idea that she believed the house was haunted, which I thought was absurd. That's all. And I don't see what any of that has to do with her ending up strangled in my backyard."

Detective Robbins was quiet for what felt like several minutes. Mia had let go of my hand and I could feel her shifting her position beside me, re-crossing her legs, adjusting her elbow on the armrest, moving her hair off her shoulders. I wondered what she was thinking, wondered why she hadn't said anything. I supposed she was waiting to be asked a direct question.

It was an unfamiliar experience to be questioned by the police. At first, I'd felt intimidated, afraid of saying the wrong thing, but now I was irritated. He almost acted as if he thought I'd strangled Charlotte myself.

Did he think that? Why would I do that? Did I strike him as a person who would kill another human being? Did he think I even had the strength? It made me want to laugh it was so ridiculous. I felt my chest spasm with an inappropriate, almost hysterical laugh. I managed to suppress it.

"We're having trouble coming up with a theory as to why she was murdered on your property," he said.

"Maybe someone killed her and brought her body here," Mia said.

"That's not what the autopsy showed."

I felt Mia stiffen beside me. I wondered if she didn't believe him, or she didn't believe an autopsy could show something like that.

"Do you have any idea why she would be in your yard in the middle of the night?" Detective Robbins asked.

"No," I said.

"Did she try to contact you?"

"No."

"And you're absolutely sure you didn't see anyone when you looked out the window, when you went into the yard?"

"I already told you, *no*."

"Now that you've had more time to think through your memories of that evening. Often—"

"I told you I didn't see anyone. I didn't hear anyone. There was no one in my yard. There were no screams."

He let out a deep, aggravated sigh. He leaned forward as if he hoped by looking at us with eager anticipation, we might remember something that would help him. After a long pause, he pushed himself to his feet. He wasn't a large man, but he acted as if this act required extraordinary effort.

"There's a reason she was on your property in the middle of the night. There's a reason she was murdered less than forty feet from your back door. Once we get the answers to those questions, we'll be closer to understanding what happened. Closer to finding out who did this."

Mia and I stood. I moved toward the hallway, but Detective Robbins remained rooted to the spot.

"I hope you figure it out," Mia said.

"That's an interesting comment. You sound as if her death has nothing to do with you."

"It doesn't," she said.

"That's not accurate. All crimes involve the community, the witnesses, the victims connected to the primary victim—in this case, her family and friends, her colleagues. In a crime like this, the entire community is a victim because it puts people on edge. There's a sense of fear that takes hold until we find the perpetrator. And in this case, it most certainly has a lot to do with both of you." He gestured toward both of us, as if it were obvious.

"It is scary," Mia said.

"My point is, you can't disengage, as it sounds like you're doing. It takes a village to solve a crime. And the two of you are key to this case."

"But we're not," I said.

"From my perspective, you're the focal point. As far as we've been able to determine, you were the last to speak to her. Your property is the crime scene. And because the community is sensitive to outsiders with money who are buying homes here for investment purposes, there's some extra attention, so you need to understand what I'm facing."

"This isn't about you." It was the wrong thing to say to a police detective. I knew that as I heard the words coming out of my mouth, but out they flowed as if my brain had come unhinged as sharply and suddenly as the screen door on my sunroom.

He raised one eyebrow ever so slightly. "I'll be back with more questions as we continue to investigate." He left the room, and a moment later the front door opened and closed.

"Well," Mia said. "That was not fun."

We looked at each other. I hoped she wouldn't suggest turning to her Tarot cards for an answer. I also wondered how he would ever find out who had killed Charlotte if he believed we were the keys to solving her murder.

17 NOW: TRINITY

*M*ia indeed wanted to consult her cards as I'd feared.

I shook my head, backing toward the doorway. "I've had enough with the cards. I need to call David. And I want to meet these neighbors who claimed they heard us shouting. Either sound travels much farther than I realized around here, or they're lying about me because they don't like *people with money*." I laughed, more bitterly than I'd expected.

"Yeah. What was that about?" Mia asked.

"Are you coming with me?"

"It's still early. Do you think—"

"I don't care."

"You go. It's better if you're alone. Less intimidating." She gave me a weak smile. "And you're the actual neighbor, not me."

There wasn't anything intimidating about Mia, or about two women introducing themselves to the neighbors, but I wasn't going to argue.

I walked down my front drive to the street, past a few large Eucalyptus trees surrounded by nicely manicured grass, and then over to their driveway. There was no fence or bordering plants to give a clear indication where our property ended and theirs began. At the sides of the houses and extending to the back, the yards were divided by an eight-foot redwood fence, but in the front, the two ran into each other in a mesmerizing flow of green. It was a good idea to establish a good connection early to understand what agreement they had regarding keeping the yards maintained and looking uniform. I probably should have done this sooner. Maybe if I had, they wouldn't have told the detective that my realtor and I were shouting at each other the afternoon before she was murdered.

I shivered as the word passed through my mind with such finality. Before, I'd still half-believed she might have fallen and hit her head. What *had* Charlotte been doing in my backyard in the middle of the night?

I walked up the front path and rang the bell of their Spanish-style house. This was one of the things I loved about this older neighborhood—all the houses were distinctive, built in different time periods as the plots of land were gradually broken up into smaller lots over the decades. It gave a sense of individuality. The streets meandered with fewer angles and there were no sidewalks. It made me feel closer to the earth.

The front door opened immediately. A man in his early sixties, dressed in a dark blue T-shirt, faded jeans, and bare feet, towered over me. He was easily six-three, his body thick and muscular. His white hair was thick and styled with gel. He smiled with warmth that reached his light brown eyes.

"Danielle! Our new neighbor is here!" He stuck out his hand as if he were shoving a bouquet of flowers in my direction. "Tom Vargas. And you are?"

"Trinity Feld." I shook his hand. It was large and warm, swallowing mine, although I'd never thought of my hands as particularly small.

"I'd invite you in, but Danielle doesn't like strangers in the house when she hasn't done a full clean." He laughed.

A moment later, a curvy, dark-haired woman appeared behind

him. She didn't offer her hand and her smile was the minimal required to not look as if I were unwelcome and she would prefer that I turn and leave that moment.

"This is Danielle," Tom said. "Danielle, this is Trinity."

"What can we do for you, Trinity?" Danielle asked.

"I just wanted to introduce myself. Get acquainted with my new neighbors."

"You're a part-timer, right?" Tom said.

"But I'm here all summer. And my husband David will be here on the weekends."

"That's nice of him," Danielle said.

Her chill made it difficult for me to bring up the detective, but I didn't want to leave without setting things straight, without finding out whether they'd exaggerated my conversation with Charlotte, or the detective had.

I wondered if Danielle had been close to Sara. Maybe she was still grieving and was less than thrilled to see someone living in her friend's home. I realized Charlotte had never mentioned how long it had been since Sara had passed away. Suddenly, I felt uncomfortable, intrusive. I felt as if I'd taken over something that belonged to a beloved friend, that I didn't belong. "I'm sorry we're meeting under these circumstances …"

Danielle took a step back, as if she wanted to hide behind her larger-than-life husband.

"I just talked to Detective Robbins. He said he'd spoken to you?"

"Yes. Nice guy. Very thorough," Tom said.

I nodded. I hadn't yet decided if he was a nice guy. I really had no opinion of him as a guy at all. To me, he was a government official who wanted something from me that I couldn't provide. "He mentioned you heard Charlotte shouting at me? Or—"

"Loud voices carry out here," Danielle said.

"No buildings and traffic to drown them out," Tom said.

"I don't recall her shouting."

"Both of you," Danielle said.

I glanced toward my house. No matter how many times someone used that word—*shouting*—I knew we'd barely raised our voices. Our tones had been sharp, possibly. But no one was *shouting*. I kept my head turned, looking at where the side fences divided our two yards.

Now I wondered if the reason we'd been overheard was because someone, and my bet was on Danielle, had been purposely listening. Someone standing behind their gate might have heard our conversation—everything from the broken hose to the speculation about the supernatural.

At this point, the details of my conversation with Charlotte had blurred in my mind, and if the detective asked me to recall exactly what I'd said, I wasn't sure I could. I only remembered her starting to say something and very deliberately stopping herself—as if she were frightened of something specific. I'd been the one to bring up the idea of some essence of the previous owner, or whatever you wanted to call it, lingering inside my house. But that was the impression Charlotte had created.

I studied my new neighbors. I didn't want to argue with them about the volume of my conversation. A disagreement didn't seem like a good way to begin a neighborly relationship. But I didn't like that the police believed I was the last one to see, and argue, with a woman who had ended up dead outside my bedroom window.

My chest felt tight, and I wasn't sure I could speak without my voice trembling. This was not the summer I'd planned for myself, for my orphaned nephew, for David. This wasn't the welcome to our new home I'd envisioned. I couldn't imagine things going any more wrong than they had. "I'm sorry you interpreted it as an argument."

"Charlotte was upset," Danielle said.

I laughed softly. "Well, I wanted to meet you and tell you how excited I am to be here. I didn't mean to start off by talking about something horrible. I'm sure the detective will find out who did this awful thing and we can move past it. I just love the house. We're really excited to get it fixed up and—"

"Fixed up?" Danielle asked.

"Yes. Fresh paint, refinishing. Some of the flooring ... and maybe open up some of the rooms so that—"

"That house is a classic. Sara restored it to its original charm. It's a little insulting to suggest it needs *fixing up*," Danielle said.

"I just—"

"It's fine." Tom's voice was louder than necessary. "A fresh coat of paint is always welcome. Thanks for stopping by, Tiffany. It was great meeting you."

"Trinity," I said.

"What?"

"My name is Trinity."

He laughed. "Of course it is. "Thanks, *Trinity*. We'll talk soon."

"Bye now." Danielle stepped around her husband and closed the door.

Walking back to my house felt like a monumental effort. My first encounter with my new neighbors couldn't have gone worse if I'd tried. I wondered if we would ever be cordial. Tom seemed friendly at first, but then, so eager to be rid of me. I wasn't sure if I'd said something off-putting or if Danielle had signaled him in some way.

I trudged up the front steps, sat on the top one, took out my phone, and called David. After a few rings, his voicemail picked up.

"Please call me," I said. "There's so much going on. The main thing is that Charlotte was definitely murdered. I guess I'm not surprised. I think I knew that in my gut, but it was still hard to hear."

Placing the phone on the step beside me, I turned my face up to the sky for a moment, then closed my eyes and rested my head in my hands as if I were gently placing it into a bowl. My life felt like a dream. The house I'd longed for sat behind me, nearly empty—an unfulfilled promise. David felt farther away every day. Even my nephew, whom I hadn't seen now for almost two weeks, felt slightly unreal. I tried to remember his warm, tiny hand gripping mine, the weight of his body when I carried him.

I felt like nothing was real. Even Charlotte's body, crumpled in the moonlight, her eyes gazing up at the sky, felt like something I remembered from a dream.

18 NOW: PETER

That dark hair and her flawless skin made me long to be back in the house, sleeping beside her. All those mornings when I'd woken to see the bright sun on the white pillowcase, her hair like smooth, creamy chocolate spilled beside me.

As I watched her sitting on the front porch, her face in her hands, the sun on her hair, I wanted to sit beside her and put my arm around her, pulling her close. I felt her against me as if it had only been several minutes since we'd last held each other. I could feel her breath against my cheek and hear her voice in my ear, feeling it vibrating in my bones.

This sharp pain in my chest, screaming that she was gone forever was a lie. It had to be. The pain, like a needle piercing me until I bled, whispered that she *was* gone. Her body had been burned to ash.

But that wasn't right.

There she was. The sun gleaming on her dark, thick hair. All of it grown back, lush and silky, so soft I could lose my fingers in it forever, feel it draped across my skin.

I hadn't made the worst mistake of my life. I hadn't left her all alone, night after night. She was still mine.

She would always be mine.

All I had to do was walk up those steps and sit beside her. Kiss her mouth, letting the moment last until eternity, until neither of us could contain our desire. We would talk. The words would flow between us as they always had, binding our souls together.

It was only a bad dream that her hair had fallen out of her head, clinging to her fingers in clumps, drifting to the floor, leaving her scalp naked and exposed, telling me what was coming.

She was right there. Healthy and full of love, her body the way I remembered it—lithe and slender, her eyes looking into mine, her hands touching me, her smile full of love, life spilling out of her.

19 NOW: TRINITY

When I finally peeled myself off the front steps, still without a response from David, and went into the house, I found Mia in the laundry room.

"I was thinking we should work on ripping up this flooring. We can pull the washer out and see if there's any water underneath. You don't want mold or worse, dry rot setting in."

"I don't think it happens that fast." I pressed my fingertips into my forehead. Her words were jarring. It was as if the visit from the detective and my unwelcoming encounter with my neighbors hadn't happened.

"Maybe not dry rot, but mold can. You don't want that nasty stuff taking root in your house. It's a health hazard. And with the little one coming." She gave me a warning look.

"I don't know if you and I can move a washing machine." I kicked the toe of my shoe at a place where the linoleum had curled up. It looked grimy on the exposed bottom. I didn't think it had come loose from the water leak. It looked as if it had been that way for a while. "I could call Brian to see if he'd be able to help."

"Not a good idea," Mia said.

"Why not?"

"Because it's weird to have the ex of a dead woman helping us in a house that used to be his. Haven't I made that clear?"

"Don't say it like that."

"Why? That's what it is. That's what he is."

"He's a nice guy."

"So? And why? Why is he so nice? Have you asked yourself that question?"

I laughed. "Because people are generally nice, that's why. You're being ridiculous." I pulled out my phone. "If you want to work on this, and I would love to do something to get my mind off murder, that's for sure. I think we need help. I don't want to be moving appliances."

"He's too interested. I don't think he should be involved. You need to hire a regular handyman. Or maybe it's time to get a contractor for the bigger projects you're talking about."

"Some of the bigger projects will be done after Ryan's here. Obviously, I can't do all of that right away."

"Fine. But you still need a handyman who doesn't—"

"I don't understand why you're so hostile toward him. Maybe you're attracted and you don't want to admit it?" I gave her a teasing smile. "It might be time, you know."

Mia had been through an ugly breakup, but it was months ago. With a guy I'd never even met. It had been a long-distance thing. She'd met him when she was on a trip to the UK, exploring her roots. It was right before my sister was diagnosed. She'd fallen hard and fast. She ended up extending her trip to spend time with Ethan. They'd had an intense relationship over video chats and text messages. He'd come to the US once, but I'd been with my sister at the time, so it hadn't worked out for us to meet up. Mia had made a second trip to the UK, and then, in some spectacular, dramatic spectacle, foretold by her Tarot cards, according to Mia, she'd caught him cheating on her.

Catching someone cheating when they were on another continent sounded complicated to me, but she said it was blatant. He'd sent her messages meant for the other woman.

Since then, she hadn't even gone on a date. She said her flirting skills had been smothered. She saw a cute guy and just didn't have it in her. She smiled, but she couldn't come up with anything clever to say, even if he started things.

"I'm not attracted to him." She gave the washing machine a shove, but it didn't budge.

"He's really sweet," I said. "He seems thoughtful."

"If you say so."

"I'm calling him."

"You're making a mistake."

"We'll find out."

She tucked her hair behind her ears and folded her arms across her ribs.

Brian answered on the first ring. I started by telling him I wouldn't accept his help unless he allowed me to pay for his time. He wanted to know what the job was. We talked in small circles on that point for a few minutes before he agreed I could pay him.

When he conceded, I told him about the leak and the water-soaked floor and walls.

"Oh, yeah. You want to deal with that sooner rather than later," he said.

Because she was standing so close to me, Mia could hear his voice. She gave me a smug look. I gave her one in return, since his agreement should cement the fact that Brian was a good guy who had met her always-fluid criteria of what constituted a *good guy*.

When I hung up, she didn't say anything, and neither did I.

After lunch, I took a nap. When I came downstairs thirty minutes before Brian was due to arrive, Mia was sitting on the living room floor with her Tarot cards arranged in front of her. I ignored the cards, gave her a neutral greeting, and retreated to the kitchen.

My mood was calm. David had texted he would *absolutely be there by Wednesday. No matter what.* He could sense how much I needed him. He knew I was strong and capable, knew I was perfectly equipped to handle all of this myself.

David: *We're in this together!*

He insisted he was aware that I wanted his input and his enthusiasm.

David: *I will definitely be there. I know how important this is to you.*

I wasn't sure he did, but I appreciated his attempt to understand.

20 NOW: TRINITY

From the moment Brian stepped into the house, I knew it wasn't going to go well with him and Mia. Forget any imagined attraction between them. I would be lucky if we managed to get the laundry room torn apart without Mia raking her nails across his face.

"Unbelievable what happened to Charlotte," he said. "And right here. In our own back—"

"You mean *Trinity's* backyard." Mia's voice was so loud I recoiled slightly.

As if he hadn't heard, Brian continued. "Sara would be …" He looked grief stricken, the very definition of the word. "I still can't believe it happened. Charlotte is more full of life than almost anyone I know. She's … she poured her heart into doing right by this house, by Sara. Everything. She treated it like it was her own. Sara would have been so pleased. That's why she chose Charlotte as her executor. With all the problems at the end …"

He shook his head.

"What problems?" Mia asked. She sounded as demanding as the detective, as if she had a right to know, as if Brian were required to answer her question.

He stared at her, stunned. "Forget I said anything." He shook his head again. "It's just …. murdered? It's such a shock. We're all shocked. No one can believe it. Everyone loved her. She was so well-respected."

"Obviously not everyone," Mia said.

"Mia!" I looked at her, but she didn't meet my gaze.

Brian leaned against the wall. He ran his hand down the molding of the doorway leading into the small, west-facing room across the hall from the laundry room. When the house was staged for sale, it had been set up as an entertainment room. "This was Sara's studio, you know."

"I didn't," I said.

"Why don't we get to the reason you're here?" Mia said. "I don't think it's helpful to talk about the woman who used to live here."

Brian looked as if she'd punched him in the face. He crossed the hall and stepped into the laundry room.

I grabbed Mia's wrist. She tried to pull away from me, but I held on tightly until she was forced to look at me. "What?"

"Be nice," I whispered.

"He should be nice. This is *your* house, not his. And not hers. Not anymore."

"Okay, but he has memories."

"He should keep them to himself."

"It doesn't bother me."

"It should. I'm trying to look out for you."

"I know." I gave her wrist a gentle, appreciative squeeze and let go.

He stood in the laundry room, staring at the floor. "So what are the plans?" he asked.

I explained what had happened with the hose.

"Have you picked out flooring? Paint?"

"I don't know. I was thinking … what do you suggest?"

"It's not his house," Mia said. "You should decide what you want. If it's too much for him, we should be hiring a contractor. He's not a tile layer or ... you should probably just rip out what's here and finish scraping the walls. We should get a licensed contractor for the rest. This is beyond handyman skills."

"You're right," Brian said. "But it was my house. And I see the laundry room as just that—a place to do laundry. Nothing fancy. I don't think you want to go to the expense of laying tile in a room that's simply a workroom. It's not a place of beauty."

"You are so wrong," Mia said, straightening her shoulders as if she were about to make a speech. "It's a key part of caring for a family. Trinity will be folding her ... well, her adoptive son's clothes in here. She'll be spending hours in this room, making things clean and comfortable for the people she loves. The room should be a pleasant environment for her."

I wished I'd met with Brian alone. There was no reason for Mia to be with us. She was making it more complicated than necessary. I was also realizing that starting in this room was a mistake. I wanted the house to have a cohesive makeover. Not a hectic, thrown together collage of painted rooms and patched up damage that was repaired as it broke.

"Maybe I need to take a step back," I said. "It doesn't need to be taken care of today."

"Absolutely not," Brian said.

Mia gave an exaggerated sniff. "I smell mold."

"I don't think you do," Brian said.

"I know what I smell."

He folded his arms across his chest. "This house does not have mold. I've spent years—"

"It's not your house!" Mia said.

"I'm aware."

"Then stop acting like it is."

"I don't think I did. I'm just saying—"

"You are. You talk like it belongs to you and you walk around like you're the man of the house."

"Maybe I'd better go," Brian said.

"Please, don't," I said. "There was a lot of water spraying out when the hose came apart and I do want to make sure it's completely dry. I really appreciate your help." I gave Mia a gentle push. "Thanks for your help, Mia. But let me handle this."

"I don't think this is a good—"

"Mia. Please."

She put up her hands. "I'm trying to—"

"I know." I patted her shoulder.

She backed out of the room, then disappeared from sight.

Brian had the good manners not to make any comments about her attitude. He told me he would rip up the floor and bring over a fan to dry out the room. I could spend the next day or so thinking about what I wanted to do while it aired out.

I walked with him to the front door. He moved slowly, as if he wanted to absorb every sight and smell within the walls of the home that used to be his. At the threshold, he paused, gripping the door-frame. After a moment, he stepped outside and turned to face me. "Is everything okay? Your friend seems really upset."

"She likes to take care of me. We've been friends forever."

He tipped his head to one side. "I'm sure Charlotte's murder is upsetting."

"It is."

"Having the police here must be stressful," he said.

"Yes."

"Hopefully, they'll find her killer sooner rather than later."

"I hope so," I said.

"You're okay here alone?"

"I'm not alone. Mia's with me."

He nodded.

"And my husband is coming. Soon."

"That's good."

"Thanks for your help."

"I'll be back with some fans. It should only take me a few hours to get that floor ripped out. The damp smell will go away once the flooring is gone. It's not really mold, just damp."

"That's good to know."

"Take care," he said.

When he was gone, I closed the door and locked it. I was shocked at the sense of relief I felt, knowing the locks had been changed and there was no way Brian could possibly have a key.

I turned away from the door, startled to find Mia standing less than three feet behind me.

"I think you're making a mistake letting him work on your house," she said.

"You've made that real clear."

"He makes me very uncomfortable."

"Clearly."

"He's going to try to remodel it to his vision, maybe to hers. He's going to insert himself and try to take over. He might even—"

"Is this your idea, or something you read in your cards?"

"You know I'm right. I know you can feel it. He touches the walls like he's running his hands over a woman's body."

I laughed. "Don't be ridiculous."

She narrowed her eyes. "Don't be blind."

"I think it's kind of sweet that he feels so connected."

"There's nothing sweet about it. He thinks it's still partially his. He's too attached. It's not healthy, and it's going to come back to bite you."

"You're being dramatic."

I went into the kitchen and turned the kettle on for tea. She wasn't going to change her mind. I couldn't understand why Mia had taken such a strong dislike to him. I was grateful to have at least one friend in my new neighborhood, now that I knew my closest neighbors were less than thrilled to have me there.

In fact, it seemed as if one, if not both of them, might have gone out of their way to plant a seed in Detective Robbins's mind that I might be involved in Charlotte's murder.

21 THEN: PETER

The neighbors gave me the side-eye when I moved into Sara's house. I guess we shouldn't have been surprised, since it had only been a week since her husband moved out. But what business was it of theirs? They didn't know what had gone on in that house before.

Anyone who has experienced the slow decay and death of a marriage knows that it doesn't end when the suitcases are packed and the locks on the front door are changed. The cracks in the walls appear and the bond is fractured long before that. Years before. The foundation has already crumbled. Love faded, then dissolved, and too often, has been slowly transformed into something dark and ugly, like a tunnel dug beneath the house that will cause its eventual collapse.

That's when everyone finally sees the damage. They react with shock and horror. What happened? Everything looked idyllic. It was so *sudden*.

But it wasn't sudden at all.

The leaving is only the final sigh.

Sara paid Brian fairly for his share of the house. She loved the freedom of owning her own home. As the months began to roll past, she made small changes, even though she and Brian had spent years remodeling. She wanted a fresh look—to create a home that fully reflected her style. One by one, she repainted the rooms. Modern tile replaced the original, but now deteriorating, sunroom floor. The front porch was redone.

Even after I moved in with her, I kept my cottage. She liked her space, and I needed room for my music. I had a large insulated second building on my property that my band used for practice. I had a vegetable garden I'd cultivated for years that I didn't want to give up.

We cherished our autonomy. For some couples, when you've both come out of deeply painful relationships, you hoard your space. For me, the woman who had walked out of my life with our infant daughter on my thirty-first birthday had left a deep hole that Sara had slowly started to fill, but that meant we were on the same page. Things between us would be easy and open, without a lot of demands. Our connection was spiritual. We didn't need it all tied up in legal paperwork and real estate.

We could be together, and we would remain individuals. We were artists. Art requires time alone, time to think, time without interruption—even periods of loneliness and what others might call boredom. At least that was my view, and Sara seemed to agree.

So we fell into a comfortable, companionable routine.

I was at her house every night for dinner. I slept at her house, but I went to mine during the day so we could both focus on our work. Every few months, I traveled for a week or so with my band, but every weekend, I was out late. I occasionally crashed at my place because I was so wired after we played, it took a long time to come down and it just seemed easier that way. I didn't think about it, she didn't seem to object.

Eventually, the chill from the neighbors melted, and they invited us over for dinner. I helped Tom put in a new fence between their house and Sara's. We hosted a block party together on Labor Day weekend. Slowly, we became friends.

The only rough spot was Charlotte.

Sara and Charlotte had been friends since college and the two of them were as close as sisters. Charlotte was not my number one fan. She called me a whiner. Not to my face. Sara told me about it, laughing. She thought it was funny. I did not. I'd never once heard a whining tone in my voice, and I had no idea what she was talking about. It was a vicious thing to say, and I kind of wondered why Sara thought she needed to tell me about it.

Because we tell each other everything, she'd said.

We told each other everything. I liked that about our relationship. It was important to her that we talked. We had great conversations. I'm a talker and our best times were spent sitting up late, on the front porch in the summer, beside the fireplace in the winter, drinking a glass of wine and talking about everything in the world.

But I didn't whine. Talking about disappointments in my music career, the way my ex had turned my daughter against me, or problems with the neighbors is not whining. I really didn't appreciate the comment.

To my face, Charlotte was all laughs and *professionally* friendly. That was the thing I didn't appreciate about *her*. She was a little full of herself in her *professionalism*. Always selling, always dressed as if she were meeting clients, slick with makeup and expensive clothes. I wondered if the woman wore a button-down shirt when she was having sex. It wouldn't have surprised me.

Charlotte and I pretended to get along for Sara. We smiled and chatted. I tried not to think about her calling me a whiner. If you ask me, she was a bit of a whiner herself, always talking about the market being soft, about how onerous the financial regulations were.

I guess it takes one to know one.

After Sara was gone, the gloves came off.

22 NOW: TRINITY

When Brian returned with the fans and tools to tear up the laundry room floor, Mia had gone to the grocery store. I was relieved I wouldn't have to listen to her critical, worried verbal attacks against him. Without his kindness, I wasn't sure how I would be keeping the house in working order right now. I could have asked for recommendations on social media and hired someone that way, but I'd had enough experience to know that when it came to reviews and recommendations on social media, one person's positive outcome was another person's hair-pulling nightmare.

I liked Brian, and I appreciated his help. I didn't care that he felt affectionate toward a house that had been his for a decade. What I cared about was that someone was on my side as I faced a detective who was close to implying I might be guilty of something simply because a woman had been murdered in my backyard.

Brian backed his truck as close to the front porch as he could. I stood watching him inch closer, recognizing his comfort with the space, his knowledge of the area that had become instinctive from years of working around the house and yard. It made me wonder what the detective had asked him about Charlotte's murder, if Brian had any insights about why she'd been wandering around my yard after midnight.

Had Charlotte planned to meet someone here? Or had she been looking for something? After the way she'd acted, as if she truly believed Sara's spirit might be lingering around this space, was it possible that's why she'd returned? Maybe she was envious of me and believed I'd had a supernatural encounter that she might also experience with her deceased friend. I certainly wasn't going to ask Brian about that. I didn't need yet another person thinking I was slightly off balance simply because I'd asked the question.

I knew as well as anyone that grief played devious tricks on your mind, made you do things you never thought you would. I could absolutely see all-business, authoritative Charlotte crumbling when no one was watching, creeping around my yard, even considering using a key she'd held onto, thinking she might come inside and have one last conversation with her lifelong friend.

I'd certainly longed for more time with my sister. We'd talked constantly in those last weeks until she no longer had the strength. After she was gone, I'd found myself speaking out loud to her. I felt a physical ache in my throat, the need to say things to her, wishing with all my heart that she could hear me.

Brian got out of his truck, yanking me back to reality.

He grinned when he saw me. "Were you worried I was going to smash into the steps?"

"No."

"You look worried."

He was misreading my expression. How many times do we look at someone's face, imagining what we see there, inferring thoughts we believe another might be having because we've guessed at what the unconscious shape of their lips suggests?

He reached into the bed of the truck and lifted out a small electric fan. He placed it on the first step. He took out another.

"Do you want me to take these inside?" I asked.

"I'll get them."

"It's no problem." I walked down a few steps, picked up the base of one of the fans, grabbed the cord that was wrapped in a neat coil, and carried it into the house.

As I walked back to the front, I met him in the hallway. He was carrying the other fan and his toolbox. I followed him back to the laundry room and watched as he plugged in both fans and turned them on low. I'd already opened the window. The fans immediately began pulling fresh air into the room.

"These should have everything dried out in no time." He opened his toolbox and took out a scraper and a hammer. He squatted and used the claw end of the hammer to grab the linoleum, pulling it off the sub flooring in strips. Some of it lifted off easily, especially where it had buckled from the water. Other pieces tore, shredding and leaving thin layers stuck to the wood.

"This will take a while," he said. "No need for you to stand here."

"I can start scraping."

He turned and grinned. "You hired me to take care of it. I'll give you a shout when I'm done."

I left him alone and went upstairs. I thought about changing the sheets on our beds, but with the washing machine disconnected, I would have to wait until the next day. I wiped down the bathrooms, read for a while, then called David. He didn't answer.

I wasn't sure if I should be angry or hurt. I really needed to find out what was in the inspection reports before I went too much further. I wanted to have an actual conversation with him. Not a hurried phone call or exchange of text messages or voice mails. I'd hardly had a chance to tell him what the detective had said, and I hadn't even mentioned our neighbors. Or had I? I couldn't remember.

I got it that he was busy when he was traveling. His schedule was completely different from normal. He was with other people all the time—meetings all day, evening meals with large groups that took forever, never alone until late at night, and then he was often catching up on email. But still. I'd found a dead woman in our backyard! I needed him. He'd promised he would be here within a few days, but I had a nagging feeling he was going to back out on that because he hadn't given me any details about his flight.

I wandered back downstairs, resisting the urge to follow the sounds of the fans and the scraping that was grating on my ragged nerves. It sounded as if there were rats trapped inside the walls, trying to scratch their way out.

Walking quickly to escape the sounds, I went into the room across from the guest bedroom at the front of the house. It had been staged as an office when I saw the house. There was a large window facing the front porch. The walls were painted burnt orange, a strange color choice for an office, but maybe she'd wanted to make it feel less corporate. I planned to transform it into a playroom for Ryan.

I stood in the center and closed my eyes, imagining low, built-in shelves along two walls. I tried to picture the color that would be the most inviting, making Ryan feel at home. Maybe a pale blue or green, with carpet the same color. I could almost see the soft color surrounding my nephew, playing with wooden blocks as he sat on the floor on a rainy afternoon.

"Trinity?"

Hearing Brian call my name made me realize it had been several minutes since I'd heard the scraping. I opened my eyes and turned. Brian stood in the doorway. Sweat stained his T-shirt around his collarbone and in a V-shape at the center of his chest. The edges of his hair were damp as well. He wiped his hand across his forehead.

"I'm finished. I'll leave the fans going and the window open. You can turn them off this evening. But it would be a good idea to keep them running for the next few days."

I took a few steps toward him. "You have no idea how much I appreciate this."

"I'm happy to do it. I enjoy working on houses. I do it for my neighbors and a few friends, too." He grinned. "A hobby that brings in a few extra bucks."

I smiled.

"I'm sorry your friend finds me threatening," he said.

I shrugged. "You give the impression you're still really attached to the house. That's all."

He sighed. "I do miss it. It's an awesome house. Sara did a lot to restore its original character. She had a great vision for it, and I loved helping her. Until things turned sour."

"Mia thinks … she thinks you feel like it still belongs to you."

"No, I got a fair deal when we split. More than fair. It's all sentimental."

"That's good."

"Our divorce was amicable. As divorces go."

I nodded.

"We were friends. I drove her to all her chemo appointments. So …" He leaned against the doorframe.

"My sister died of cancer, too. I know how it is."

"I'm really sorry to hear that."

"It's brutal." I folded my arms around my waist as I felt the sharp burst of pain that sometimes accompanied memories of her suffering.

"It is. No one who hasn't watched it happen can really know," he said.

I shook my head, my throat and eyes too clogged with tears to say anything.

"Anyway. I'm really sorry for your loss," he said.

"Thank you," I whispered. "Yours too."

"I appreciate that," he said. "When you're divorced, people assume there's no loss. But there is." He patted the doorframe sharply, then stepped into the hallway. "I'll be back Monday. Does that sound good? Should be well dried by then."

"Yes. Thank you so much."

When he was gone, I wanted him to return. I felt as if it was the first real conversation I'd had since Jennifer had died. At the same time, that thought made me feel as if I were betraying my husband, as well as Mia.

A few minutes later, I saw a shadow pass by the window. I looked up. Tom and Danielle stood on the front porch. Danielle was peering in the window, her hands cupped around her face so she could get a better look at the room, and me.

23 NOW: TRINITY

I let out an involuntary yelp when I saw Danielle staring at me. She didn't move, didn't seem to register any shame that she was looking into my house, and had been caught in the act. I walked to the window and still she kept staring in at me. What did she expect to see? The room was empty.

I turned and went into the foyer.

Before I reached the front door, the bell rang.

I yanked open the door.

Tom stood there, smiling as if he were making a friendly, neighborly call and was about to hand me a plate of cookies to welcome me to my new home.

"Trinity! It is Trinity, right?"

"Yes. What can I do for you?"

"We just wanted to drop by and say hello. Danielle saw Brian over here and was curious to see what you're doing with the place."

Danielle appeared beside him.

"Hi, Danielle." I kept my voice steady. "Were you looking for something specific in my front room?"

"No." She smiled. "You don't have any furniture."

"I told you, I'm doing a few updates first. The house needs some TLC."

She glared at me. "TLC? What's that supposed to mean?"

"Nothing major. Just fixing things up. Calmer color schemes, some new flooring."

"Sara put a lot of work into this house over the years. A lot. She did it all herself. She poured her heart into it. And quite a bit of it was recent. I don't see the need for a do-over."

I didn't care whether she saw the need for anything. This was my house now. I could do whatever I wanted. I could knock down all the walls and create a single great room on the first floor, painting the remaining four walls a lurid purple. I could paint the exterior sunset orange and plant bird of paradise flowers all over the front garden with their bright orange blossoms and purple tongues to match.

Tom put his arm around his wife's shoulders. "Sara was ill for a long time. There were probably a few things that were neglected."

Danielle wriggled out from under her husband's comforting arm. "Sara was an artist. The house is stunning. And it has historical value. I hope you aren't planning to destroy its character."

I continued staring at her, trying to think of something to say that would get rid of them without creating a hostile relationship. Although maybe it was impossible to have a cordial, neighborly connection with a woman who resented that I wasn't someone else.

I wanted to be sympathetic to the loss of her neighbor, who had obviously been a good friend. But I didn't understand why she felt she had to attack me to cope with her feelings.

"Things were a little strange here," Tom said. "It was a weird situation."

"Don't," Danielle said. "Sara was a beautiful person. You have no right to judge her. Especially now, when she can't speak for herself."

"I'm not judging her. I just thought Trinity should know."

"She doesn't need to know. It's the past."

"I think she does. Since Brian is doing work here."

"Is that why you dragged me over here?" Danielle asked.

Tom sighed. "I thought you wanted to see how she was fixing the place up?"

Were they going to stand on my front porch and argue with each other? I felt uncomfortable, but I was curious to know what they were talking about.

"She's not going to let us inside. Besides, there's nothing to see. The house looks empty. What has Brian been working on?" She fired the question at me as if she believed I was up to no good. Almost as if she thought Brian and I might have plotted Charlotte's death and were now getting our alibis straight. I felt a shiver at the solid ice in her tone.

"As I said, the house needs some TLC. The washing machine hose broke and there's water damage."

She glared at me.

"Brian was always good about staying on top of things," Tom said.

"He's been a huge help," I said.

"It was a strange situation," Tom said.

"Don't start up on that again, Tom. Why are you so obsessed with other people's sex lives? It's sick."

"I'm not obsessed with their sex lives. But it was weird."

Danielle grabbed his arm. "I will not let you bad mouth her. I'm sick of it. Why can't you let it go? Sara was my friend. And she was a sweet, good person. She deserved to have love in her life. She just had a hard time finding the right man."

I desperately wanted to ask. At the same time, I was equally desperate to get Danielle off my porch. I was not going to invite her inside to give her any further details about my plans for the house.

"We were hoping to see what you've done," Tom said. "But it sounds like you're not ready."

I laughed. "Not even close. So far, it's been all repairs. The water damage. And the back screen door fell off." I let out another half-hearted laugh.

"When is your husband coming? Shouldn't he be doing all this? Instead of Sara's ex-husband?" Danielle asked.

"He's traveling," I said. "And I'm paying Brian to do the work." It sickened me that I'd fallen into explaining myself to her, but I felt attacked. The explanation tumbled out of my lips before I could stop it.

"We should let you get back to it." Tom took Danielle's hand and gave it a gentle tug.

"I really did want to see what you've done."

"I haven't done anything," I said. "Beyond repairs, and dealing with a murder in my backyard." I started to close the door. "Your husband is right, I should get back to it. Thanks for stopping by." I stepped away from the door.

Danielle opened her mouth, but said nothing.

I probably wasn't going to have a friendly relationship with them. I could hope for better with the neighbors on the opposite side, or possibly those behind me. There were other homes along the quiet, sparsely populated street.

Danielle had been determined not to like me before I'd even met her. I was living in a home where she believed I didn't belong.

24 NOW: TRINITY

*W*hen Mia came home, she and I spent the rest of the day making a plan for tackling my renovation projects. It was my idea to sit down with my notebooks and paint chips, Pinterest open on my tablet, which was propped up in front of us. I needed to purge Danielle from my head. I also wanted to forget about what Tom had said about Sara's relationships being a *weird* situation.

Despite faint stirrings of voyeuristic curiosity, I didn't care to hear gossip about a woman who had passed away and the man who was helping me fix my house. It had nothing to do with me. My vision for our home was to make it a peaceful retreat from a world that was racing toward technological submersion. It was to be a place where the little human being entrusted to our care could experience the outdoors. I wanted him to thrive and learn here. I'd seriously considered not having a TV in this house. I knew David wouldn't let me go so far as to not have an internet connection. In fact, I was pretty sure I couldn't live without that either, but I wanted to live in a way that wasn't constantly inhaling pop enter-tainment and content from the internet instead of the natural world.

Gossip and neighborhood rumors were not something I wanted to get involved with.

I needed to refocus.

The murder and the police were horrible enough.

I needed all of that out of my head.

Because some of the updates I had in mind would require a contractor and I didn't want to get started on that until David and I went over everything together, face-to-face, my plan was to start with the rooms where we would only be painting or staining the natural oak molding. We could strip wallpaper and scrape old paint. That alone would keep us busy for several days.

Even though I liked the authentic period feel of wallpaper, I knew I didn't want it in my home because it made the small rooms feel smaller. One of the features of the house was that it had a lot of rooms—four bedrooms, a kitchen and separate dining room, living room, the sunroom, and the two smaller rooms that would become the playroom and either a family room or possibly a home office for David. It wasn't a large house, so the rooms were small, and I planned to spend a lot of time thinking about the right color schemes and furniture to maximize the space.

After poring over my plans, we ate leftover spaghetti and green salad for dinner, talked for a while about the neighbors and Mia's disappointment over a canceled cruise to Acapulco that she'd planned with friends from her gym. We went to bed early.

A cold breeze across my face woke me in the middle of the night. I pulled the blankets around my neck, curling my head toward my chest and my knees up toward my hips. I missed having David beside me. But he'd traveled for extended periods before, and I hadn't woken every night, feeling cold and alone, overwhelmed by weariness while my body refused to sink back into sleep.

There was no doubt the murder was disturbing me on a deeper level than I'd realized. Maybe I was entering a new phase of dealing with the loss of my sister—the awareness that I would be living without her for the rest of my life.

I closed my eyes, trying to take a long, slow breath.

Again, I felt the cool breeze across my face.

I opened my eyes and sat up. I'd shut my bedroom window before going to bed because the night air had been unseasonably cool. Every window and door on the first floor was closed and locked because I'd checked them all before coming upstairs, and Mia had gone up to bed a few minutes before me.

I pushed off the covers and got up. I grabbed my phone off the floor. Twelve fifteen. I picked up my hoodie from the foot of the bed, shoved my arms into the sleeves and my phone into the pocket. I stepped into the hallway and walked toward the room at the front of the house where Mia was sleeping. The door was closed. Even if she had her window open, I wouldn't be feeling the breeze with that much intensity.

I went to the top of the stairs and stood there for a moment, wondering if I should wake Mia. If a door or window was open, did I have the courage to go down myself? It was possible she'd woken earlier and gone down for a glass of water or a snack, although I couldn't imagine her opening a window. She was feeling as overly cautious as I was.

Maybe it was just a drafty old house, and this was the coldest night since I'd been here. Maybe the door to the basement was open and there was enough cold air down there to cause a draft.

I'd never been a fearful person, and it made me a little annoyed with myself that I was allowing anxious thoughts of Charlotte's killer to race through my mind. Just because Charlotte had died in my yard didn't mean her murder was connected to my house. There *could* be a serial killer. It was something people feared and thought of too easily, even though it was actually somewhat rare. Still, it wasn't unheard of.

The detective hadn't said a word about anything like that. As far as I knew, there had been no other murders in the area before Charlotte's, so the coincidence of a new serial killer arising out of nowhere and choosing my backyard seemed a bit far-fetched. But I wasn't up-to-date on local crime. And serial killers moved around, didn't they?

Thoroughly disgusted that I was still arguing with myself when I could have gone down, checked the doors and windows and been snuggled back in bed by now, I turned on the light, pulled my phone out of my pocket in case I encountered an intruder, grabbed the railing, and walked quickly down the stairs.

At the bottom of the stairs, I no longer felt the breeze. I turned toward the living room. In the shadows beyond the light coming from the stairwell, I saw the faint shape of a person standing near the arched opening to the kitchen. I screamed. My phone started to slide out of my hand. I stooped slightly and managed to grab it with my other hand as it fell against my bent legs. I straightened, but whatever I'd seen was no longer there.

Upstairs, Mia's door crashed open and her feet thudded down the stairs.

"Trinity? What's wrong? Are you okay?"

A moment later, she was beside me. "What happened?"

"Someone's in the house." I spoke in a low, trembling voice. My hands shook as I tried to keep my phone from sliding away again. "In the kitchen."

She moved quickly to the opposite wall, reached around the arch, and tapped the wall switch to turn on the kitchen light. I crept up behind her. The room was empty. The basement door, visible in the small pantry area, was closed.

"Are you sure?" She walked past me and went into the sunroom. I heard the door wiggle as she yanked on the knob. "It's locked. Why do you think someone's in the house?" She returned to my side.

"I saw him ... or her."

"Where?"

"Right there." I pointed to the archway.

"Maybe you were sleepwalking?"

"I don't sleepwalk."

"You did one time. Remember?"

"That was years ago."

"Well ... there's no one here."

"I felt a breeze."

She looked around. She checked the living room windows and moved the drapes. "They're closed." She did the same with the kitchen windows. She walked down the hall. I saw light spill into the hallway as she entered the other rooms, checking windows.

When she was beside me again, she patted my shoulder. "I think you're on edge. From her murder. I am too. Let's get some water and go back to sleep." She returned to the kitchen, filled two glasses with water, handed one to me, and waited while I took a few sips.

Then, she nudged me toward the stairs, turning off lights as we went.

I climbed the stairs slowly, more certain than ever that I had not been sleepwalking. I had clearly seen someone standing near the archway.

In my room, I sent a text to David.

Trinity: *Are you definitely getting here Wednesday? I need you!*

25 NOW: TRINITY

I thought I'd gotten up early, showered, and shaken off my scare from the middle of the night. But when I came downstairs at six thirty, Mia was seated at the table with a cup of tea in front of her. She jumped up.

"Sit down. What kind of tea? Peppermint, cinnamon, or green tea?"

"Peppermint. I can get it."

"No, sit down. We need to talk. I was awake for a long time, thinking about what happened last night."

I laughed. "I don't know what there is to talk about."

"The thing that happened." She placed a mug in front of me, the string and tag trailing onto the table. She sat across from me and pushed the bowl containing her used tea bag toward me.

"I still don't know what there is to talk about."

"I wonder if you did see someone."

"I know I did."

"I'm sorry I tried to make you think you were imagining it."

"You didn't make me think that."

"But I tried to," she said.

I shrugged.

"I think Brian might have a key to the house," she said.

"How is that possible? I changed the locks."

"I don't know. Maybe he knows the locksmith."

I laughed. "Be serious. I hired a professional locksmith. I'm sure she doesn't go around handing out spares to anyone who asks."

"Not just anyone, but someone who might be a friend."

"Do you know how crazy you sound?"

"I'm just trying to find an explanation for what you saw."

"I appreciate that." I pulled the bag out of my tea and dropped it into the bowl. I took an experimental sip to see if it had cooled enough. It hadn't, but I sipped more anyway. It calmed me.

"He knows this house inside and out. Maybe he didn't get a key. Maybe he somehow left one of the window locks loose or something so he could jimmy it open. Who knows? The point is, I think it was him. I think he's upset that he didn't get this house. Property values have skyrocketed since he and Sara were divorced."

"So?"

"He probably thinks he deserved some of that."

"Why would he think that? He got a fair deal when he sold it and he moved on. He owns another home."

"He loves this house. It's written all over his face every time he walks in the door."

"He has a sentimental attachment. Marriages are complicated, even after you're divorced. Some people are still friends, and they obviously were, so he has good memories here."

She placed both her hands flat on the table. She tapped her fingers lightly, as if she were playing the piano. "What if he murdered Charlotte? Because he thought he got a bad deal? She was the executor of the estate. And she sold the house. She got a huge commission. Maybe that upset him. A lot."

I laughed.

"It's not funny."

"I'm not laughing at that. I'm laughing at how you've made up this theory out of nothing. How would killing Charlotte get him anything?"

"People don't always kill to *get* money. Sometimes it's just pure rage. Strangling someone? Think about it. Maybe they were arguing, and he just grabbed her and started choking her and he couldn't stop."

I shook my head. I took a sip of tea. "No."

"What do you mean, *no?*"

"He's a sweet, sensitive guy."

"You don't know what someone is capable of."

"He didn't kill her and he doesn't have a secret key to the house. I don't know what I saw, but I don't want to talk about it."

"What are you going to do?"

"About what?"

She waved her arm around. "About all of it. The murder and … how can you live here, knowing someone was murdered in your backyard, knowing that someone, maybe that same person, was inside your house?!"

"I'm not going to overreact to midnight scares. I'm trying to move past it. I'm expecting the detective to find out who did it. I expect it will have nothing to do with me, nothing to do with my house. Then David will come and we'll seriously start our remodeling. And in a few weeks, we'll bring Ryan to come and live here and we'll have a beautiful summer together. By next year, this will all be ancient history and we'll have a beautiful summer home. That's what I'm going to do."

Mia pushed her chair away from the table. She carried her mug to the sink and dumped the remains of her tea down the drain. "Do you want toast? Maybe some yogurt with strawberries?"

"Sounds good."

She pulled a few slices of bread from the bag and moved the toaster I'd brought from home toward the edge of the counter. She popped the bread into the slots and pushed the button. As I watched the bread descend, I thought about her wild idea that the locksmith had provided a spare key to Brian.

It made sense that Brian might want to come inside and sit in the dark with his memories. But the idea that a qualified locksmith would hand out a key to a friend was absurd.

We spent the rest of the morning at the home supply store looking at paint colors and hardware for doors and kitchen cabinets. By the time we were finished wandering the aisles, I'd decided I wanted to look online for suppliers offering hardware and light fixtures that were more unique and designed to echo an earlier era.

Although Mia didn't bring up her accusations of murder, the damage had been done. I felt as if someone had taken a meat cleaver to my brain. Part of me saw Brian as a sweet, thoughtful man who still had tender feelings of friendship toward his deceased former wife. Another part of me feared it was too coincidental that he was so available and eager to help, and that he might have had a complicated relationship with his deceased former wife's best friend.

It would have been so easy for him to wait unnoticed on my property. Who knew the layout and best routes for coming and going better than the man who had lived and worked to maintain the place for over ten years?

I didn't know which part of me I trusted and which part of me had fallen into distorted thinking.

26 NOW: PETER

$\mathcal{I}$ really wanted to know what was going on inside that house. In all the time I'd been watching, there had been no moving van. I'd seen a small box truck pull up to unload two beds and a few other pieces of used furniture, but that was it. Not nearly enough to fill the house. And the furniture was pedestrian. It lacked the classic style that would do the house justice.

That house had a spirit, it always had. And now, it broke my heart, wondering what was going to happen to it. The best years of my life had been lived between those walls, the best hours, the most precious moments. And I realized now that while I was living with them, I'd hardly noticed they were the best.

I was so very *busy*. I was planning my career, writing songs, performing.

Yes, I was loving Sara. We did some work on the house. She had big plans. She wanted to bring in more light, she said. Replace some of the windows with picture windows. I didn't have the skills for that, but I just needed to share her vision and maybe help out a little, since I was living there almost full time. My house had become a music studio more than a home.

I did share her vision, but I was busy.

I got comfortable, too comfortable. She did too, but of course neither of us recognized it. We still had incredible times. We traveled, we gardened, we carried on long, deep conversations. We had amazing sex. We cooked together. But I was absorbed by my work, the band, the creation as well as the logistics of it all. She was too, although I was busier. Performing four nights a week takes a lot out of a guy. Not that I resented that, I loved it. Every single minute. I thrived on it, but it's intense. Almost like another relationship. I hadn't seen that at the time.

Music isn't an art form that you create alone and then present your finished work to the world. At least not for me. I needed to see people move with the music. I needed to see it fill their bodies, watch their lips form the words, often unconsciously speaking my thoughts back to me. But mostly it was the subtle movement of their bodies. I could feel it in my bones.

It was almost like sex.

When I explained that to Sara, the first person I ever told that to, she got it. Sort of.

And so, like any relationship, there was too much taking each other for granted. And some of the things she wanted for that house didn't happen the way she wanted them to. Maybe that was what I didn't fully get. That house was her sanctuary. It was part of her. She wanted me to feel that with her. She *needed* me to feel that.

After she was gone, I didn't feel so busy. I felt as if I had all the time in the world. For regret. So much regret.

You would think I would have had a wake-up call when she got sick. At first, I did, but then, she was sick for so long that, too, became familiar. The cancer had an ebb and flow to it. They found an alternative drug therapy, which brought fresh hope, and then the disease flared up and hope dissolved. The cancer abated again and once more, hope sprouted like bulbs in the spring.

When it all finally became too much for her poor, frail body, it almost didn't seem real. Surely it would turn around again. This couldn't be it. She was too young. She'd fought back too many times and succeeded. This couldn't be the end. Even when it was so very clearly the end, I don't think I ever truly believed she was going to die.

I felt my throat constrict, my eyes blur slightly as Danielle placed an oval serving dish with two pieces of pork tenderloin in the center of the table. Bowls of salad, lightly buttered green beans, and small roasted potatoes surrounded the pork. Beside it she put a gravy pitcher with extra sauce.

"Smells delicious," I said.

She put her hand on my shoulder and gave it a squeeze. I patted her fingers. I felt at home.

From where I sat at Danielle and Tom's dining room table, I could see the front porch of Sara's house. I knew I shouldn't be calling it Sara's house, but that's what it was to me. How could it belong to someone else? Sara lived inside every room, in the garden, in the pond that used to be filled with dark blue water. I was certain, if I'd been allowed into the bedroom upstairs, I would feel her breath on my neck, even now.

I closed my eyes and tried to push the tears back into my skull. It was embarrassing for a grown man to cry. Especially when he was being served several perfectly cooked pieces of pork tenderloin. I breathed in the aroma of the meat, and that did the trick. Sara had been a vegetarian.

I appreciated Tom and Danielle's friendship. They'd mostly been Sara's friends, and like it had done with some of her other friends, I'd expected everything to end after her ashes were scattered. But they weren't like the others.

They especially weren't like Charlotte. Icy cold to the core. Smiling and polite, even though I knew she loathed the sight of me after my breakup with Sara. She was nice for Sara's sake, but the moment Sara took her final breath … wow. Charlotte might as well have chopped off my right arm with an axe.

At first, Tom had indulged my memories of Sara. But now, I could feel him working hard to get me to *move on*. He wanted the bitterness washed away. He'd lost patience with me recounting Charlotte's sins, cheered on by Danielle—the outrage Danielle and I shared over how I'd been treated. Tom did his best to steer the conversation to neutral topics.

"It was wrong," he said now, when Danielle murmured that perhaps Charlotte had been murdered because I wasn't the only one she'd treated with such cruelty. "But it's over, so let's—"

"It will never be over," Danielle said.

"You're only hurting yourself. Stirring it up over and over. It won't change the past."

"I can't stop thinking about it," Danielle said.

"You're not helping Peter," Tom said.

"He needs to express his feelings. It's not good to bottle them up."

I did need to express my feelings, but I saw Tom's point. Maybe the constant re-living of the pain and the disrespect was keeping me in the past. That's what my therapist said. So far, she hadn't told me how I was supposed to stop re-living the past, but she was adamant that it did have to stop.

"Plenty of feelings have been expressed," Tom said. "I don't think there's anything new to be said on the subject."

"I wonder who killed her," Danielle asked, as if this were a change of subject. "Maybe she's done worse."

"It might be opportunistic," Tom said, "and have nothing to do with her life."

"I don't think so." Danielle cut a piece of potato in half and put it in her mouth.

"You're just speculating."

While they talked over and around me, I sliced the pork and ate it. Danielle was an incredible cook. Sara had been too. She'd made vegetables, and even tofu dishes, taste like they were being served in a four-star restaurant. But this pork was melting on my tongue. I was so satisfied, I didn't care if we talked about baseball all evening, instead of my favorite topic—Sara's house and how I'd been rudely evicted, kicked out onto the street without adequate time to grieve.

"The new owner is remodeling," Danielle said.

"I know." I took a bite of pork, followed by another roasted potato.

"It's her right," Tom said. "It's what all new homeowners do."

"The house looked great the way it was," I said.

Danielle sighed. "Sara had beautiful taste."

"She had a truly artistic soul." I picked up my wineglass and took a sip. It was Sara's favorite, and I appreciated Danielle's attention to that detail. "Whatever the new owner does will take away some of its personality."

"You don't know that," Tom said.

But I did. I absolutely knew that. You can't improve perfection.

27 NOW: TRINITY

*A*fter leaving two voicemails and sending four text messages to my husband, I wasn't sure whether to be worried, hurt, or annoyed. And so, I circled wildly through the three emotions as if I were on one of those rides at the county fair where the box you're sitting in is thrust in one direction, then spun wildly back and around, then thrust furiously forward in a different direction, whipping your head on your neck in a way that can't be good for your spine.

All I'd heard from him was that he still hadn't booked his flight. No explanation. No apology.

He'd told me before I left to come to the house that it was going to be a crazy summer. Organizational changes in his company, a big name new client they were trying to close a major sale with, back-to-back travel. He would try to be at the house for a week here and there. But he couldn't promise. I knew I had no right to be annoyed, no right to be hurt, for that matter.

But I was. I was because of the subtext, although I wasn't sure if that was the right way to characterize it. David hadn't been one hundred percent on board with this house. He wasn't sure we should have a second home. He worried it would fracture our social life. He believed Ryan needed one place to settle and call home. He thought that as Ryan got older, and if we had kids of our own, they wouldn't want to leave their friends for the entire summer every year. According to him, it would completely squash all family travel.

We needed to expose Ryan to other cultures and let him see the country, he'd said. Not squat in one place, weeding a vegetable garden and feeding ducks. That wasn't a well-rounded childhood. I thought it was. At least for the early years. Ryan didn't need to see the Mona Lisa and the Parthenon when he was seven years old.

In David's mind, this house was my thing. I hated he viewed it that way, and once he'd spoken those words, I felt it every time he failed to show interest in my plans and every time he didn't return my phone call right away.

At the same time, he was sending mixed messages. He'd gone out of his way to make sure the purchase was taken care of while I was with my sister. He'd spent hours at the house with the inspectors. He'd signed the papers, faxing the legal documents that required my signature, and stayed on top of all the details to ensure the house would be ours.

I didn't understand where his head, or more importantly, his heart, was.

Mia walked into the living room as I sat staring at my phone, as if cradling it in my hands might cause a heartfelt message from my husband to appear on the screen.

"What are you doing?" she asked.

I put my phone down beside me. "Nothing."

"I'm going for a run." It was obvious from her shorts, sports bra, running shoes, and the phone holder strapped to her upper arm. Her hair was in a braided ponytail and she smelled of sunscreen. "Is everything okay?" she asked.

I nodded.

"See ya." Her shoes squeaked on the hardwood floor as she walked down the hallway and out the front door. I heard her talking to someone, then there was silence, followed a moment later by a knock on the doorframe.

I went out to see the front door standing open. Brian was on the porch. Mia, obviously postponing her run to keep an eye on him and an ear on what he had to say, waited on the bottom step.

"I won't stay long." He handed me a package wrapped in pale blue paper. There was no bow or card. "Nothing fancy, but I thought I should wrap it." He laughed.

"Come in." The invitation was instinctive, even though my thoughts whirled over my momentary suspicions of the previous day. Now, they appeared wildly paranoid as I considered his kind smile and his light blue eyes that looked utterly innocent behind his dark-framed glasses, as I remembered his gentle understanding of my grief.

He glanced over his shoulder at Mia, her arms folded, her hip cocked to one side, staring at him. She looked poised to climb back up the stairs and follow him if he decided to enter the house. "I just wanted to drop this off. I guess I'm spoiling the surprise, so maybe I shouldn't have wrapped it, but it's a book that was helpful to me after Sara died. I thought you might get something out of it. It's about grief, but from the perspective of losing someone to cancer."

"Thank you."

He took a step back. "Hope it helps."

"I appreciate it. Are you sure you won't come in? I could make tea."

He looked at Mia again. I felt an irrational desire to walk down the stairs and shove Mia off the bottom step. I wanted to talk to Brian about what I'd witnessed in the middle of the night.

I wondered if he *had* been in the house, but maybe there was nothing sinister or threatening about it. He'd been inside, possibly more than once, but it had nothing to do with Charlotte's murder. Maybe he was just missing what had been. Missing a marriage that had gone wrong, regretting what had happened, wondering what might have been between them—so many complicated feelings when someone dies. Especially someone you who you think is going to be part of your life for decades to come. You think there will be plenty of time for your relationship to evolve and change. You don't expect all those opportunities to be gone forever.

Maybe the house comforted him. The few possessions of Jens that I'd kept brought me enormous comfort. It was almost impossible to explain what they meant to me.

Mia probably couldn't understand that. If I could ask him, without Mia's disapproving, worried, suspicious glare, maybe he would tell me the truth.

I called out to her. "Aren't you going for a run?"

She didn't answer.

"I need to get going." Brian moved away from the door. "Talk to you soon." He walked down the steps, steering a wide path around Mia. A moment later, he was inside his truck, pulling away from the house.

Mia started a slow jog down the driveway. It almost looked as if she planned to chase the truck all the way down the driveway, following him until he was out of sight.

28 THEN: PETER

Two artists should be simpatico. That's what Sara and I thought when we started out. Everything is the same. Your work is your passion and a part of who you are in a way that's not quite the same with people in other professions. Because with art, the work comes out of something inside your heart. It sounds pompous, I suppose, arrogant, to someone who's passionate about the legal profession or teaching or practicing medicine. Even to a professional athlete or someone who owns a hair salon.

But it is different. She and I knew that.

It turns out, there's a world of difference between sculpting and performing music on a stage.

Sara did not understand why I didn't come home after my gigs were over.

"I thought you stayed late to talk to me because it was *me*. Not because you categorized me with your other groupies," she said.

"I never considered you a groupie."

"Whatever."

"I need to interact with my fans," I said.

"No, you don't."

"When you go to art fairs, or spend time at the gallery, you interact with fans."

"Sure, but it's not every weekend. Four nights, every single week of the year."

"If they wanted that much of your time, you would."

"I would not, Peter. They don't own you."

"I don't feel like they own me, they feel connected to me."

"You need to set some boundaries."

"My music speaks to them and they appreciate the interaction. I'm wired anyway. It's not like I can come home and fall asleep. I need to talk. I need to come down. I need to let the energy dissipate."

"Why can't you do that here? With me?"

"You're asleep."

"I could wait up."

It wasn't the same. I did want to be with her. But I also wanted to be with my fans. I needed to be with my fans. It was important to engage. It helped keep my creativity fresh, it helped me know what resonated. I'd thought she understood that. I knew that if the people who bought her work wanted to talk to her for hours, she would do the same. It was just different.

Writing songs touches people in a different way than a visual piece of art does. Put those words to upbeat or haunting notes and it moves people in a way that transcends everyday life. Music connects people to each other and to memories and experiences. It's meant to be shared. I knew she knew that, and I didn't understand why she didn't want me to have that. Why she didn't want my fans to have that?

"I need you," she said.

I put my arms around her and pulled her close, resting my chin on the top of her head. "I need you, too. More than you'll ever know. But I also need this. Can't I have both? I feel like you're …" I couldn't finish. I wouldn't say that to her, but I felt like she wanted to take part of it away from me. I felt like she had a subtle desire to own my music. That might be harsh, but I felt it, or I thought I did.

"Charlotte said—"

"Why are you talking to her about this?" I pulled away from her, looking at her face, twisted into ridges of pain.

"She's my best friend. We share everything."

"I thought I was your best friend."

"You're my partner. She's my best girlfriend. It's different."

"Why would you talk to your girlfriend about us? About me?"

"That's what girlfriends do."

I'd been aware of that. On some level, I knew this. But it felt like a betrayal. Already Charlotte wasn't a fan. I couldn't imagine this would endear me to her. She was a real estate agent. What did she know about art at all, much less music, and how fans connected with a musician who wrote songs that touched their hearts?

"Charlotte thinks you need the attention."

"I'm not interested in Charlotte's opinion about what I need. And she's wrong."

"Is she?"

"Yes, she is. You should at least know that from some of your collectors."

"Maybe. But it's so much. All four nights, every week?"

"There are a lot of people."

"Some of them are the same every week. I've seen them."

"Are you jealous?"

"Charlotte said—"

"Leave Charlotte out of it, okay? This is our conversation."

"I won't leave her out of it because she has some good insights. And you're not here and I needed someone to talk to. So please stop interrupting me."

I took a few steps away from her. I shoved my hands into my pockets.

"She said the fact that you need to be there every single night, that you can't draw any boundaries at all, that *every* fan takes priority over me, makes it obvious that you need constant reassurance. You should feel good about your music *while* you're writing it —that's the creative act—*while* you're practicing, *while* you're performing. You shouldn't need to listen to them tell you how great you are after it's over. The fact that they come and listen at all should be enough."

"Should it? Well thank you, Charlotte Hughes, or should I call her Dr. Hughes? I wasn't aware she was a psychologist."

"Don't mock her. She's trying to be helpful. It's worth thinking about."

I would certainly be thinking about it. I would be thinking about how this woman I hardly knew was trying to worm her way into my relationship with the woman I loved. Maybe the reason Sara was feeling this way was due to Charlotte's *insightful* whispers in her ear about what was wrong with me.

I wished there was a way to shut her up, but I'd spent enough time around Charlotte to know that silencing her was a hopeless desire.

29 NOW: TRINITY

$\mathcal{M}$ ia returned from her run fired up to finish scraping the mural off the dining room wall. "We need to get going here. Summer is passing us by. And I can't stay forever."

I looked up from where I sat on the couch. I slid my finger into the book Brian had given me to hold my place.

"What are you reading?"

"A book about grief. It's for people who lost someone to cancer."

"Aww, sweetie." She crossed the room and sat beside me. She put her hand on my leg. "I'm sorry if I haven't given you much chance to talk about your feelings."

"It's fine. If I need to talk, I will."

She nodded, sliding her hand off my leg. "Sorry if I'm stinky." She laughed gently. "Is that what he gave you?"

"Yes."

"You probably shouldn't have accepted it."

I dogeared the corner of the page and placed it beside me, inching away from her. "Don't be like that. It's really helpful."

"You shouldn't let him manipulate your feelings."

"He's not manipulating my feelings. He understands what I'm going through." I sighed and stood, grabbing the book off the couch.

"Do you want to work in the dining room together?"

I nodded.

"I'll take a quick shower and we'll get going," she said.

I pulled my phone out of my pocket. I thought I'd felt it vibrate, but the screen was dark. I tapped it to be sure. No messages.

"What's wrong?"

"Nothing." I shoved the phone into my pocket.

"You look upset. I'm sorry if that word is harsh, but he—"

"I'm upset about David. I'm having a hard time getting hold of him. I thought he would be here in a few days, but it's looking like maybe not. I'm really ... we were supposed to work on the house together. It's hard to stay motivated without him here. I don't want to just do these small projects. There are bigger things that need to be taken care of. And he'd talked about—"

"I thought this house was your thing."

"It's for our family."

"But it's your idea. You're the one who wants to have a rural existence and go off the grid and all that."

I laughed. "I don't want to go off the grid. I just think kids benefit from doing things that aren't all organized and adult-driven and screens all the time. But we're supposed to be fixing up the house together. David and me, as a couple, a family."

She stood. "Don't be so needy."

"I'm not needy."

"You sound it, a little. I don't want to be mean, you just ... he has a demanding career, right? You're always telling me that. So fix up the house and surprise him."

I supposed I could do that. But I'd wanted to create something together. How did I know what he wanted? He said he didn't care, but I knew that once he saw it, he *would* care. He had ideas that would suddenly become important if things weren't to his liking.

"Come on." She lunged toward me, almost knocking me back. "Get excited, Trinity. You could surprise him. What if we could get the house all fixed up before he got here?"

"That's not possible. And the inspection reports are at home. I need to see them, or he at least needs to have time to discuss them over the phone because I think there are some things that need to be—"

"Don't focus on the negative. Think about the things we *can* do. I'm here to help, and we can get a lot done." She rubbed my arm. "You've had a lot of setbacks. A murder in your backyard!? That's a lot. The police asking you questions as if they think you had something to do with it? It's awful. But you have a beautiful new house and a little boy coming into your life and we need to get inspired and busy and fill this place with positive energy."

She was making me smile. She was right about everything. She usually was.

"David's busy with work. That's his job. This is yours. And mine, at least for now, is to help you and support you. So let's get to it. Pretend David doesn't even exist."

"That's an awful thing to say."

She looked at me for a moment.

"I don't want to do that. Why would I want to do that?" I asked.

"Maybe that wasn't the best way to say it. Sorry. Let me take my shower. You grab the scrapers and tarps and masks."

"I do hate that mural."

She laughed. "Me too. So let's get rid of it. Who wants a painting of musicians all around your dining room? And it's a little amateurish."

I agreed. I didn't want to criticize someone's art, but Sara had been a sculptor. I'd searched online for photos of some of her figures and they were exquisite. I wasn't sure why she'd taken to acrylic paints on her dining room wall. Boredom, maybe. Or she might have done it to get ideas for her sculptures. Either way, it was strange and it would feel good to have that be the first thing removed from the house, the first step toward making it fully ours.

"We need to move the bookcases to get at the rest of it," I said.

"It's strange that she had bookcases in the dining room."

"Maybe she displayed her sculptures in them or something," I said.

"But the shelves are so low to the floor, you wouldn't really see them while you're eating."

I shrugged. "Help me push them away from the wall before you shower."

There were six four-foot bookcases, with a single shelf and a double set of glass panels that opened up and slid back like those on legal bookcases. We each took one end of the case closest to the glass doors that opened into the kitchen, tugging to move it away from the wall. The case refused to budge.

"Why is it so heavy?" Mia asked. "It's empty. It shouldn't be this hard." She gave it another tug, but the case remained rooted to the floor.

I knelt and opened the glass panel at the bottom. I peered inside. "It's bolted to the floor."

"No way."

I nodded.

"Why?"

I laughed. "How should I know?"

"It can't be for earthquake protection."

"Maybe it was. If it had fragile sculptures."

"They aren't tall enough to fall over in an earthquake."

I ran my fingers over the head of the bolt, then sat back on the floor and crossed my legs.

"It looks like you need to make a run to the hardware store." She backed toward the doorway. "You do that while I shower. Okay? It's only a minor setback. Half an hour."

When she was gone, I looked around the room at the bookcases. I wasn't sure I knew how to remove bolts. I knew for a fact that Mia didn't. I pulled my phone out of my pocket and texted Brian. As my fingers tapped the screen, I was acutely conscious of how irritated Mia would be, but I didn't care. I wanted to make forward progress, and this was the fastest way.

Clearly, my husband would not be around to help. I was good with a scraper and sandpaper, a pro at taping and rolling on paint, precise and perfectionistic with corners and edges when painting a room. But Brian had offered to help, and he was probably the one who had installed the bolts. Why make something more difficult than necessary?

Time was racing by and before I knew it, I would be picking up Ryan and bringing that adorable, tow-headed boy with the sweet smile to live here. I wanted a warm, inviting home for him.

As I stared at the ring of musicians surrounding me, I wondered: Would I be able to provide that, or was I bringing my sister's precious child into a place haunted by death and murder?

30 NOW: TRINITY

*T*hree minutes after I sent my text message, Brian replied he was still in the area and would stop by. Two minutes later, he knocked on the door.

As always, I was struck by the fact that his chic but studious glasses and his slim build made him look more like an accountant or a software engineer than a handyman. Of course, he'd never said he was a handyman. It was something he did on the side. And maybe by on the side, he meant he liked to work on this house in particular. Possibly, he'd done the maintenance work even after he and Sara divorced.

As soon as he walked into the foyer, I heard Mia's footsteps on the stairs. "This is a surprise." Her voice was cool.

"Hi, Mia." Brian was trying hard to overcome her icy tone.

As if the conversation had already begun, he said, "Sara was cautious to a fault. She bolted all her furniture to the walls and floors. She moved to California from the east coast when she was in her early twenties. Her first earthquake freaked her out." He laughed. "Not like those of us who loved them as kids and don't think they're any big deal, right?"

I wasn't sure we thought they weren't a big deal. If you'd lived through a quake that caused any kind of damage, you learned to bolt bookcases and cabinets to the wall. I imagined David and I would be doing that, especially with a child in our house.

"I can get those taken care of for you," Brian said.

Mia was standing beside me now. "You and I are capable of removing bolts, Trinity."

"Are we?"

She turned and glared at me.

Despite her annoyance, Mia followed us into the dining room. Both of us watched while he began removing bolts as easily as if he were extracting a straw from a coffee drink. With a few flicks of his wrist and a quick zip, zip from a power tool, the bolts came out. Mia and I were able to ease the bookcases onto the tarp and drag them to the center of the room without scratching the floor.

"Are you planning to keep them in the dining room?" Brian unplugged the cord, wrapped it into a neat twist, and placed the power tool in his box.

"I haven't thought about it," I said. "Probably not. They make it feel crowded and I can't imagine having enough things I'd want to display in them."

"Do you want them at all?"

"I'll have to think about it."

"Do you want me to help you move them?"

"This is fine, for now." I gave him a grateful smile.

He flipped the latches on his toolbox closed.

"All good, then. Anything else I can help with?"

"I don't think so. Can I make you a sandwich?"

He glanced at Mia. "I don't—"

"I'd love to hear about the history of the mural before we obliterate it," I said.

He smirked.

"So it has a history?" I asked.

"Oh yeah."

"Then I'm definitely making you a sandwich."

"It's only eleven thirty," Mia said.

"By the time they're made, it will be close to noon."

"Do we eat at the strike of twelve?" Mia asked.

"Why not?" I went into the kitchen and pulled the loaf of bread out of the cabinet. I opened the fridge and began putting condiments on the counter. I removed bottle caps from three beers.

Brian sat at the table. Mia remained in the dining room doorway, picking at the label on her bottle.

I sliced tomatoes, pickles, and avocado. I spread mayo on the bread and placed turkey and cheese on top. "I assume Sara painted the mural?"

"Yes. She liked to dabble in painting, although she never displayed her work. She did a lot of sketching and painting to play around with ideas for her sculpture." He took a sip of his beer. "The mural was something that happened after I was gone."

I layered tomatoes and pickle slices over the turkey.

"When she hooked up with Peter—"

"Who's Peter?" I asked.

"The guy who came after me. A musician."

"Ah," said Mia. "The mural is a tribute."

Brian gave a short laugh. Maybe he was relieved that he'd captured Mia's interest. "You could call it that. He plays with a band —he's the lead guitar—in bars around the county."

"Is one of the figures him?"

"Sure. Probably. I never looked at it that closely," Brian said.

Mia turned into the dining room. "Which one?"

"I don't really know."

Mia returned to the doorway, pulling one of the double doors closed. "There are a lot of guitar players."

"Yeah, I don't get it. There must be some reason for that. Maybe different facets of him?" He shrugged.

I placed the strips of avocado and lettuce on the sandwiches and covered each one with its second slice of bread. I cut through them with a large knife that was surprisingly sharp for one I'd bought for a few dollars at a discount store when I'd bought the minimal amount of supplies for our new kitchen.

"I expected a better story," Mia said. "Something more dramatic. Or ..."

"Or what?" Brian asked.

She shrugged.

We sat at the table and ate our sandwiches. When the food was gone and our beer bottles empty, Brian thanked me for lunch and left.

I resisted the urge to point out to Mia what a nice guy he was. She'd softened a little, maybe she would stop with the attacks now.

We returned to the dining room, and by dinnertime, it looked as if the mural had never existed.

"Now we'll never know which one was her lover," Mia said.

"Does it matter?"

"We should have taken a photo."

"I'm trying to make this my house ... our house. I don't want to document what was important to someone else."

"Someone who's dead," Mia said.

"You didn't have to say that."

"We got a lot done. But we could have removed the bolts ourselves. We could have started sanding if we hadn't wasted an hour and a half socializing over lunch. And made ourselves tired and dulled our energy with beer."

I didn't respond. I was happy with our progress. And I was happy to know the history of the room before I wiped it out of existence. Room by room, this place would become mine.

By the time David arrived, I would show him a significant amount of progress. Although I was getting nervous about the inspection reports. I hoped I wasn't doing cosmetic work over some serious issues that would need to be undone once my husband arrived with the details about our home's past. It frustrated me that Charlotte hadn't entered the digital age, that all the reports were on paper. It hadn't been that way when we purchased our home in

Cupertino. David had complained repeatedly that Charlotte insisted he print and locate a fax machine to send her our financial documentation.

For someone so young, she was strangely averse to email. Maybe it was her rural roots, or maybe I was stereotyping her and she simply liked tangible objects. Not unlike me.

31 NOW: TRINITY

Something felt strange when I walked into the kitchen to make coffee the following morning. I couldn't say what it was. Not right away. I filled the carafe with water and poured it into the receptacle. I put coffee into the filter, watching my hand tremble for no apparent reason.

I glanced around the kitchen. Nothing was out of place. Why was I feeling this way?

Something was making me feel tense and uncomfortable. I closed the lid of the coffee pot and turned it on. I washed my hands to remove the grounds that clung to my skin like microscopic insects. I still felt uneasy.

Backing away from the sink, I glanced toward the dining room. Through the glass panels in the doors, I could see the room just filling with light from the sun coming through the window that looked out toward the backyard. The room looked different. The mural was gone, although that wasn't it because I couldn't see the walls clearly due to the lack of light.

I crossed the room and opened the door on the right, putting my hand on the doorframe to steady myself.

All the bookcases were back in their original positions. I reached into the room and turned on the overhead light, thinking my mind was playing tricks on me. The light confirmed what I'd already seen. The bookcases were lined up against the walls. The walls where the mural had been scraped away were painted with strips of pale blue paint. They didn't seem to mean anything. There was no design, none of them were shaped into anything recognizable, just a series of random lines interspersed by a few globs that half-resembled drops of water ... possibly.

I took a few steps back, feeling light-headed and slightly sick to my stomach.

Had we moved the bookcases before we'd gone to bed? I had no recollection of doing that, but I couldn't think of a single reason why they would be back in their original spots unless we'd moved them and I'd somehow blotted out the memory. I continued staring, trying to make sense of what I was looking at.

It didn't seem real. Not the strips of blue paint, not the repositioned furniture.

Was I dreaming? Imagining things? Losing pieces of my memory?

Maybe Mia had moved them. But why? Why would she rearrange things like this?

I tightened my grip on the doorframe. I gasped for air, the words circling in my head—*Mia moved them, Mia moved them, Mia moved* ... But my rough breathing told me I didn't believe this. We planned to sand and paint the walls today. There was no way she would have moved the shelves into their original positions.

I turned off the light, closed the door, and backed away from the room.

As the coffee burbled and the aroma filled the kitchen, offering me comfort and promise of a strong jolt of caffeine, I hurried past it, almost running down the hallway. I raced up the stairs and knocked hard on her bedroom door, calling her name.

She opened the door, freshly showered, her hair smooth as silk, her makeup already done. "What's wrong?"

"Did you move the bookcases?"

"Of course not."

"They're back where they were."

"Why?"

"I don't know why! That doesn't even matter. Someone was in the house. Again."

Her eyes had a blank appearance, as if she were staring through me, as if she didn't want to know who might have come into the house, didn't even want to think about it. She blinked, then refocused her attention on me. "Let me see."

"You don't believe me?"

"Yes, I believe you. I want to see."

I turned, and she followed me down the stairs. "There's paint on the walls. Blue streaks. And something like raindrops."

"That's …"

"That's what?"

We entered the kitchen. I opened the dining room doors and turned on the light.

"Oh, wow." She stepped into the room. She walked to the far wall and touched one of the blue streaks. "It's dry."

"What does that mean?"

"That it happened hours ago, I guess." She turned to face me. "It must have been Brian."

"I don't think so."

"Who else?"

"Why him?"

"He's the only one who knew we moved them."

"That doesn't mean he did this."

"He's the only person who keeps coming around. And Charlotte … he's scary."

"There's nothing scary about him."

"You need to call the police. Right now."

"I'm not calling the police on a sweet guy who's helping me fix things around the house."

"Someone was in your house! They vandalized your walls and moved furniture. We're not safe. If someone has access, we could wake up dead any day."

I laughed hysterically. "If we're dead, we won't wake up."

"It's not funny. You know what I meant."

"I don't think it's funny. I hate this. I'm scared too, but I'm not … do you think she …?" I'd never believed in the supernatural. I didn't even enjoy watching horror movies. They seemed silly to me, and although I got scared, there was always a part of my brain laughing at myself for even the slightest shiver of fear.

I felt exactly that now. Part of my brain was imagining that Sara was angry we'd destroyed her mural. Another part of my mind was laughing at me for believing some unseen force was moving furniture. It was ridiculous. I was a nutcase for even speaking the words. Even to someone like Mia, who made decisions based on admittedly beautifully drawn, and historically valued, but a wholly superstitious deck of cards. A collection of cards that she chose to interpret in any way she wanted, depending on how they were flipped over on the table, or her mood on any particular day.

"What I think is that somehow, Brian Price has a key to a house that he thinks should still belong to him. And he's smiling and helping you and acting like your good friend. But he wants this house back. And he's trying to freak you out, or maybe scare you all the way out the door. Either way, someone was in here while we were asleep in our beds and extremely vulnerable. Please, call the police. If you won't do it for yourself, do it for me. Because I'm scared. Will you do that for me? Your oldest, best friend?"

"What are the police going to do?"

"Keep an eye on the house? Take fingerprints? I don't know. Please?"

"His fingerprints would already be on the shelves from yesterday."

She heaved a deep, put-upon sigh. "I'm scared, and I know you are, too."

I was, but I still couldn't be quite sure what was scaring me—a physical intruder, the idea of a murder in my backyard, or something else.

What's going on, Jen? I whispered in my mind. *What's going on?*

32 NOW: PETER

*C*Watching her move in and out of the house, seeing glimpses of her through the windows, made me ache to be inside those walls with her. If I closed my eyes, I could see every part of that house. I could see what she was doing inside each room.

My gaze followed her as she cooked, while I sat at the table sipping a beer, watching her chop vegetables with such love and care it was as if each one were the most precious item she'd ever handled. My attention followed her when she placed our meal on the dining room table and sat across from me, a smile on her face that told me I was the only thing she needed.

I felt as if I could see her walking into her studio, closing the door behind her. There was no desire to follow her inside. She and I were the same—we knew that creating something out of nothing required time alone without another pair of eyes, without another voice intruding upon our thoughts and our space.

Inside that house, in my dreams, I saw her on the couch in the evenings, watching TV, reading on her tablet. I saw her moving around, tidying up, almost always with her feet bare because she was never comfortable wearing shoes.

And then we climbed the stairs together. She went first, and I followed, watching the sway of her hips as she moved slowly upward. We took off our clothes and slid under the covers and found each other in the dark.

I couldn't see inside the second story, but I knew every inch of its rooms. Just as I knew every inch of her body, her face, every hair on her head.

She looked anxious. I wanted to hold her and tell her everything would be okay. Recently, she looked frightened, and there was a quickness to her movements that said she wasn't paying attention to what she was doing, because her mind was somewhere else.

Most of all, she looked lonely. I could remove that loneliness. If only she would let me inside.

33 NOW: TRINITY

$\mathcal{C}$alling the police was the last thing I wanted to do. What if the same detective came out? He already looked at me with a negative attitude because someone had murdered Charlotte Hughes right outside my bedroom window. Even if that detective didn't show up, if detectives didn't handle minor calls like this, what would a regular cop do about it? They would ask whether we'd locked all the doors and windows. They might suggest we get a security camera. There wasn't really anything else they could do.

How do you prove, hours after the fact, that your house was secure? How did we prove we'd moved the shelves, and they'd been returned to their original positions? And what did that matter to a police officer? It sounded silly, even in my own thoughts. Nothing had been taken. There was no damage to my property.

To the two of us, seeing those shelves standing innocuously against the walls was terrifying. We knew for certain someone had been inside the house, but no one else would experience that visceral fear. No one but Brian. Maybe. He hadn't been sleeping in the house.

So what if there were strips of paint on the walls? It was obvious they were being prepped for a new coat of paint. Maybe we'd painted a few test strokes. The random stripes of color hadn't damaged a freshly painted wall. There was no threatening message scrawled in red.

I could imagine a police officer standing in my dining room, giving us a small, patronizing smile. He would tap notes into his phone, tell us to call if anything else happened. He would leave and do absolutely nothing. My address would go into their file as the site of a murder and a house to watch out for because it was inhabited by people who made nuisance reports.

After filling two mugs with coffee, I handed one to Mia. I took mine out to the backyard. I walked down the steps and out into the yard. I walked slowly across the patchy lawn, past the well, which I managed to avoid looking at, to the edge of the empty pond. Looking up into the oak tree beside it, I was overcome by a desire to climb the tree, nestling onto one of the lower branches, snuggling up close, wrapping one arm around its trunk, leaning my head against the rough, solid bark.

When I returned to the house, Mia was waiting. "Are you calling them?"

"I don't see what that would accomplish."

"Someone was in your house! A woman was murdered in your backyard." She lifted her hands slightly. She looked as if she wanted to grab my shoulders and give me a solid shake.

I placed my coffee mug on the counter and covered my face with my hands. So many conflicting feelings rushed through me, I couldn't sort them out. I wanted her to stop talking, to stop looking at me as if I had to do something right this minute.

"What's wrong?"

"I'm not sure—"

"Not sure about what?"

"I'm trying to think." I lowered my hands away from my face.

She was glaring at me. "What is there to think about? I don't—"

"I need a minute." I picked up my mug, took a sip of coffee, and walked out of the kitchen. I went upstairs and closed my bedroom door. There wasn't anything to think about with the police. I wasn't calling them. I'd already worked out how they would respond. I needed her to stop talking, stop telling me what to do.

The person I really wanted to talk to was Brian. He'd spent time in this house. He'd helped us move the shelves. He would understand. I didn't want to acknowledge to myself that I was entertaining the idea that maybe something was going on here beyond what was normal and rational.

Mia was probably right. It was entirely possible, and far more likely, that Charlotte's killer had been in the house and meant to torment us. At the same time, I was absolutely certain I'd checked all the locks. I saw a flicker of doubt when I said that to her. Those flickers in her eyes caused me to doubt myself, and I didn't like that.

I hated the fact that my choices seemed to be either complete lack of trust in my own memory or a willingness to believe in paranormal phenomenon. I didn't like either choice. I was also confused that Mia wasn't leaning toward the latter, given her willingness to believe the things she did, things that I considered as unbelievable as the idea of a dead woman's spirit tormenting me for removing her mural.

All I wanted was a chance to talk out my thoughts without being shoved in one direction or another, and Brian seemed like the kind of person who would be willing to do that. I pulled my phone out of my pocket and sent him a text message.

I stayed in my room, sipping coffee, looking out the window at the abandoned well. Hiding from Mia, if I was honest. Brian had answered my text immediately, and a little over an hour later, I heard the doorbell.

Leaving the mug on the dresser, I rushed down the stairs, but Mia beat me to the door.

"What do you want?" she asked.

"I'm here to see Trinity."

"We're in the middle of something," Mia said.

I stepped around her. "I asked him to come over." I moved onto the front porch.

"Why? You were going to … I thought we agreed we need to deal with …"

I smiled at her effort to remind me about her desire to call the police without letting Brian know what had happened. I regretted that she and I viewed him so differently. I was used to pouring out all my feelings and secrets to Mia. I was used to getting solid advice from her, sympathy when I craved it, silence when I needed it, outrage when I wanted it. Despite her too frequent offers to solve my problems with the Tarot cards, the thoughts and suggestions that came out of her own head were usually brilliant. But for some reason, something was off between us since she'd come to stay in my new house.

It might have been the stress of Charlotte's murder, or my frustration and hurt over David. Maybe it was my grief, or the apprehension I felt over becoming a mother, or whatever I was about to become in Ryan's life. Maybe it was simply that we hadn't seen each other much while I was with my sister. Had the experience of losing Jen changed me so dramatically that I was now an entirely different person? Was our friendship going to require some remodeling as surely as the house did?

It hadn't occurred to me until that moment, but neither did I have time to think about it right now.

I wanted to talk to Brian. The need was growing inside me like a gnawing hunger. "Let's go for a walk," I said.

"Trying to be rid of me?" Mia asked.

"No. I just want to get some fresh air." I walked down the steps without turning to look at her.

"You aren't going to …" Again, her voice trailed off. I think she knew I was going to tell him.

Brian and I walked down the driveway to the quiet street and turned right, headed away from Tom and Danielle's house, as if by mutual agreement. We walked on the gravel shoulder in quiet companionship until we reached the cross street.

"Why don't we walk in the park." Brian pointed to the kids' play structure across from us, surrounded by an endless sea of green and mature trees that partially hid several picnic tables and two other enormous, brightly colored play structures.

We crossed the street and started along a path that looped around the perimeter of the park. I told him everything that had happened, starting with the sounds we'd heard while Mia was putting out the Tarot cards. He listened without comment.

When I was finished, he still said nothing. By this time, we'd circled the park and were back at the street leading to my house. We crossed again, heading home.

Finally, he spoke. "What are you asking me?"

"First, I guess I'm asking whether you agree with Mia. The police said nothing about a serial killer. Although to be fair, they don't know about the cards, or the shelves being moved."

"Right."

"What do you think?" I asked.

"I'm not sure, to be honest. A serial killer seems like a big leap to the worst thing imaginable."

"I know."

He was silent again as we turned onto my street.

"Are you going to make me say it?" I asked.

He laughed gently.

"Did you … have you, ever experienced anything …" I laughed. "… not normal, in this house?"

"No."

I laughed again, louder, with a slight edge of hysteria. "You answered that quickly."

"Because I didn't have to think about it."

"Do you think …"

"I don't believe in that kind of thing," he said.

"Neither do I!"

"It's your grief talking, making you wonder. You might be hoping …"

"I know. I know that." My voice caught. "But I don't understand what happened."

"Do you want me to check the locks? To be sure everything is working correctly?"

"That would help."

We didn't say any more about what had happened or about the supernatural, which I was honestly glad to put out of my head. At the same time, he found all the window and door locks were working perfectly, which was what I'd expected. If something was broken, I would have noticed when I'd locked up at night.

I did not believe in the supernatural. I just wanted an explanation, and I didn't have one. I didn't want to call the police, and I didn't want to believe Brian had been inside my house. Now that I'd spent time talking to him, I had an even better feeling about him. There was no way he was trying to frighten us away.

I wasn't that naïve, not that easily conned.

We stopped at the bottom of the porch steps.

"I can't explain it," he said. "But I do think you should tell the police. Leaping to a serial killer is a bit fantastical, but because she was killed on your property, they should know about this."

I gripped the railing beside me. I hated unanswerable questions. I suppose everyone does, it's not as if I'm special for wanting to understand what's going on around me. But the lack of ability to come up with anything to explain this was making my head ache. I pressed my hand to the back of my neck, massaging the base of my skull.

"One thing I do know," Brian said. "There's always an explanation."

I laughed weakly.

"Do you want a hug?" he asked. "You look like you could use one."

I nodded. "Actually, I could."

He put his arms around my back, and I did the same. We hugged each other briefly. He patted my back and released me. We smiled, and I wondered if my smile looked as frustrated as his.

When he was gone, I turned to go up the steps. For some reason, I looked up. Mia stood at the window in Ryan's future playroom. She was staring at me with a look of absolute terror on her face.

34 NOW: MIA

The only way I could explain Trinity's sudden explosion of naïveté was her grief. Something about watching her sister die must have broken her.

I was absolutely certain that Brian Price wanted something from her. I might not have been right about what that something was, but he wasn't there to be a nice guy. He wasn't just helping her make home repairs and start on her remodeling project for a house that he thought he should still have the rights to, or whatever it was that guy thought.

And although I wasn't dead certain he was a killer, I wasn't convinced he wasn't.

How could Trinity almost trip over a corpse in her backyard and not be scared out of her mind? There was a guy she didn't know creeping around her house, and she acted as if that was absolutely fine. I didn't understand why she trusted him so completely. She knew nothing about him.

These thoughts were keeping me awake every night. I laid on my back, staring at the ceiling, trying to figure her out. I tried to remember what she used to be like. I tried to remember how things used to be between us, but my mind was blank.

So many things had happened in our friendship over the past few years. And while her sister was dying, we'd hardly talked at all. We'd seen each other even less. There had been lots of text messages, but it's so easy to misunderstand and misinterpret things, enormous things, when you're texting. All the things that don't get said start to pile up until there's a mountain the size of Everest between you.

No one close to me had ever died. I'd lost my mom, in a way, to early-onset Alzheimer's. So I knew about grief. But it was probably a lot different when you lost someone your own age. Someone young. That's probably a lot different.

She just wasn't acting at all like I'd expected her to.

Every time she opened her mouth, she said something that surprised me.

I think her mind was on her sister's little boy. That had probably changed her quite a lot, too. Maybe I didn't know her at all anymore. It was possible we were now total strangers. The two girls who had been best friends through elementary school, and then held hands as we rode the waves of all the high school drama. The friends who got drunk together for the first time and told each other when we had our first kisses and first had sex and first fell in love and first got dumped, although Trinity never got dumped ... were those girls dead and gone?

Were we strangers? Pretending to be friends?

I'd decided to call the police. She didn't seem to know how to protect her own self, so I realized I had to do it for her. Someone had been in her house, she didn't deny that.

Since I was sleeping there too, I wasn't going to just brush that off and not worry about it. I'd already done a reading and been guided to trust my instincts. It was a weakness of mine that I often didn't trust my instincts, and a common theme in my readings was that I needed to return to my true self.

I called the non-emergency number and told them I needed to report an intruder. They asked if someone was in the house at that moment. I said, no. They asked if I felt safe. I said, yes. They told me someone would be out within two hours to take a report.

Now that it was taken care of, I turned my thoughts back to Trinity—trying to understand this new version of my friend. It was disturbing to know she'd texted that man without telling me. She'd been almost secretive about it—covering her face with her hands, then running upstairs as if she couldn't wait to escape me. I suppose that's how it is when someone is hiding from the truth. She couldn't be around me, so she'd hurried out of the room and cowered inside her own with the door closed.

The next thing I knew, he was ringing the doorbell.

Watching Trinity and the dead woman's ex walk down the driveway, whispering to each other like lifelong confidants, was so disturbing and hurtful. But mostly disturbing. What did she want from him? What could he possibly tell her that might help with this situation? Unless he confessed that he'd been the one to break into her home and move the furniture. That he was the one watching me do her reading, standing so close he'd been able to see even the third card, the future card, the one Trinity hadn't seen.

They were gone a long time. After a while, I went to the front window and looked out. They still weren't back. I stood there, hardly blinking, as if staring down the long driveway would make them materialize.

And then, just as I'd imagined, they did. Walking beside each other almost like an old married couple.

They walked more slowly as they approached the house. They stopped at the bottom of the steps and talked for a few minutes. Then he put his arms around her and held her for what seemed like forever. I felt as if a knife went through my heart.

What was he doing? What was *she* doing? I knew she was upset that David kept changing his plans, but this was awful. Was she thinking about … she wouldn't? I couldn't imagine her betraying David like this. He was an amazing guy. Yes, he worked a lot, but this? I wanted to pound my fist on the window. It was him. I'd known this guy wanted something. I'd known it the minute I met him. And I hadn't even needed to do a reading.

When I saw that, I felt things might be worse than I'd imagined.

Thankfully, she came into the house without him.

I decided not to confront her. It was better to keep this to myself. She'd seen me looking at her. Did she realize I'd also seen that? I wasn't sure. I waited for her to say something, but she was silent. She had a strange expression, something I couldn't interpret. She walked past me, headed toward the kitchen.

She opened the dining room doors and stared at the bookcases lined up against the walls. Her jaw was tight and her head thrust forward slightly, as if she'd expected them to be back where we'd left them the night before.

She turned to face me. "Brian thinks I should call the police."

"Does he?"

"He said it seems like a big leap to assume a serial killer."

I laughed. "You told him what I said?"

"It's not a secret."

I shrugged.

"But he said because of Charlotte's murder, they should know."

"Well, yes. What have I been—"

"So you were right. I'm going to—"

"Now that Brian has given his stamp of approval?" I asked.

"That's not it."

"I already called them." I turned away from her. I thought about pouring a glass of wine, but if the police were coming, it probably wasn't a good look to be sipping wine. Especially before lunchtime. I should have been relieved she agreed they needed to be called, instead of feeling upset that she looked to him for guidance instead of me.

But it still hurt.

35 NOW: TRINITY

a short, slim female cop, who didn't look large enough or strong enough to chase and tackle a teenage girl if circumstances called for it, much less an adult male, knocked on the door. Her name was Chelsea Matthews, which sounded very un-cop like, not that I knew what a cop's name should sound like. I invited her inside, and she followed us to the living room. Mia stuck to my side as if I were incapable of telling the story of what had happened without her beside me to give clarifying insight into every detail.

As it turned out, Mia didn't give any clarifying details. She let me do all the talking.

Chelsea—I suppose I should have called her Officer Matthews, even in my mind, but once I heard her first name, and every time I looked at her thin wrists and her small feet and her curly hair, I couldn't think of her as anyone but Chelsea—didn't interrupt me as I told her the first story about the night Mia had been doing the Tarot card reading.

When I was finished, she gave me a sympathetic smile. "So it does sound like you might have a rat or a mouse problem. Do you know how to recognize their droppings?"

"There were no droppings."

She nodded. "They can be hard to find. Especially for mice."

"That's fine, for the sounds we heard. The concerning part was the cards."

"It's easy to get yourself spooked when you're playing occult games. Like Tarot cards. Or Ouija boards."

I expected Mia to object to her labeling the cards as part of the occult, a dark, dismissive label Mia objected to, but she remained silent. Was I going to defend the cards for her? I didn't feel inclined to do that, but Chelsea was making us sound like silly teenagers who talked ourselves into thinking we were hearing and seeing things because we were in a suggestible mood due to our belief in occult games.

"I don't believe in any of that," I said. "Mia enjoys them, but—"

"It sounds unsettling," Chelsea said in a condescending tone that she tried to infuse with a soothing quality. "But the fact you were already on edge from being in a new, unfamiliar house, worrying about when your husband was going to arrive. And given that someone was murdered here ... it's perfectly understandable that you would think—"

"We didn't imagine it," I said. "The cards were laid out in a very specific order."

She nodded. "You said there was another incident?"

With less confidence, my voice sounding flat and uncertain, I told her about the bookcases being moved and the paint on the freshly sanded walls.

Her reaction was almost identical. Condescension, an attempt to placate me, dismissal. "I think the stress of what you've gone through is tremendous."

"It's not stress. Someone was in my house. We didn't imagine any of this stuff."

"If you checked the locks, unless someone else has a key, I don't see how—"

"It would be helpful if a patrol car could come by to check on the house a few times at night."

She smiled. "Even if there was an intruder—"

"Not if—"

"Let me finish, please." Her smile tightened. "A patrol car won't be able to help much. Someone entering your house is going to be careful not to be seen. And the odds of that happening at the same time the patrol car is in the area are slim to zero." She shrugged. "I really think these incidents are caused by—"

"I'm not imagining this. It's a little insulting that you're treating it like I'm dreaming, or having a psychotic breakdown, or whatever you want to call it."

"I'm not diagnosing your mental health," Chelsea said. "I'm just trying to take the information you're giving me and find an explanation. I'm not exactly sure what you're expecting. Do you think someone is breaking into the house every night? Or are you trying to suggest you think your house is haunted? Because the previous owner passed away?" I could see her fighting a smile, perhaps with a giggle right behind it.

"I don't think ... I don't know what I think. I just know that—"

She stood. "Please don't get upset. We'll definitely keep a record of this. In case there are more ... incidents. But you haven't reported a crime. And there's nothing I can do to ensure you don't have any more disturbing experiences, or to—"

"It seems like *because* of Charlotte's murder, it would be worth putting an officer out front to watch my house."

"I'm sorry, but we don't have enough officers to do that." She pulled a card out of her pocket and handed it to me. "If anything else happens, please call me."

"Why?"

"If it escalates, or ..."

I nodded. If it escalated. What did that even mean to her? I had a feeling a lot would have to happen for them to do anything at all. She left a few minutes later.

In the end, I almost wondered if Mia let me do all the talking so that I was the one who looked foolish, explaining that with all the doors and windows securely locked, checked twice by both myself and my houseguest, someone had been inside my home two different times. Once to peer over our shoulders from some unspecified place in the room, noticing the Tarot cards, then placing them in the same order so that we'd be scared out of our minds by the supposed message displayed there. This person had been so determined to upset us, they'd returned a second time to move furniture for no particular reason and roll a few stripes of paint across the wall.

I'd sounded like a lunatic, and Chelsea had treated me like one.

36 NOW: TRINITY

*T*hat evening, I made stir fry pork with bamboo shoots, carrots, and green beans with a healthy dose of red chili sauce. We opened a bottle of *good* Chardonnay, according to Mia.

"I wonder if I should do a new reading?" Mia said as we sat down to eat.

"No."

She sighed. "That thing with the police officer was really—"

"It didn't help that you were completely silent."

"You were explaining everything really well. I didn't want to say the wrong thing."

"She thought I was a nutcase."

"I don't think so." She took a sip of wine. She poked her fork into a piece of pork and ate it. "This is really good."

"Thank you."

"Even if you don't want a reading, let's try to put all of that behind us. We need some positive energy." Her smile was genuine. She looked relaxed and happy, glad to be eating a delicious meal and drinking wine.

"We do." I lifted my glass, and she did the same. We clicked them against each other.

"It's such a beautiful sound," she said.

I nodded.

"To old friends."

"To best friends," I said.

"The best." She gave me a tearful smile.

We clicked our glasses again.

After we ate, we refilled our glasses and went out back, determined to enjoy the peaceful, spacious yard with no thoughts of what had happened there. The sun had just gone down, and the sky was inky blue. The air was warm and soft and it felt as if we truly did have some positive energy flowing our way.

"I wish I had lawn chairs," I said.

"I'll get you a set tomorrow. As a housewarming gift."

"Not yet, but thanks for offering. I was thinking of building a patio area near the pond, maybe with lattice overhead that I could train wisteria to grow through. I might want wicker with cushions."

"It will still be my housewarming, okay? Just let me know when." She looped her arm through mine and we walked across the grassy area to the pond. We stood there and sipped our wine. By the time our glasses were empty, it was dark. We went back into the house, watched a movie on my tablet, then went to bed.

I slept well.

In the morning, as always, the first thing I did was check my phone. There were no messages. I got up and put on my hoodie, missing my long soft robe from home and wondering why I'd thought there was no room in my suitcases to pack it. Surely I could have tucked it into a corner, or managed to squeeze it into my duffle bag.

I went downstairs. The kitchen was dark, the coffee maker sparkling clean. I gazed out at the backyard, realizing that I no longer looked out there and imagined my plans for the enormous yard that had sparked memories of years with my sister and brother on our grandmother's farm, even though my yard was a fraction of the size. Now, I looked out, half expecting to see Charlotte's body still lying across the covering on the unused well. Our walk to the pond the previous evening had helped, but looking out now, the image of her crumpled body flashed across the backs of my eyes yet again.

I turned away and began making coffee.

Before going upstairs for my shower, I glanced out the front window. Mia's car was gone. I realized she must have gone to get food for breakfast. And now, I also realized she was probably buying fancy coffee drinks and I would be pouring the fresh coffee I was brewing down the drain. Or I could pour it into another container and save it for iced coffees later in the day.

When I came back down from my shower, my guess was proven right. Mia stood beside the kitchen table, beaming. She was dressed in workout clothes, her hair tied up in a ponytail. On the table were two oversized coffee drinks, a plate with croissants, and a bowl of strawberries.

"It's not a very robust breakfast for a day of scraping and painting, but we can have an early lunch. Should we eat in the sunroom?" she asked.

We moved two of the kitchen chairs to the sunroom, and although it wasn't the most comfortable arrangement, the treats made us forget the straight-back chairs without a table and we talked about how the room might be decorated.

"Let's go check out the pond again," I said. "After we work on the dining room and get the playroom and guest room painted, I'll be stalled until David gets here."

"Why is that?"

"The one thing David did mention from the inspection report is that there's a beam in the living room that needs replacing. And we'll be doing some remodeling in the kitchen. So I was thinking my next step might be hiring someone to work on building a patio area beside the pond."

"This is all feeling a little haphazard." Mia licked croissant flakes off her fingers. "It doesn't sound like you've planned it at all."

"I want to do as much as I can before Ryan comes. I'm taking care of the low-hanging fruit as fast as I can. My brother and sister-in-law's baby is due at the end of July. So I have to move fast. I want to get the rooms that I can fixed up to make it welcoming for him. The room where you're sleeping will be his. Once the guest room is painted, you can move down there and—"

"I'll probably need to get back to work before you get that far." She stood.

"Sure. I didn't mean to assume you were staying forever to help with all my random projects."

She laughed. "Let's go figure out your patio. I hope you're planning to hire someone experienced with patios. Not Brian."

"Of course."

We took our coffees and went out. The morning air was already warm. It smelled like freshly cut grass with the slight aroma of jasmine. It must have come from behind Tom and Danielle's fence, because there was none growing on my property.

We started across the yard. Mia was just ahead of me.

After a few steps, she stopped so abruptly, I almost crashed into her. Coffee sloshed in my cup and bubbled up through the tiny cutout oozing across the lid.

"Why is it like that?" she asked, her voice shrill.

"What?"

She pointed. "The cover."

I moved to her side. My fingers tightened on the coffee cup, squeezing more coffee out so that it ran down the sides and dribbled around my fingers. "I don't ..."

The cover to the well was moved away from the opening, lying upside down on the dirt.

"Do you think Brian was working out here?" Mia asked.

"I don't know. I don't know why he would be. I don't ... we're going to have this filled in as soon as we can."

"It's really unsafe," Mia said.

"I know that. But the latch was secure. It's not easy to get off."

166

"But not impossible," she said. "Obviously."

"I just don't understand why someone ... why anyone would ..." I took a few steps closer. I had an overwhelming need to look down into the depths of the well. I don't know if I expected to see water, if I thought a wild animal might have fallen inside. It was almost like the urge to step close to the edge of a cliff, or the feeling of standing at the dangerously low barrier on the balcony of a high-rise hotel, wanting to look down, sometimes almost wanting to climb over, just to see what it felt like. I shivered.

"Are you okay?"

I nodded.

"It probably doesn't mean anything," Mia said. "It's strange. It's creepy that someone was in your backyard. Again. Maybe the person who reads the water meter has to—"

"I doubt that. In the middle of the night?" I shivered again.

"It might not have been—"

"We were out here after dinner."

"Oh." She put her hand to her cheek, then lowered it to her side.

I stepped closer to the well. Mia moved with me, as if she felt the same compulsion I did. We both peered into it at the same time. And at the same time, we screamed and stumbled backward. Both of us dropped our coffees on the ground. The lids popped off and coffee spilled out.

"Oh, my God!" Mia screamed. "Oh, my GOD! Who is ...?" She began sobbing and screaming. She grabbed me, hanging on like a small child, like Ryan had after I'd taken him into my sister's bedroom so he could kiss her goodbye, when I'd taken him to the park later and tried to help him understand that this had been his last goodbye.

I felt the punch of that to my solar plexus yet again as I held Mia, crying in my arms. I wasn't sure whether I was crying for the broken body at the bottom of my well, or for Ryan, or my sister, or my own broken heart. Maybe I was crying for everyone at once.

37 THEN: PETER

I loved Sara so much. I believed our love was transcendent, a kind of love and multi-faceted connection that most people never experienced. And I wanted to be with her every night. But my work happened at night. And the problem with being an artist is that people with regular work hours will never understand that. Not in a hundred years.

In the eyes of many, I was out partying all weekend. Playing music with my buddies. Drinking beer, or so they assumed. Gone until long after midnight. How could that be a job?

In the opinions of some, I was *abandoning* the woman I loved.

Even though Charlotte Hughes didn't work so-called business hours herself, she thought my hours were an unbearable burden on Sara. A good man would be there at night. A good man would cook nutritious meals for his partner, who was battling cancer. A good man would definitely not be hanging out in bars, playing lively music, partying while his beloved soul mate was chewing CBD gummies to control the nausea caused by chemo.

The animosity started before we even got to that point.

The day Sara told me her plan for chemo, Charlotte was there.

As if it was no longer the two of us. Somehow, without me noticing when, we were a *team* of three. And soon, four.

"Don't be a child, Peter." Those were the words Charlotte hissed at me as we stood in the sunroom while Sara sat out in the backyard by the pond, gazing up at the sky, thinking about things I wanted her to share with me. Instead, I had to listen to Charlotte hissing, literally, into my ear.

"This is an all-hands-on-deck situation. I'm Sara's best friend and she needs me here. You need to put your feelings aside and do what's right for her."

"That's exactly what I'm doing, Charlotte. But you need to understand, you're not in charge here."

"I absolutely am. Sara needs an adult to take responsibility for her care."

"What's that supposed to mean?"

"Someone who can be here for her."

I wasn't going to dignify that insult with any response whatsoever.

"And that person is me."

"I live here. I'm her—"

"I know what you are."

I also didn't know what that was supposed to mean, but she obviously wasn't inclined to explain herself. I didn't want her to. What it meant was that she was showing her true colors. The woman was a class-A, self-important bitch. A control freak. Sara didn't need someone *taking responsibility*. She was a fully functioning adult. We didn't need Charlotte crawling all over our home, acting as if she lived there.

"And another thing ..."

Now she was pointing her index finger at me. I wanted to grab it and fold it down with her other fingers.

"We need to get along. For Sara. You need to treat me with respect and speak to me in a pleasant tone of voice. No more sarcasm and snide remarks or any of your other passive-aggressive bullshit. Is that clear?"

"That goes both ways," I said.

"I've always treated you with respect."

"Is that what you're doing right now? Speaking to me in a pleasant tone of voice?"

"I just want you to be clear about how things are going to be around here. I'm stressed out and maybe that's showing in my tone of voice. You should understand that and show a little compassion for once in your life."

I could not believe this woman. Everyone else was wrong all the time. And she was right. No arguments, no discussion.

"I'm going to stay over when you're hanging out with your band and all that."

"I'm not *hanging out*."

"Whatever. I'll be here for her," she said.

"It's not necessary for you to stay over."

"She shouldn't be alone. If she needs anything, someone needs to be here," she said.

"She's not dying. Sure, she'll be tired and not feeling great, but she doesn't need a babysitter. I'm here all day. Of course I have to go to work, but I'm here. All day long, every single day."

"I'm telling you how it's going to be. This is for Sara, so please stop arguing. You need to put her first."

"I've always put her first."

"Have you?"

I glared at her. I wanted to walk out of the room. I wanted her out of our house. I couldn't believe Sara had agreed to let Charlotte spend the night whenever she had her chemo treatments. Maybe she hadn't. But how could I ask now? I wanted everything to be calm and peaceful for Sara. Whatever she wanted, whatever she needed, was absolutely okay by me. But Sara should be telling me this, not Charlotte.

Sara and I were partners. We shared everything, and we knew

every nuance of each other. We didn't need this other person telling us how to live our lives, how to manage this horrible thing that had walked in and decided to make itself at home in Sara's exquisite body.

I wanted to murder this invasive, horrifying beast we couldn't see, visible only on scans of the inside of her body. But I couldn't do that. So I think a small part of me wanted to take it out on Charlotte. I wanted to pry our house key from her fingers, drag her out the front door, and lock it behind her.

I wanted to tell Sara we would fight this alone, the two of us against the world, and the monster.

38 NOW: TRINITY

*I*t made me sick to look into the well again. But I had to. Because after we'd calmed down, I began to doubt what I'd seen. It was a deep hole. Narrow and dark. It was so deep that if it weren't for the sun hitting a ghastly white face streaked and mottled with colors, I didn't have the stomach to describe, we might not have seen to the bottom. Was that really a body down there? Bent and broken? Was that awful thing a man's face? I thought it was a man, legs and arms in horribly unnatural positions against the sides of the enclosure, grotesque shadows barely visible at twilight.

What had I seen, really? Was it something I imagined because I'd feared the danger of the well, left unattended for decades, with nothing but an iron cover and a thick bar that slid beneath a metal ring? Maybe I'd remembered a fragment of a nightmare in which someone had fallen in, and now I'd imagined it, my mind spinning out of control when I saw the cover had been removed.

But why would Mia have seen the same thing? Both of us had screamed in terror, then grabbed onto each other, sobbing.

I took my phone out of my pocket and turned on the flashlight. I held it over the opening. My hand shook so badly the light danced off the sides of the hole, ricocheting from side to side as if I were trying to put on a light show inside the abandoned well.

It only took a few seconds, despite my shaky hand, to confirm what I'd seen. I moved away from the side and turned off the light. Another sob rose from my belly. "How could this happen? I don't understand."

"Could it be him? The killer? He came back for us and somehow he …" Mia stopped.

I wondered if she'd stopped because she was scared, thinking about what might have happened, or she realized how foolish her theory sounded.

The fact that the cover had been secured when we'd been out there only twelve hours earlier suggested that the man lying in a crumpled heap at the bottom had removed it himself. But how had he fallen in? Had he lost his balance with the effort of pulling the cover away from the opening?

I called 911, dreading what was to come.

While we waited for emergency services and the detective to arrive with his inevitable, persistent questions I wouldn't be able to answer, but would surely get under my skin, I called David. I was stunned when he picked up. We'd exchanged so many voicemails, and I'd sent so many text messages that sat unanswered for hours over the past week and a half, I couldn't speak when I heard his voice.

"Are you okay?" David asked for the second time.

"No."

"What's wrong?"

"There's a … a man's … a man's body. In our well."

"A … what?"

I described our experience of walking across the yard and seeing the uncovered well.

David was quiet for several minutes. "That's … I don't know what to say. I'm so sorry, Trinity. This is so … no matter what I say, it's not enough."

"I know. When are you coming?" My voice sounded weak and needy, but I didn't care.

"I'm cancelling the rest of my meetings. I'll book a flight. Now. As soon as we hang up. Okay?"

"Okay."

He told me to text him after the police left. He asked whether I had any idea who it might be. I told him I couldn't look. It was too awful. I would let the police tell me.

I half expected to feel a sick sense of déjà vu, but it wasn't like that. It felt like a dream, or a movie, as if this were all happening to someone else and I was watching from a distance, wondering what was going to happen next, noticing how horrible it was, but aware of a certain detachment from my feelings. It seemed as if I'd felt too many things in such a short amount of time that I'd used up all my feelings.

Mia and I stood in the sunroom, watching them haul the man's body out of the well. Watching, but not watching. I didn't want to see what they had to do, and I didn't want to see the remains of a human being dragged out of that narrow hole like a bunch of debris that had been left in there for years, rotting in the water. Maybe it *had* been there for years, maybe someone had simply pulled the cover off so we could see what was hidden below the ground of my beautiful new home. A home that was starting to feel like a house of mirrors.

But if that were the case, wouldn't we have noticed? Wouldn't there have been a terrible odor, some obvious signs? Bones and missing flesh? I was sure I would have noticed that. I shuddered, my whole body convulsing as if an electric shock had surged through me.

"Are you okay?" Mia put her arm around me, pulling me close.

I nodded, my head rubbing against her shoulder.

"Whatever horrible things you're thinking, stop."

"I just …" I moved away from her, closer to the large windows that made up two of the four walls, allowing the room to fill with light from sunrise through the middle of the afternoon. I looked out, despite promising myself I wouldn't pay close attention. We should have gone into the living room to wait for the detective to arrive. There wasn't anything good that would come out of watching this horror show.

And then, I saw them lift the body out, already encased in a black bag. I felt my shoulders relax, relieved that I wouldn't have to see what I'd been dreading all the time we'd been standing there. The men and women beside the well grabbed the bag and carefully lowered it to the ground.

As one of them stepped back, something caught on the opening of the bag glittered in the sunlight, then came loose and dropped to the ground. Just before it fell, I saw what the sunlight had captured —the lens in a pair of eyeglasses. Distinctive, stylish black frames. I felt like I'd been punched—the second time since I'd lived in my new home. A hard fist to the bone of my solar plexus. The air went out of me and I doubled over, gasping.

Mia put her hand on my back, then grabbed my shoulders. "What happened? What's wrong?"

"It's ... those are his glasses."

"What?"

"Brian. I saw Brian's glasses. It's him."

She gasped, then coughed at the sudden intake of breath. "You can't be sure."

"I know it's him."

"But he ... lots of people, hundreds, thousands of people wear the same kind of glasses."

"It's him."

The doorbell rang. I removed her hands from my shoulders and walked out of the room.

When we were seated in the living room, once again facing Detective Robbins, a wave of exhaustion washed over me. It left me more drained than I recalled feeling in my entire life. I didn't have the strength to answer his questions. I didn't want to hear him ask me things I didn't know, insisting I must have seen and heard things I hadn't. I couldn't stomach his certainty that I wasn't in touch with my own memory.

He plowed ahead, asking us to explain every step of how we'd found the well uncovered and the body inside. He asked us the same ridiculous questions about hearing people arguing, raised voices during the night. Screams. The sound of the cover being removed. He asked us whether we'd seen anything, if there had been other sounds that had disturbed our sleep.

"Why do you think two people have been found dead on your property in the past ten days? One of them, very possibly both, the victims of murder?"

"I have no idea! Aren't you supposed to tell *us* why?" I asked.

He gave me a look that said it was his job to ask questions, our job to answer questions, and, if such things can be read into a simple scowling facial expression, that he was not used to hearing questions from the people he spoke to.

"I've only investigated five murders in the last sixteen months, and two of them have been at your house. In the past two weeks."

"That's not my fault."

He didn't say anything.

"It's not," Mia said. "It's not her fault."

I was annoyed that she'd felt she had to back me up, as if my word wasn't good enough on its own. I was even more upset that she'd found a way to isolate me, suggesting that she had nothing to do with it, that this was solely my problem. Maybe it was.

"It raises a lot of questions in my mind," Detective Robbins said. "You're new in the area. You bought a home that you only intend to use for a few months during the year. You move in, without your husband, whom you keep insisting will be joining you, but he isn't anywhere to be seen. And now two people are murdered on your property. It's a very atypical situation. And when situations aren't typical, I start asking questions."

"Well, I can't answer your questions. My husband is traveling for work, which a lot of people do, so I don't see why you think that's so unusual. And I don't think buying a summer home is all that unusual either."

"Around here, it is."

"Things change, even around here," I said.

He grunted softly. He studied us for a moment, then got to his feet. "I understand you called the non-emergency number to report an intruder yesterday."

"Mia did," I said.

"But you believed there was an intruder?"

"Yes."

"And you were concerned that this person might have killed Ms. Hughes?"

"It's possible, don't you think?"

"Anything is possible," he said. "It's also possible it's unrelated. Or that there was no intruder."

"Did you read the report?" I asked.

"Yes."

Because he said nothing more, it sounded as if he thought I was a kook who believed a ghost was moving things around in my house. Or more extreme—that I thought the spirit of a dead woman was committing murders on my property, that maybe she was coming for me.

Of course, who knew what he was thinking? All I really knew was what he'd said—the things that had happened in and around my home weren't normal, and that was causing him to ask questions about me. And possibly Mia, but his attention was directed at me.

Did he really think I was murdering everyone who came to my house? And then calling the police because I thought there was a ghost on the premises? What *was* he thinking? I didn't like the way he was looking at me.

39 NOW: TRINITY

The moment Detective Robbins was gone, I closed the door from the living room to the sunroom, so I didn't have to see another minute of what was going on in my backyard. The detective had said they would be finished by the end of the day.

Mia and I sat for a while on the front porch steps and talked about what had happened. Mostly, we talked in circles because we couldn't make sense of anything. She had been so certain Brian was the one who was creeping around inside my house, certain he was Charlotte's killer.

"This doesn't mean he wasn't, obviously, but it does seem less likely. And I guess it means he can't do anything to us now. But also, I won't believe for sure it's him until the police tell us that."

"It's him." I pointed through the Eucalyptus trees clustered at the front of my property, spilling over into Tom and Danielle's yard. Brian's truck was parked across the street, not visible from any of our windows, but now in plain sight from where we sat. "Did you see it when you went out for coffee?"

She stared, then closed her eyes, trying to remember. She shook her head. "I don't know." She opened her eyes and rested her chin in her hands. "It doesn't matter. Someone is killing people in your backyard and someone was inside your house." She stood and leaned her hip against the railing. "Are you *still* planning to stay here?"

I nodded. "I ... yes. I have to."

"You need a security camera. I don't know why you didn't ... why *we* didn't think of that right away."

I felt my mouth open as if it were operating independently from my brain. Why *hadn't* I thought of that? It was so obvious. We had a security system at home. And eventually I would have done the same here. But because I hadn't fully moved in, it hadn't occurred to me. My thoughts had been flitting out of control, like a bee drunk on too much nectar, unable to focus on anything for more than a few minutes.

"Let's take care of that right now," she said. "And this afternoon, we'll get back to work on the house. I'll strip the wallpaper in the guest room and you can—"

"I'll paint Ryan's playroom. I think that would make me feel better." It seemed disrespectful. Kind of awful. But sitting around thinking about murder was not an option. I had a child to think of. A child who had already experienced the worst loss imaginable. He was all that mattered. Creating a home for him.

"Yes." Mia clapped her hands and grinned. "Something positive. And, I don't care what you say, and you don't have to participate, but I'm doing a reading for this house. And for you." She sat beside me and gave me a hug.

While I spent time going over camera features with the sales guy at the electronics store, Mia grew increasingly bored. Finally, she left to run a few other errands, telling me to text her when I was finished.

A few hours later, we returned home with a large, thick plastic bag filled with two small cameras and the supporting equipment needed to keep a digital eye on my house. One camera would be installed above the front door, its range extending down the driveway, and the other at the back door. We'd decided it wasn't necessary to put one near the laundry room entrance at the side of the house. The front camera would have a wide enough angle to see anyone approaching the yard on either side. A technician from the electronics store was scheduled to come out the following day to install the equipment. I tried not to beat up on myself for not thinking of a security camera the moment we'd seen the Tarot cards laid out on the living room floor.

Famished, we ate lunch, changed into work clothes, and got to it.

As we worked, we called back and forth to each other across the hallway, although the rooms were just far enough apart that we couldn't always hear the other. So as I scraped the burnt orange off the playroom walls, sanded the plaster, and painted the first coat of a beautiful sky blue, I placed my tools on the floor every fifteen or twenty minutes and walked across the hall to check on Mia's progress.

"You're not going to finish today if you keep stopping to inspect my work," she said.

"I need companionship," I said. "I'm really glad you're here, have I mentioned that?"

"Only about ten times today." She laughed and peeled off a long strip of paper, made goopy by the removal solution. She dropped it into the garbage bag where she was collecting the waste.

"It feels creepy to be fixing up the house when a forensics team is digging up my backyard."

"This is supposed to be taking your mind off it," she said.

"It is. Sort of. But I feel …" I shivered. "Guilty or something."

"Guilty? Why would you feel guilty?"

"Two people have been murdered right outside my window. And I'm listening to my favorite playlist and painting a whimsical room for a child as if everything is completely normal."

"It's not your fault they're dead."

"I know that. But I've never known anyone who was murdered. And it just feels … I don't know. It feels wrong, somehow. It's upsetting."

"We have to do *something* to keep busy. We can't sit around and try to solve the crime."

I knew she was right. I agreed completely, but it still bothered me. It felt cold and selfish. But maybe all of life was that way. Every moment of every day people were suffering all over the world, and those who were not,carried on as if it wasn't happening. Maybe there wasn't a choice. Otherwise, you sank into a puddle of grief and you were no longer a living being. You might as well be dead yourself. Or was that rationalization?

"Stop thinking," Mia said. "I can see in your eyes that you're overthinking again." She peeled the thin rubber gloves off her hands. "Let's do a reading. Right now."

"That's not the answer."

She gave me a sad look, as if she felt sorry that I didn't have something to hang onto, as if her deck of cards could be counted on to make everything okay. She gave me a hug. "Then go back to your music and your painting. I'll do it for you."

She let go of me and gently pushed me out of the room, across the hall, and into Ryan's future playroom. As I inhaled the aroma of fresh paint and let the soothing blue that already covered two of the walls wash over me, an image flashed through my mind—Ryan, David, and I walking through a toy store, picking out blocks and cars, oversized pillows and small play figures to fill this room.

Mia left me alone.

I painted the other two walls, my thoughts lost in my favorite songs, feelings more optimistic about the future with each streak of paint that covered the scraped and sanded burnt orange.

When Mia returned, she gushed over the transformation of the room. She was smiling as if she'd just had the best sex of her life. "I have great news for you. The future of this house will be filled with love and romance and an abundance of happiness. I know you don't believe me. That's your choice, but knowing that makes me feel absolutely incredible." She gave me a confident grin, then slipped out the door.

A moment later, I heard her singing to herself as she returned to stripping wallpaper.

40 NOW: PETER

*W*atching her care for that house filled me with a warmth I couldn't describe. The feeling was close to desire—strange and intensely personal. Something I could never tell another person. There was a tenderness in the way she applied paint to the walls, in the careful, steady movements of her arm when she sanded the plaster, pausing to feel it with her other hand to check that her strokes were even and the results were creating a smooth surface.

The house was almost an extension of her, as if it had grown up around her, a second skin. It seemed to hold her breath in its walls and her heartbeat in the rhythm of the sun passing through its windows every day—first pouring through the sunroom and living room windows facing east, then spilling sideways across the windows at the back and filling the front porch at midday, and finally warming the kitchen and the west side late in the afternoon.

It wasn't only the house. She was there in the dreams she'd had for the garden and the growth and shape of the trees, and that tranquil pond near the back of the property.

I knew every inch of it, like I knew the inside of my own mind, the contours of her body, and the shape of our relationship, the notes and words of every song I'd ever composed. Even those that were never performed for another pair of ears.

All of this gave me a comforting feeling as I sat on Danielle and Tom's living room couch, watching Danielle pour white wine into three glasses. She offered a toast, but the words drifted past me, and the moment she finished speaking, I couldn't have said what they were.

Danielle settled in the chair facing me. Tom stood by the window, blocking my view of the house. As if he knew. As if he wanted to stop me from looking.

"I would never wish death on anyone," Danielle said. "Murder is ugly. The worst crime."

"Then let's not talk about it," Tom said.

"We have to. It happened right next door," Danielle said.

"We don't have to," Tom murmured.

"It's almost like they asked for it, though," Danielle said. "Both of them."

"No one asks for it, and you shouldn't say things like that. It's—"

"The thoughts are there. I can't help that. I'm just being honest and saying what I think. I'm not going to lie."

I appreciated Danielle felt what I felt. Of course, all I heard echoing in my head was Charlotte's assessment of me—whiner. But I wasn't that. I was a man so deeply in love I sometimes couldn't see straight, and when you can't see straight, you make mistakes. Maybe I made a few. Maybe I made a lot of mistakes. I loved two things in life—Sara Linden-Price and music. To my never-ending regret, a regret that will follow me to my grave, I behaved as if I loved music more.

At least, that's how I made Sara feel. But I also needed to make a living. It was an impossible choice. A choice that only the devil can offer.

"It was terrible what Charlotte did to you," Danielle said.

"I appreciate so much that you recognize that."

"But it's time to move past it," Tom said. "We've beat it to death. It's over. The house is sold. You're never going to come to terms with your loss if you keep picking at the scab."

"Maybe he doesn't want to come to terms, Tom." Danielle took a huge swallow of wine. Gulping it as if it were a glass of water.

Tom stared at her with a look that was hard to decipher. Shock? Or disgust?

I'd been in an absolute state of shock when Charlotte spoke to me. Even when you know someone is going to die, even when death's fingers are so close you can see the woman you love slipping away from you, feel her body shutting down, the shock of that final breath is like a punch in the heart.

My heart was bleeding, aching, splattered all over the ground when Sara stopped breathing.

The bed where her body had lain was still warm. I knew because I was sitting at the foot, my hand burrowed beneath the sheets, my eyes closed, my cheeks wet with tears. I heard Charlotte's voice. There were no tears in her throat, no ache that softened the volume.

"You have two weeks, Peter. After that, we're changing the locks."

I said nothing. I didn't know who *we* referred to, but I assumed it was Brian. The two of them were thick as thieves. An appropriate description at that moment. Possibly, *we* also included other friends of Sara's who had been part of their gang during the years Brian and Sara were married. The group that had Friday night wine parties until Sara started spending her Friday nights gently moving her body to my music, letting my music shape her sculpture. But they hadn't known that. It was likely they still didn't, despite the mural on the dining room wall.

"Did you hear me?" Charlotte asked.

I still didn't speak. The tears dried as a deeper, burning, all-consuming pain took their place. Leaving this house meant leaving Sara behind. Leaving us behind.

How would I live without this space where we'd been together?

Of course I knew she was gone from the earth. But how could I sustain myself without eating in the dining room where we'd laughed over the five-course meals we'd cooked together? How could I rest without lying in the bed where our bodies had been wrapped around each other for countless nights? I would never walk into her studio and see her bent over a lump of clay again, never sit on the front porch to watch the sky grow light in the morning or dark in the evening.

Of course, I hadn't imagined I would stay there forever. Although it was possible I'd had fleeting dreams of buying the house. Maybe. If I could manage. But when the woman you love is dying, you aren't working out real estate transactions.

But this?

"Peter! Look at me. We need to get this settled. Now."

I didn't look at her. My eyes remained closed. "Now? Really?"

"Peter?" Danielle's voice was kind, breaking the echoing memory of Charlotte's vitriol.

I took a sip of wine.

"Are you okay?"

"Hey, buddy," Tom said. "You gotta let this go. It's gonna kill you. Sara wouldn't want this for you."

"Sara didn't want me kicked out of the house, either."

"Fair enough," Tom said. "But it's over. You have to get past it and stop brooding over it. Stop talking about it."

"He needs to process his grief," Danielle said.

Soon, they would be off in a conversation of their own, talking about me as if I weren't there, as they had several times before.

"This isn't grief," Tom said. "This is resentment. Charlotte's gone now. It seems like a good time to put it all behind you."

"Not until he's ready," Danielle said. "You can't rush this. It takes time."

"I think there's been plenty of time," Tom said.

He was wrong. There would never be enough time. But in a

strange mockery, there was also too much time. All I had was time. Time to think and remember and regret. To remember that we hadn't had enough time, and remember all the time that Charlotte had stolen from me.

41 NOW: TRINITY

$\mathcal{A}$s I descended the stairs in the dim, pre-dawn light, I was overcome by the aroma of fresh paint. It smelled like a new beginning. I turned at the landing and hurried down the last section of the staircase, landing in the hallway with a thud.

Although I couldn't wait to look at Ryan's playroom in the morning light, I needed coffee first. While I waited for it to brew, I imagined him sitting on a soft, sky-blue carpet, playing with a wooden train set, the tracks winding in a complicated arrangement around the entire room. I would sit beside him, rebuilding the track as he pulled it apart. I'd spent enough time with him to know that at his age, pulling apart tracks, knocking down towers of building blocks, and smashing sand castles made from overturned buckets were his favorite activities.

Thinking about him in this house was both exciting and frightening. I worried he would feel disoriented and scared outside his familiar environment. I planned to bring all his furniture and toys. His bedroom upstairs, just a few yards from where David and I slept, would be painted the same pale yellow as his bedroom in my sister's home.

The more I considered it, the more I wondered if it might be better for him to stay in this house full time for a while. Moving him here for the last two months of the summer, followed by another move back to our home in Silicon Valley, might be traumatic. I wondered how David would feel about that?

Holding a thick white mug in both hands, the steam from the coffee warming my face, I walked slowly toward the front of the house. I stepped into the playroom and froze. My fingers turned stiff, then numb, and the mug slid out of my hands. It crashed to the floor. The ceramic splintered into several pieces and hot coffee splashed across my bare feet and ankles. I screamed at the pain, and two of the four walls leering at me.

They were burnt orange. The pale blue color I'd painted yesterday was gone.

I screamed again, backing out of the room, stepping on a sharp piece of ceramic that pierced my heel, tearing a gash that felt like it had cleanly sliced off a chunk of my flesh. I cried out with a different kind of pain, feeling the warm blood oozing out, causing my foot to skid on the slippery stuff.

Grabbing the doorframe, I lifted my foot to see the wound. Blood dripped onto the floor. I tried not to look at the dark, hideous orange, glaring at me like a sky enraged with the blazing sun and smoke from a forest fire. Half sobbing and screaming, I hobbled into the hallway so I didn't have to see it.

Mia, coming around the corner from the stairs, crashed into me.

"What's wrong? What ... you're bleeding? What happened?" She pulled a tissue out of her pocket and knelt to press it to my foot. It was immediately soaked with blood.

"The paint," I whispered.

She looked through the doorway into the room. "What's wrong?"

"I painted the entire room."

She shook her head. "No."

I limped away from her, dragging my heel, and the bloody tissue stuck to it, across the floor. "Yes, I did."

"I think you're misremembering. You started painting, but you—"

"Don't do this, Mia. I've had enough. I don't need you doing this."

"Let's get this cleaned and bandaged. You're really upset, and you're getting blood everywhere. We need to make sure this is clean."

"I'm fine. Except for the room! I painted the entire room, and now half of it's the same color as before."

She stood. "You stay here. I'll bring bandages and stuff. Do you have a first aid kit?"

"No."

"Well, let's see what I can manage."

She left me and went to the kitchen. A few minutes later she returned with a bowl of water, several hand towels, paper towels, anti-bacterial hand soap, and painter's tape. "I'll clean it up. We can bandage it with a towel for now, and I'll run to the store for ointment and some real bandages. I hope you won't need stitches."

"I painted the entire room. You saw it."

"I didn't see all of—"

"Yes, you did."

She turned her attention to pressing paper towels to my heel, soaking up the blood, washing the cut, then wrapping the towel around it and securing it with tape.

"I painted the entire room. I know you saw it. I don't know why you're pretending you didn't."

She rubbed my ankle gently. "I'm not pretending. I just wonder if you're forgetting? You've had an unbelievable amount of stress—the murders, David's constant schedule changes. And you're still grieving, don't forget—"

"I haven't forgotten I'm grieving! And I know what walls I painted."

"You came into the other room so many times to check up on

me." She laughed, somewhat mechanically. "I don't know how you think you would have had time to paint the entire room."

I shoved myself away from her and pushed myself to my feet. "Stop talking about it. I painted the room and now half of it's the same color as before." I started into the playroom, intending to look for a can of the burnt orange paint.

"Don't go in there with bare feet! You'll slice yourself up again."

I stopped and limped back to the doorway. "Please go get me some bandages. I need to get dressed. The guy is coming at ten to install the security camera."

"I'll be back before then." She tried to touch my arm.

"Stay away from me."

"I know you're upset."

"I'm upset because you're treating me like a lunatic. I know what I did. And now, I'm actually more upset—I'm starting to think you painted the room to freak me out."

"I would never do—"

"Maybe you want to upset me so I'll agree to a card reading or something. I don't know. Just go get my bandages." I turned and limped to the stairs. I climbed slowly, making sure not to put pressure on my foot. At least I was no longer scared. Now, I was angry. Angry and confused because I had no idea why Mia would try to frighten me with such a ridiculous trick. Maybe it was all about trying to get me interested in her cards.

Whatever her reason, I felt unsettled and utterly betrayed.

42 NOW: TRINITY

*E*ven with the security cameras installed, I didn't feel any more secure. Because now I felt as if one of the people whom I trusted most in the world had turned against me. I didn't understand why she'd played such a cruel trick on me. After my shower, I'd searched the entire house. The only thing making me wonder whether I was rushing to judgment was that I didn't find a can of burnt orange paint anywhere.

While I hunted for the paint, I'd tried to come up with a reason for Mia's betrayal, but my mind remained empty. There was no reason for her to want to torment me like she had. I was miserable, half crying, drifting around the house, wondering why she was taking so long to purchase a few bandages and a tube of antiseptic ointment.

I texted David, but of course, there was no response. I was starting to think—not starting, I realized I'd felt for some time—that he was avoiding coming to the house. He hadn't wanted to buy it, but after he'd risen to the occasion and taken care of all the details, I thought he'd come around.

Now, it felt passive aggressive to leave me here on my own for so long. Two people had been murdered here! Would he even show up when I went to pick up Ryan to bring him to his new home? Ryan hadn't seen David since Jen's memorial service. Re-establishing a connection was going to be as challenging as acclimating him to his new home.

I was completely and utterly overwhelmed. And alone. I felt like everyone had abandoned me.

By lunchtime, Mia still hadn't returned. The bleeding had stopped hours earlier, but the towel was stiff with dried blood. I unwrapped the makeshift bandage and put the towel in hot water to soak. I washed the cut again and looked at the wound. It wasn't nearly as deep as I'd thought based on the pain I'd felt and the amount of blood. At least I didn't feel the need to go to urgent care to ask about stitches. I re-wrapped it and settled on the couch.

I called my sister-in-law for an update on Ryan, which calmed me. I didn't tell her anything about what had happened. There was no reason to pass on stories of murder and intruders and issues with my husband. She placed her tablet in front of Ryan and I sang Twinkle, Twinkle Little Star to him. Four times. That, and seeing his smile of recognition, did wonders for me.

Things with David would work themselves out. I reminded myself that I always felt disconnected from him when he was over-seas. As much as I needed his emotional support, his presence wouldn't change anything. Undoubtedly, he recognized that and was focused on getting work done so he could put that aside when he was here.

Mia and I would work things out. What she'd done was beyond cruel, but she'd been my friend forever. Maybe her stupid game had been her own frightened reaction to the murders and the fear of violence, of someone being inside the house. She'd given up her time to stay with me, to help me fix up the house. And she hadn't let any of these horrifying and strange things scare her into leaving.

Thanks to my security camera, I saw her car pull into the driveway a few minutes after two o'clock. I hurried to the kitchen and used the leftover coffee that I'd stuck in the fridge while it was fresh that morning to make us two iced coffee drinks.

When she came into the house, the front door closed gently, as if she wanted to show she was being meek. Gentle. She wanted to start over. But despite my realization she was my lifelong friend who was probably feeling as upset as I was and had simply acted out, I was still angry. Starting over wasn't as easy as a careful closing of the door.

I met her in the hallway—halfway, as it were. "I made iced coffee. Do you want some?"

She gave me a grateful smile. "That sounds good. I'm really sorry I was gone so long. I should have texted. I had some things I needed to take care of. Let me fix your foot first."

As she cleaned my cut and put on a proper bandage, we didn't talk much. The accusations and hurt hung silently around us.

"There." She patted my foot. "That's much better."

"Thanks." I pulled my sock back over my bandaged foot.

Mia slurped the last of her coffee and pushed the glass to the side. "I know you're really upset with me, but I'm just trying to figure out what's going on here. I told you the cards said there would be happiness in this house. What I didn't tell you was—"

"Please don't start with the cards. I'm not in the mood."

"I need to tell you this. I know you don't take it seriously, but they've been right ninety percent of the time. More than ninety percent."

"You've kept track?"

She waved her hand in the space between us. "You know what I mean."

"Yes. You made up that number."

"Will you just listen? You've had so, *so* much stress. Losing your sister was …" Her eyes filled with tears.

Despite being upset with her, I felt her love. She was my oldest friend. She'd never lied to me. I couldn't recall her ever lying to anyone.

"It was awful," Mia said. "More than most people have ever faced at our age. And you don't know what that does to your mind."

I felt my neck stiffen. "I'm not going crazy."

She put her hand over mine. "Let me finish. You've been through so much. And then Charlotte murdered right in your backyard. And the pressure of becoming the mother for a little boy who has no idea what happened in his life. It's ... well, it's a *lot*. And I wonder if you've been sleepwalking."

I laughed.

"You did once, remember?"

"When I was twelve."

"Hear me out. Stress might have caused you to do that. It's a genuine factor. Maybe ... maybe you moved the bookcases. And repainted the room. And maybe ... this is so hard to say, but I really have to. Maybe you caught Brian in the house, or saw him out back, and you pushed him into the well."

I shoved my chair away from the table with so much force it tipped over, crashing to the floor. I stood, backing away from her. My skin was hot, my eyes so full of tears I couldn't see her face. "I can't believe you said that. I can't believe you even thought that!" I was edging toward the door, not watching where I was going, not paying attention to my foot, which was stinging as I put too much pressure on it. "That's the worst thing anyone has ever said to me. I would never, ever ... not in a million years. I would never do something like that. Never!" I was screaming now, my hands clenched into fists so tight they ached.

"In your *sleep!* We do strange things in our dreams. Terrible things, sometimes. We're not responsible. You've been thinking about Sara's spirit being in the house, talking about it, having dreams you probably don't even remember about your sister, about ... it's just too much for your tired, hurting heart. Your mind can only take—"

"Stop! Stop talking. Just stop. You're making this up. You just make up all these things, you look at those stupid cards and they don't mean anything and you make up whatever you want and you think it's a message and it's not! So don't act like you know something about me, that you have some kind of special *insight*. You don't have any idea what's going on inside my head." I was sobbing so hard my throat was raw and my chest ached. I couldn't look at her. "I want you to leave. I want you out of here."

"I can't do that, Trinity. I won't do that. I'm your best friend. I love you, and you're so fragile. I won't leave you alone. I know you hate me right now, and that's okay. But I'm not leaving you."

I ran out of the room and up the stairs. I slammed my bedroom door and fell onto my bed.

I cried for a long time.

Just before I fell asleep, the most awful thought passed through my mind. What if she was right? What if I had pushed Brian into the well?

43 NOW: TRINITY

*M*y unplanned nap was tortured with dreams. It was one of those wakeful naps in which I felt I was sleeping, yet aware of the images flashing across the screen of my mind—the hidden part of my brain telling wild stories to my conscious mind.

Part of me wanted to sleep, to fall into a dreamless state, to escape. Another part of me wanted to wake and drag Mia out of the house so I didn't have to listen to another amateur psychological analysis of my state of mind, so I never had to see or hear about a Tarot card for the rest of my life.

Yet she was my closest friend. My forever friend. Almost like a sister. She'd always told me I was like a sister to her. I'd never said that in return, of course, and that had probably hurt her. I already had a sister. Now ...

Finally, my thoughts dissolved, and I slept.

An hour later, I woke with calmer thoughts toward Mia. I washed my face. As the cold water ran off my skin, I decided there were too many years and too many good things between us to let a few horrible, misguided, thoughtless comments cut us apart forever. That wasn't what I really wanted. Now that I'd learned the harshness of *forever*, I was not about to become the type of person who cut friends or family out of my life because of misspoken words and wounded feelings. People who loved each other talked about their hurts. No relationship ran smoothly day in and day out. We all said and did thoughtless, hurtful things. She was as scared and confused as I was. Searching for answers.

Yes, this was beyond anything I'd experienced. It required a lot more from me. It would require a lot more from her, but it wasn't impossible.

I found her in the sunroom. She'd arranged the cushions from the living room couch on the floor. She was leaning against the wall, holding a glass of white wine.

She looked at me and gave me a pleading, hopeful smile. "Do you want a glass of wine?"

"No thanks."

I pulled one of the cushions away from her side so it faced her and sat down cross-legged.

"I'm so sorry," she said.

"I don't sleepwalk."

"Even if you did …" She took a sip of wine.

"I don't."

"Definitely not to that degree. For that—"

"You don't need to say anymore."

She nodded. "I was trying to think of something. Anything. It was stupid."

"Right now, there isn't any explanation. Hopefully, Detective Robbins will get some answers."

"I'm not counting on that," she said.

"Why not?"

"How can he? Two people? In the middle of the night? It's not like anyone left fingerprints. I'm sure they wore gloves to move the cover to the well. It just …" She took another sip of wine.

"I hate it when you tell me what I'm thinking or feeling," I said. "Or when you think you know my future."

"I get it."

"I don't think you do."

"I absolutely do. Can't you accept that I've had experiences you haven't? I want to share those with you and you refuse to give me any credibility. So that's really hurtful too. Have you ever considered that?"

I hadn't. And I hadn't meant to hurt her. But did that mean I had to pretend to buy-in to the idea of fortunetelling cards? I couldn't do that. I would never do that. So I wasn't sure what the answer was. Maybe if she stopped shoving them down my throat. Who was at fault here? Me for refusing to honor her beliefs, or her for trying to force me to participate in her ritual? I was certain it was her. I could accept her consulting her cards for her own life. But not for mine.

The doorbell rang, excusing me from having to answer. Maybe she knew my answer because I'd said nothing. I'd never considered that I was hurting her every time I rejected a reading. And now, I wasn't sure how this conversation would change anything.

I pushed myself to my feet and went to the front door. Detective Robbins stood on the porch.

"May I come in?"

Why was that always his request? He never said hello or how are you or I have an update for you. In fact, apparently, I wasn't deserving of any updates on the murders committed in my yard. Maybe there were no updates. He appeared to be as clueless as we were. And for that reason, he wanted to come in. He wanted to ask more questions. He wanted to find someone, somewhere to give him the answers he couldn't figure out himself.

Maybe there were no answers. Maybe we would never know.

I moved back into the foyer. He stepped inside, closed the door behind him, and followed me to the living room as if this were a ritual we now lived by.

We settled in our usual places. Mia came in and sat beside me. It was the strangest feeling because the stern gaze of the detective had the effect of washing away every prick of hurt and animosity I'd felt toward her. I wanted to take her hand and squeeze it. Without a word exchanged between us, without any more discussion of cards or the horrible suggestion that I'd inadvertently killed a sweet, kind man, I felt as if she and I were teenagers again. Best friends who would stick together until the end of our lives. So close that no hot boy, no mean girl, no ugly words or terrible mistake would ever split us apart.

Without the slightest tremor of doubt, I did take her hand. She squeezed my fingers, and we held on tight.

The detective looked at us as if we were, indeed, children. Two little girls in a lot of trouble.

"I've just finished speaking to your neighbors."

"Tom and Danielle?" I asked.

"All of your surrounding neighbors, but yes, the Vargas's as well."

"I haven't met any of the others yet."

He raised his eyebrows and tapped a note into his phone, as if my failure to meet my other neighbors indicated a flaw, maybe even a criminal tendency. Perhaps it told him I was a person who kept to herself, and therefore, a person who had dark secrets that drove her to keep those around her at arm's length.

"They told me they'd spoken to Mr. Price on ..." he checked his phone. "Saturday. Mr. Price told them he thought something was *off* about the occupants of this house."

I laughed. "Okay."

"You think that's funny?"

"A little."

"Why?"

"Because it doesn't mean anything."

"Why do you think that?"

"Because something being *off* can mean anything in the world, or nothing at all. I can't possibly guess what he might have meant by that."

"Something bothered him enough to comment to your neighbors."

I shrugged.

He directed his attention to Mia. "What do you think it means?"

"I read Tarot cards. Maybe that made him uncomfortable. A lot of people don't understand the practice." She gave my hand a gentle squeeze.

The detective studied her as if he expected her to say more.

"Is that the only question you have?" I asked.

"Neither one of you saw or heard anything the night Mr. Price fell, or was pushed, into the well?"

"No," I said.

"No," Mia said.

"I'm finding it increasingly difficult to believe that both of you are sleeping in this house and have heard nothing when one individual was strangled and another fell to his death less than forty feet from your window."

"It's really frustrating that you keep asking us the same questions," I said.

"I think you're not telling me everything."

"You have no reason to think that," Mia said.

"In my experience, there's always someone who sees or hears *something*. And you two were right here."

"We were asleep," I said.

"And aside from the Tarot cards, you can't think of any other reason why Mr. Price thought something about you was off?"

"No. Because I have no idea what he meant." I didn't know, and I also felt betrayed. I thought Brian and I had a connection. I'd thought he was my friend.

44 THEN: PETER

*C*harlotte and I had what can only be described as a masquerade through Sara's first cancer surgery and the three months of chemo that followed. We took turns cooking for her and taking her to her chemo treatments. We spoke to each other with the utmost courtesy. We made concessions, and we went out of our way to laugh at each other's jokes, to show interest in the other's work, and to be helpful when the other needed it.

Every gesture and word a grand, elaborate show for Sara.

I never knew whether Sara believed it was real or not. She and I didn't discuss it.

Once she was in remission, I felt I could breathe again. Sara felt she could breathe again.

Charlotte went home. The house was ours. Sara gained weight and her hair grew back. She was sculpting, and I was writing more songs than ever.

Then everything fell apart.

It was like watching a slow-motion car crash—someone shows you the crash in slow motion, then rewinds it and shows it to you in real time. There's a disoriented feeling that you're not watching the same event. It's moving so slowly you feel as if you can do something to prevent the inevitable. But in real time, you blink, and everything explodes.

That's what happened to us.

I was out every night on the weekends as I'd always been, but this time, Sara couldn't handle it. I think being sick had changed her in ways I hadn't recognized. She looked the same, with her thick, luscious hair and curvy body. Her laugh was the same, and her thoughts, at least those she shared with me, felt the same. Her art had shifted, but not dramatically. Her sculptures were still filled with life and grace, but maybe, looking back, they became a little more ethereal, a little more … I couldn't put my finger on it.

She wanted me more. She needed me more.

She loved my music as much as ever, but she didn't love that music meant fans and that fans wanted and needed me. I think she tried to let me have that, and she wanted me to have that. I don't really know.

It was a fall evening. We were sitting on the front porch drinking tea that she'd brewed from loose leaves, something she'd gotten into it when she was sick—treating it like a ritual of some kind. She liked measuring the tiny leaves into the strainer, heating the water to the specified temperature, and pouring it slowly and lovingly over the leaves. She thought it tasted like the nectar of the gods. I couldn't honestly tell the difference, but I did love watching her do it.

"This isn't working," she said.

"Did you get leaves in it?" I asked.

"I'm not talking about the tea."

"What?"

"You and me."

"What's not working?"

"I can't live like this. I need a whole person."

"What does than mean?"

"Exactly what I said."

"You have all of me. My entire heart, my—"

"You aren't here. I want someone holding me when I fall asleep every night. Life is too short."

So maybe I did know what had changed. She'd faced the reality of death. I thought I had too, with the scare of cancer, but maybe not in the same way. Obviously, not in the same way.

"But I ... I can't be a musician without—"

"I know. And I've thought about that every which way, but I just can't do it. There are other ways. You could record, you could arrange for dinner shows, afternoon performances, come home earlier. I don't know, but I do know what I need, and it's clear you can't give it."

"What are you ..." I put my tea on the ground. I couldn't drink it and have this conversation. Was she breaking up with me? What was she saying? It seemed both completely obvious and totally confusing.

"I want you to move your things out. I don't want to be together anymore."

"Don't you love me?"

"I do, but it's too painful. Loving you is too hard."

"That doesn't make sense. I can ... you need to give me a chance. We can work on a compromise."

"You knew this was hurting me, and you've had months, more than a year. You managed when I was sick, but now, everything is the same as before."

"But that's because you were ... it was an extreme situation. Music is my life. And my livelihood, you know that. You can't—"

"It was extreme. But life is an extreme situation, don't you think? I've given it a lot of thought. More than you can imagine. And I've made my decision."

"Without talking about it?"

"We've talked about it a thousand times."

"But not like this."

"I don't want you to change because you think you have to, because you're forced into it. You had to want it, and clearly, you didn't. You don't. I do love you, Peter, but I just can't." She stood and went into the house.

I stared out at the Eucalyptus trees. I felt as if all the life was draining out of me. I felt as if I'd made the worst mistake of my life, but I couldn't even figure out when I'd made it.

45 NOW: TRINITY

I stood on the front porch and watched David's rental car turn into the driveway. Just when I was succumbing to irrational thoughts that he might never show up, his text message had arrived, saying his flight had landed and he would be there in less than an hour.

His international flight landed in San Francisco and he'd taken another flight to Monterey airport so he wouldn't be stopping by our house in Cupertino. That meant I still would not get a chance to read the inspection reports. Of course he would be able to give me an overview from memory, but I'd wanted to read the details myself. At the same time, I wasn't sure why I was thinking about home repairs and remodeling when it sounded like Detective Robbins was deliberately searching for evidence that pointed to Mia or myself as the person who'd murdered two beloved and respected members of this community.

He wouldn't find any, obviously. But he was looking, and it made me tense that he didn't seem to be putting a lot of effort into trying to find out what had actually happened. It also seemed as if he was now going to rely upon things people said rather than physical evidence, since they had none of that.

He must have talked to everyone who was acquainted with Charlotte and Brian. Maybe their lives were simple and straightforward and there was nothing to suggest why anyone would want to kill them. So without anything in their own lives to invite hatred or revenge or jealousy great enough to cause murder, he had to come up with another scenario.

Was it as simplistic as turning on the newcomer? Assuming that the stranger, the outsider, the one who was different, the one *with money*, was suspect? It seemed like such a cliché—something from a badly written TV series.

David parked his car and climbed out. He almost looked like a stranger. At the same time, he was the man I'd ached for over the past three weeks, longing to have him beside me in bed at night, thoughts and feelings piling up inside my head that I desperately wanted to share with him.

I ran down the steps, reaching the car before he'd closed the door. I wrapped my arms around his waist and he held me close as I pressed my face into his shirt, inhaling the smell of him, feeling the solid strength of his bones and muscles.

He laughed. "You're going to crush me to death."

Barely able to breathe, I finally loosened my hold. He bent down, and we kissed, just for a moment, then longer, until I felt my stomach melt and my legs turn soft.

He let me go, and we walked toward the front steps, my head resting against the side of his chest.

I talked so fast, things tumbling out of chronological order as I leaped from Brian's death, to the neighbors, to the broken washing machine hose, to Charlotte's body lying on the well, the perfectly displayed Tarot cards, the re-painted room, the uncovered well with Brian at the bottom. When I was finished, we were upstairs in the bedroom. I was gasping for breath, unbuttoning his shirt.

"Let's wait," he said. "There are some serious things going on here. Should we talk to Mia?"

"She won't have anything to add." I continued working on his buttons.

"I missed you too." He laughed softly, covering my hand with his. "But let's not go crazy. What if the detective comes back?"

"I don't think he will today."

"Why don't the three of us go out to dinner and talk this through, and we can save this …" he kissed me gently, "…for later."

I sighed. "I thought you—"

"I do. I really missed you. But I want to know all the details. Every single thing." He buttoned his shirt.

I moved away from him and sat on the foot of the bed.

"We need to get this sorted out before you bring the kid here."

"Don't call him that."

"Sure. Let me jump in the shower, and you make a reservation. Somewhere nice."

An hour later, we were seated at a corner table with a flickering candle. A white tablecloth was draped over our legs and large, thick menus stood open in front of us. The aroma of beef filled the room.

David ordered a bottle of Cabernet. Each of us chose our steaks and side dishes, starting with salads, and the server left. His easygoing smile was a surreal contrast to the conversation we were about to engage in—discussing murder and trying to figure out if we truly needed to be concerned that the detective could actually arrest one of us simply because he wanted to pressure us with more of the same questions, insisting we knew more than we'd said.

"There's no evidence," David said. "As far as we know."

"If there was, wouldn't he have asked us about it? He thinks I had an argument with Charlotte, but he hasn't mentioned it again."

"All he does is repeat the same statements—*you must have heard something, are you sure you didn't see anything?*"

"He wants to unsettle you, so you'll say something to implicate yourself. He thinks you killed them. He thinks he can make you uncomfortable enough that you'll say something that will give him a road in. And like I said, he—"

"How can he think that? Why? There's no reason."

David shrugged.

I felt as if David wasn't quite on my side. I wasn't sure why I felt that. I cut into my steak, edging close to tears, although I couldn't pinpoint what was making me so miserable. Why didn't I feel he was supporting me? He insisted there was no evidence. Although I hadn't needed him to tell me that. In some ways, he was treating me like a child. Coming in at the last minute, understanding nothing about what had happened, because he hadn't experienced any of it, telling me I didn't really need to worry.

Why were we even here, eating this elaborate dinner with Mia, when all I'd wanted was to be alone with him?

He and Mia continued talking about the things that had happened. She told him all the details with great dramatic effect, giving him gruesome descriptions of the removal of Charlotte's and Brian's bodies. She explained the discovery of the Tarot cards laid out by some unknown hand, as if that somehow solidified their message.

He lapped it up as eagerly as he salivated over his medium rare steak and the silky Cabernet. Looking at the red stain on his lips, I felt as if I didn't know him.

Yet, later in bed, he was the man I'd loved since the night we'd first met. That incredible night when he'd listened to me talk, ignoring Mia and his friend, gazing into my eyes, attentive to every word I spoke, as if I were the most fascinating woman in the world.

46 NOW: PETER

*E*ating dinner with Danielle and Tom had been a regular thing since Sara died.

Danielle was the only person who felt something of what I felt. The injustice. The outrage, and when you're feeling waves of emotion too powerful to surf, it helps to have someone there who feels the same, instead of people telling you to *pick yourself up* and *let it go* and *move on* and *get a grip, dude.*

The day had been hot and all their windows were open, so we kept our voices low. The houses had lots of space between them, yet it constantly surprised me how easily voices carried.

I took a sip of chilled Pinot Gris and noted the new car in front of Sara's house. A white late-model sedan.

"Who does the car belong to?" I asked Danielle. Tom was outside, grilling sausages and peppers for a meal we would eat on their shaded back patio.

"The husband," she said.

"He's real?"

She laughed. "I was starting to wonder that myself."

I held up my wineglass and looked at the pale liquid. I preferred

red wine. That's what Sara and I usually drank. But Danielle often served white, and they were so nice to invite me over all the time, I wasn't going to complain. It was nice to eat real food too, instead of subsisting on snacks and takeout as I had been.

"Do you think she pushed him into the well?" Danielle's tone was so bland, it took me a minute to process the words. She spoke as if she were asking whether I wanted my salad before dinner or on the side with my sausage and peppers.

"No."

"The detective does."

"Why on earth would she do that? She hardly knew him."

"Maybe an accident?" Danielle shrugged one shoulder. "Or, maybe not. Sometimes the smallest things can trigger people. You never know what's buried inside that can light someone on fire— cause them to do things you'd never imagine."

"She wouldn't be able to—"

"She's tall."

"But she's thin."

"Thin and wiry. Strong. And adrenaline accounts for a lot. It's possible."

"But why?"

"I don't know why. Who knows what's going on over there? People with all that money."

"You're not making any sense." I took a sip of wine.

"I think I saw something."

"Saw what? When did you see something?"

"The night Brian died. I saw two people out there. Sort of hanging onto each other."

"Are you sure?"

"I think so." She took a sip of wine, nervous, like a mouse nibbling at a cracker crumb, looking around frantically, worried it might have inadvertently wandered into a trap.

"You *think* so?"

"I took an Ativan." Her cheeks turned red, and she took another anxious sip of wine.

"So you weren't really awake?"

"I was awake. I looked out, and there was someone, or two someone's. I'm not really sure."

"Did you tell anyone?"

She nodded. "I told the detective."

"Did he take you seriously? With all that—*I think* and, *I'm not sure*? Plus, the Ativan?"

"I didn't mention that."

"The Ativan?"

"Any of it. Police don't like uncertainty."

"How do you know?"

"I just know. They need reliable witnesses. And that woman is disrespecting Sara's memory. It looks like she's also disrespecting her husband. Out there kissing another man in the middle of the night when her husband is ... wherever he was. At first, I didn't think she really had a husband. I thought she was lying, because she kept saying, *oh my husband is coming*, but he never showed up." She shrugged.

"What did you tell the detective?"

"I kept it simple for him. They like things simple. I told him I saw two people out there hugging each other. Passionately."

"How did you see over the fence?" Danielle and Tom's sprawling Spanish-style house was single story. I didn't see how she would have seen anything.

"I heard something. So I went outside. That's what made the Ativan kind of wear off a little, I think."

"And you climbed the fence?"

She laughed. "No. There's a small space between the boards."

"And you could see two people in the dark, past her garage and the trees, and all that?"

"Why are you arguing with me, Peter? Someone killed him in

her *backyard*. Someone murdered Charlotte in her backyard! What's going on over there? We've never had a murder anywhere near here. Then she moves in and now two people are dead. It's terrifying. I know they were awful to you, and maybe … this is a terrible thing to say … maybe it's not a huge loss, but it's still terrifying. I can hardly sleep. Even with my Ativan. And I saw *something*."

"I just think you should be careful what you say to the cops. If they arrest her, if they find other evidence, you'd have to testify at a trial."

"They would have other evidence by then. So it wouldn't be a big deal." She took a large swallow of wine.

I wondered if she was supposed to be drinking so much wine if she was taking Ativan on a nightly basis. I knew you shouldn't take it at the same time, but was it okay to drink wine all evening, then pop Ativan before bed? It didn't seem like a great idea.

Tom came into the room to tell us the sausages were ready. Danielle took my glass for a refill and we went outside to eat. Tom immediately steered the conversation to baseball, then gardening, then my music. It sounded as if he'd written a script before I arrived.

Later, while he was clearing the dishes and making coffee, and Danielle was scooping ice cream into bowls, a thought wandered across my mind. It wasn't the first time. It was a thought I shouldn't have had, but thoughts rise up, and who can ever say where they come from? Our shadow self, some would say. I don't really know. But the thought that came to me was that maybe Brian got what he deserved. He stole Sara from me when she had only a few months remaining in her short, precious life. The only thing Brian had to offer was his reliability. He might as well have been a rooster, crowing because the sun came up every morning.

I was the one who connected with Sara on every level. She knew that. I don't think she meant to choose reliability, I think she was scared. In fact, I don't think it, I *know* it.

And I didn't see that. I'll pay the price for the rest of my life.

My other, more practical thought was that I hoped the detective was more careful with his police work, that he didn't take Danielle at her word. At the same time, I didn't want to get involved. I really did not want to get involved.

47 NOW: TRINITY

*D*avid dragged his feet, literally, scuffing the heels of his shoes on the pavement as we walked down the driveway. After our strange but intense reunion the night before, I'd thought everything was good with us. Sex had been amazing—not like the first time, or our wedding night, both of which were overburdened with too much expectation—but like it had been during the first months we were together.

I felt connected to him on every level, and the way he'd held me after, I was certain he felt the same. But when I suggested we go for a walk, he acted as if I'd asked him to grab a shovel and start filling the open well with dirt, digging up hard-packed clay and dumping it into that fifty-foot hole until his hands blistered and his shoulders ached.

"I'm beat. I woke up at six London time. I have a headache. I'm—"

"We haven't had a real conversation for weeks. I really need to talk to you."

"About what?"

"About everything. We need to make plans for Ryan. I need to hear the details of the inspection reports. I never had a chance to read them and I want to know what—"

"Do I really need to deal with all that right this minute?" He held up his hands, palms facing me. "I just got here. What's the rush?"

"I'm picking up Ryan July seventh. And I'd like—"

He sighed.

"What's wrong?"

"I don't need all this pressure. And going for a walk right now? I've been working non-stop."

"Then walking will be good for you. It's not like you were doing physical labor. You should get out in the fresh air."

"Don't tell me what I should do."

"What's going on? Why are you so moody?"

He seemed to pull himself up, readjusting the expression on his face as if he'd realized how combative he was being. He put his hand on the back of my neck. "I'm tired, Trinity. Jet lagged. Like I said, I woke on London time and never went back to sleep. I came down-stairs at five. Mia made coffee. Maybe I should have tried to sleep more, but I was just too wired."

"Let's go for a walk. I won't get into all the nitty-gritty details. We'll just relax and be together. You can tell me about work. Walking might help you sleep better tonight."

We walked to the corner without speaking. We continued in semi-companionable silence for a while. I tried taking his hand, but he brushed it away. "We have to move to single file too often for hand-holding," he said.

We crossed the street to the park.

There were so many things I wanted to say, but now I felt as if I had to keep them to myself. I had to be careful not to *pressure* him, whatever that meant. I waited for him to tell me about his work, but he said nothing for quite a while.

"What was the situation with this Brian guy?" he asked finally.

"Falling into the well, or—?"

"No. Why was he working on our house?"

"Charlotte recommended him."

"But he used to own it?"

"Yes."

"And you were pretty cozy with him?"

"What?"

"He gave you a book?"

"About loss."

"That's aggressive."

I laughed sharply. "Aggressive? How is a book about dealing with losing someone to cancer considered aggressive? That's the last word that comes to mind."

"He was someone you hired to work on our house. Why was he giving you gifts?"

"Because he lost someone he cared about the same way I lost Jen!"

"They were divorced."

"I don't believe this. Why are you bothered about it? He was really kind to me. We had a good talk."

"Is that right? And then he tried to hit on you?"

I stopped. David kept going. I lunged after him and grabbed his wrist. "What's wrong with you? He didn't hit on me. He hugged me. Besides, that was before he gave me the book."

"That's a lot of explaining. For a hug. And a book."

"Oh my God. What are you talking about?"

"Did you fuck him?"

I clenched my teeth. I wanted to punch him. What was wrong with him? And if that's what he really thought, why was he so angry? Shouldn't he be hurt? "Where is this coming from? You are so far off base, I can't believe I'm even talking about it."

"Am I off base?"

"What did Mia tell you? I assume this is coming from her?"

"She thought I should know. She's worried about us."

I felt a rush of emotions I couldn't easily sort out—anger at Mia, confusion at why she would tell my husband such a ridiculous story, why she would lie to my face, pretending we were sticking close to each other while she was going behind my back. And David.

"She is way off base. And so are you."

"You seem really upset." Now his voice and his expression were cool, completely in control.

"I am. This is nonsense. Brian was a nice guy who was helping with the house."

"Why was he so eager to help?"

"I was paying him, for one thing! He does handyman work on the side. And he loves this house, and he liked having a chance to—"

"Mia thought that was really disturbing."

"I know she did. But that's beside the point. I can't believe you don't trust me. I can't believe she would make up a story like this."

"Where there's smoke, there's fire."

"Oh my God, David. I have not cheated on you. It would never even cross my mind."

"Never? Mia said you were standing there hanging onto him as if he was the best thing that ever happened to you."

"That's not true. She misinterpreted what she saw."

"How is that possible? Why were you hugging him? It must have been intense."

"He's dead!"

"Did you kill him? Because he was going to tell me what you did?"

Tears rushed to my eyes. I felt like I *was* losing my mind. He seemed to be making up stories as he went along. Or had Mia told him all this? Had these ridiculous stories come out of her cards, invented simply to stir up trouble between David and me?

"I would never cheat on you. It hurts that you would think I could, that you believed her for even half a second."

"You had yourself wrapped around him like a snake that wanted—"

I turned and started running. I ran even faster as my thoughts spun more wildly. What was happening? I felt like I'd been plucked out of the life I'd known and placed in a world I didn't recognize, forced to live another life where neighbors hated each other for no reason and people were murdered on a regular basis and marriages splintered into a thousand pieces because of a lie.

48 NOW: TRINITY

I felt as if I could run forever, that I wanted to run forever, past my house, and out into the countryside, as far as I was able, running until the sun went down and I couldn't see where I was going. Running would allow me to break free of the things David had said, the things Mia had whispered, like a worm in his ear, a spy inside my own home, watching me and then crafting a dark interpretation, as if she were reading my life like her cards, weaving a story out of her imagination, making believe it meant whatever she wanted it to mean.

How could everything solid be spinning so far out of control? How could I be living in this place where nothing seemed real and everyone had lined up against me? The only people who loved me and were on my side were dead.

And when had I begun thinking that the people in my life were either for me or against me? That wasn't the way I'd ever viewed my life or any of the people I'd invited into my heart.

By the time I reached my street, my legs had grown tired and my pace slowed.

Instead of flying past my house as if I could run from my thoughts and the things that had happened, I slowed and turned into the driveway. I climbed the front steps and went into the house.

"Mia!"

I was greeted by silence. Her car was out front, so I knew she was there. I charged through to the sunroom, but it was empty, as had been the living room and kitchen when I passed by. I glanced into the backyard but didn't see her out there.

I retraced my steps and started up the stairs. "Mia! I need to talk to you." My words echoed up to the second floor, but disappeared into nothing.

I walked to the front bedroom, regretting that I'd allowed her to sleep in the room that would belong to Ryan. It felt as if she might have filled it with negative energy. I didn't want to think that, I didn't believe that was even possible, but I didn't like that she seemed to love and care for me one minute, and inexplicably turned against me the next.

Had she?

Or was my husband exaggerating? Had he given in to his own paranoia based on nothing more than a passing comment?

I turned out of the bedroom, wondering where she'd gone.

I stood in the hallway, listening for sounds of activity. Had I missed her in one of the front rooms downstairs? I'd charged into the house shouting her name, maybe she hadn't answered and I hadn't slowed enough to pay attention.

I moved toward the stairs. As my foot touched the top step, I heard the flick of a playing card snapped into position. The sound came from our bedroom. I turned and went into our room.

Mia sat cross-legged in the center of our bed. Her cards were spread out before her, some of them leaning against our pillows. Her head was tipped slightly, her hair covering the side of her face as she stared with intense concentration at the card she'd placed in the center of a diamond-shaped layout.

"What are you doing?" My voice was sharp and loud, but she didn't lift her head.

"Reading the cards."

"I can see that! Why are you in our bedroom? On our bed! Please pick them up and get out."

Her head remained bent over the cards.

"Mia!"

"I need to think. It's the same card. Again. And in a more prominent position. We need to take this seriously. I know you don't, but I really wish you'd—"

"Get off my bed, Mia."

I moved toward the bed and picked up three of the cards closest to me.

"What are you doing?" She grabbed at my arm.

I stepped away from her toward the head of the bed. I scooped up the cards lined up along the pillows.

"Stop. You're damaging the energy. Please stop."

I pushed the rest of the cards toward her crossed ankles in a messy heap. I sat near the head of the bed, still holding the others. "What did you tell David about Brian and me?"

She looked at me, her eyes glassy. "Why did you do that? Can't you respect what I'm doing?"

"It's not respectful to come into our bedroom without asking, to sit on our bed, to—"

"I needed to be close to the core of your energy."

I slapped the other cards on top of the pile in front of her. "Stop talking about the cards. What did you tell David about Brian and me?"

She looked down. Her long, thin fingers traced gentle strokes across the top of the jumble of cards. She began arranging them into a stack, carefully nudging each one into place, pausing to stroke the images on a few.

"What did you tell him?"

"I told David he should come home. That I was afraid Brian was trying to seduce you."

"Why would you do that? It wasn't anything like that, and you know it."

She looked up at me. "I do not know that. I didn't know that, and I still don't." She reached into her deck and, without seeming to look, she pulled out the card with the snake on it. She waved it in my face. "If you'd paid attention ..."

I yanked the card from her fingers.

"Be careful."

I placed it facedown beside me. "He wasn't trying to seduce me. And even if he had been, I would never—"

"I know that."

"Then why did you tell David I had?"

Her eyes grew wide. Her lips parted slightly. "I didn't tell him that."

I had no idea who to trust. Telling her what David had said felt like giving her a window into our marriage. Maybe she'd told him more, maybe she hadn't. Maybe she was downplaying the sordid details she'd built up around a perfectly innocent, comforting hug. Maybe she truly had seen something in Brian that I hadn't. But either way, whatever David was thinking about me, and our marriage, I didn't want to discuss it with Mia.

Occasionally, I'd talked to her about my marriage, but I didn't tell her our secrets. Not that we had dark or shameful secrets. We weren't hiding terrible things from the world, but every relationship has private aspects that are part of a deep and lengthy connection. To me, sharing those risked weakening the bond.

The same was true of my friendship with Mia. David didn't know every single secret and memory Mia and I shared. Some things were an integral part of who we were. I didn't deliberately hide them. I just felt they belonged only to us. A moment in time that would be spoiled if it were shared.

49 NOW: TRINITY

*M*ia packed away her cards. I decided not to say any more to David until I'd had time to think. The three of us made sandwiches while having a stilted and unnecessarily detailed conversation about the meat, cheese, and veggies we wanted included.

We ate on the front porch, sipping beer. We forced ourselves into polite conversation about London and discussing how soon Mia might be able to rebook her trip to Acapulco. No one mentioned the remodeling. David said nothing about the inspections, and no one asked a thing about Ryan.

I'd arrived only two weeks earlier, thinking I would throw myself into this project and be ready to welcome my nephew into a place where he would heal and continue to bond with me. Now, I was terrified that the atmosphere surrounding our new summer home would damage him irrevocably. I hadn't had an imagined conversation with my sister in days, as if I were afraid to tell her what was happening. Afraid she would be disappointed in me, concerned about the wellbeing of her son.

Of course, none of that was real, but it weighed on me. That poor little boy had lost his mother. He'd only had one parent to begin with. He was alone in the world, and David and I had promised to fill that void. And now, I felt as if I would be ushering him into a house of mirrors.

I took a long swallow of beer and turned to look at the house next door. The massive picture window in their living room, almost a wing of its own, jutting out at the front, looked directly at my front porch. It was far enough away that it didn't feel invasive, but if I thought about it, they had a panoramic view of my porch, as well as my entire front and side yard.

After lunch, I went out to the garage. There was a small table in the back corner where a few gardening supplies had been left—a shovel, a garden spade, a weeding tool and pruning sheers, and a pair of women's gardening gloves. I could imagine the outrage I would get from Danielle if she saw me wearing what I could only assume were Sara's gardening gloves, but there was no way she could see the pond with the eight-foot redwood fence that surrounded both our backyards.

I walked out to the empty pond, pulled on the gloves, and inserted the weeding tool into the soil near the roots of a dandelion that came up past my knees. Once I'd loosened the roots, I tugged it gently out of the ground, feeling immense satisfaction when the entire root structure came with it. I worked my way along the edge of the pond, pulling enormous weeds and grasses that were a bit more challenging than the dandelions, even though they were turning brown in the summer heat. Their roots were deeper and entangled with each other, creeping everywhere so that pulling them out required more force than I'd expected.

I was perspiring, but feeling industrious and pleased that I'd succeeded in emptying my mind of some of its tension, when I looked up to see David walking toward me. I straightened and waited for him.

"The detective is here."

I sighed.

"He wants to talk to you."

He didn't need to say that. I was already removing the gloves.

Inside, I washed my hands in the kitchen and stepped into the living room, where Detective Robbins stood near the window.

"I'd like to speak to Ms. Feld alone," Robbins said.

"I don't keep any secrets from my husband."

"In fact, we should use a room with more privacy," the detective said.

"It's not—"

"Just you, Ms. Feld."

"Why?"

"I'd like to ask you some questions without input from anyone else."

"I don't see why I—"

"This isn't a negotiation." He stepped around me and started toward the front of the house. "There are several rooms with doors, any one of these will be fine."

"There's no furniture in those rooms yet," I said.

"We'll manage."

I walked away from David without looking at him. As I entered the playroom, the detective closed the door and moved toward the front window. He sat on the edge of the front windowsill, stretching his legs out to prop himself up. "Make yourself comfortable."

It was impossible, but I did my best, mirroring his posture at the side window.

"Why isn't your house furnished, Ms. Feld?"

"That's what you brought me in here to ask?"

"Just curious. You've been here for several weeks and it seems uncomfortable to have three people staying in a house without furniture."

"There's furniture."

"Just curious. It seems strange. Anyway. There's a witness who saw you the night of Mr. Price's murder. You were observed in an intimate position with him. In your backyard. This was sometime after one o'clock in the morning. So, approximately one hour before he died."

"That's a lie. What witness?"

"I don't need to tell you that right now."

"Yes, you do."

"I don't. Did you have an encounter with Mr. Price in your backyard that night?"

"No."

He made a note on his phone.

"This witness is quite sure."

"I don't care. And I don't think anyone can be quite sure about anything they see in the middle of the night. Unless they're standing right there."

"How do you know this individual wasn't standing right there?"

"Well, I ... they would have spoken to whomever they saw and realized it wasn't me. Because I wasn't there."

"I'm picturing a scenario in which you were outside with Mr. Price. There was a disagreement. Your husband was coming to the house and Mr. Price wanted to tell your husband about your relationship. You argued, and you pushed him. He lost his balance and slipped into the well. If he didn't die on impact, he died from his injuries because you left him there."

"That's ridiculous. Even if something like that could ever happen, which it didn't, the well was covered and secured when I saw it that evening. Who uncovered it?"

"That's a good question. Maybe you regretted your relationship. Maybe it wasn't an argument, but you set him up. You enticed him out there and—"

I got off the windowsill and crossed the room. "You're just making up stories because you have no idea who did this." I put my hand on the doorknob.

"I'm not finished," he said.

"I'm done."

"Do you prefer to do this with an attorney?"

I turned to face him. "I don't need an attorney."

"That's what I thought. At least for now."

His threatening tone infuriated me. He was making up lies, trying to intimidate me. My choices were to get an attorney or submit to his interrogation. I wasn't sure which was the worse choice. Both were repugnant.

"These aren't stories. It's what we do when we conduct an investigation. We take the information we have from witnesses, the evidence—"

"You don't have any evidence, that I'm aware of. Or witnesses."

"We do now."

"Not to the murders."

"Interesting that you're lumping both murders together."

"I'm not … what's your point?"

"We take the information we have, even if it's only bits and pieces to start, and we build possible scenarios. Theories. These provide additional routes for us to pursue."

"In other words, you make up a story and you look for facts you can force into your story."

He stood. "We have an eyewitness who saw you in your backyard with Brian Price moments before he was murdered. You were in a position that suggests you had an intimate relationship with a man you weren't married to while your husband was out of the country. If there's anything you'd like to tell me about your relationship with Mr. Price that you haven't, please consider telling me now. This is also a good time to tell me any details you haven't mentioned about that night, before I find them out myself. The same goes for Charlotte Hughes."

He waited for a moment, then crossed the room and opened the door, stepping back so I could leave first. As if he were a gentleman.

50 THEN: PETER

Two months after Sara asked me to leave, the cancer returned. She waited another entire month before she told me. By then, she was back on chemo. She'd asked her ex to move back into the house with her. He was *graciously and heroically, lovingly and with utmost tenderness and care*, according to Charlotte, driving Sara to chemo every three weeks and caring for her after.

"He's an incredible man, a remarkable human being, to do that for his ex wife," Charlotte said, tears sliding around the surface of her eyes.

It was unclear what it meant that Brian was living there. Were they a couple? I couldn't be sure.

Once, I saw them walk across the yard, Sara carrying a plate of cookies, headed to Tom and Danielle's for dinner.

They walked side-by-side, but they didn't seem to be in step. They looked like brother and sister, almost. Another time, I saw them going home from a small party at the neighbors' across the street. As they ran across the street, Brian took her hand. But *he* took *her* hand. Did it mean anything? What was going on in that house?

Were they back together, or was he helping her with her treatment? A ministering angel, as Charlotte said.

I wanted to write songs about how I felt, but it seemed like a betrayal of Sara. Eventually I did. They were never performed in public, all those words and the accompanying tunes that flowed out of me without effort. I didn't think about whether they were any good, I didn't think about them in terms of my livelihood.

They were raw me.

Everything I'd done wrong with Sara. But also, the choice she'd given me. Music or being there for her. It was an impossible choice, and I knew I'd made the wrong one, but the other one might have killed me as surely as the cancer was now killing her.

No one else appeared to be aware of that. Maybe because they were so close, inside the house with her.

I was the literal outsider. I saw how thin she was, I noticed the skeletal look of her face, as if her skull were trying to assert itself.

I could see that when she smiled, it was the most tremendous effort she'd ever put forth.

And I could see it in her heart. How her sculptures were changing into something more surreal.

Being outside of her life made me feel like a stalker. I was always watching them. I knew her schedule better than I had when I'd lived there. Because then, I'd been at my place during the day. Now, I was always around, out of sight, but paying attention in a way I never had before.

She was becoming someone I knew inside and out because I was observing her gestures and the expressions on her face. I was listening to the movements of her body and the rhythm of her hours and her days, all with my eyes.

If Charlotte had known, if Brian had seen me, even if Sara had become aware, they would have designated me a first-class creep. But I was stealthy and kept out of sight.

In some ways, just being close to her was enough. It was a pain I could hardly endure—being cut out of her life. But it was a pleasure I cherished—to continue watching over her, knowing she needed me, even if she wouldn't admit that to herself, and didn't have the courage to tell the people who were so focused on her physical well-being, they ignored her spirit entirely.

51 NOW: MIA

*T*he day Trinity bought the security cameras, I'd left her alone with the sales guy while I went to purchase some additional security. Real security.

We needed better protection than a camera. At least I did. Trinity refused to believe me, even though she'd sat right beside me and listened to the police speak the same words I had—telling us they weren't going to do a fucking thing to protect us. She did not believe me, that I hadn't crept downstairs in the darkest hours of the night to repaint half that room its original color. She'd wanted to blame me for trying to scare her.

Why couldn't she see the obvious? Someone had been inside the house again. I hadn't slept well since the night an unknown hand laid out the Tarot cards. Now, I wasn't sleeping at all. Knowing that someone was coming and going from the house with absolute freedom was terrifying. I wasn't going to end up at the bottom of a well. I was either going to leave Trinity alone in the house, which wasn't an option, or I was going to protect myself and her.

Trinity would never understand me buying a gun, but she'd always had a man in her life. I had not. And a woman alone, even when she has men in her life from time to time, looks at the world a lot differently than a woman who moves from relationship to relationship and then is swept away in a whirlwind romance, engagement, and marriage to a guy like David Feld.

Maybe Trinity was comfortable sitting around waiting for David to come and be her rescuing knight, but I needed insurance.

The gun was loaded, and I'd been sleeping with it under my pillow. It wasn't the safest choice, but what's the point of an unloaded gun safely locked in a box? By the time it was ready to use, I might be dead. When I'd come to stay with Trinity, I'd thought I knew what was going on in the summer home she had such dreams for.

Now, I had no idea what was going to happen. Now that David had arrived, now that Trinity was being eyed by the police as a suspect in Brian's murder, maybe Charlotte's, for all I knew, anything could happen. Anything. No matter what I'd expected when I'd come to help her decorate, no matter what I'd thought my cards were telling me, the future had turned into something completely unpredictable.

And I supposed I'd learned, for the first time in my life, that the future is always unknown.

You can make all the plans you want. It doesn't matter. Life happens. Other people make their own plans and they don't invite you to participate in that planning. Suddenly, you're caught off guard. Your closest friends have secrets and dreams you know nothing about.

The only one you can rely upon is yourself. That's a lesson I should have learned when I was ten years old. Why hadn't I?

When I was ten, my father decided he didn't want to be our father any more. That was it. Everything was in my mother's hands. And she did a spectacular job. But still, no one had seen it coming.

One day we were playing soccer in the backyard, my dad and me on one team, my brother and my mom facing us down. My dad and I were winning. Even though my brother was older, I ran faster. And I had my dad on my team! He coached me on having a good strategy for when to kick and when to dribble the ball. He coached me on when to go left or right, when to pass and when to keep the ball to myself and go for it all the way.

We won the match. We cheered and high-fived each other.

After the game, my brother was actually a good sport, for once. So it wasn't that. My dad hated it when he was a sore loser, but that day, he wasn't a sore loser. My brother said, *good game*, just like my dad had taught him.

We all walked three blocks to the ice cream shop and got sugar cones with round scoops of ice cream.

The next day, my dad was gone for work before my mother had time to get up and make the coffee. In front of the coffeepot was a note.

When I came into the kitchen. It was dark. She hadn't started cooking our eggs. She hadn't poured our orange juice. She was sitting at the table crying. The note was still on the counter in front of the coffeepot. All it said was—*This wasn't how I planned my life.*

That was it.

Gone. Done.

So my mom's plans changed without her permission. She got a job as a receptionist. My plans changed without my permission—no more dance classes. I don't know if my brother's plans changed. It was hard to say because he stopped talking. He didn't say a word to my mom or me for three solid months. When he finally spoke again, he didn't have any plans, and he never said a word about my dad.

My cards have helped me figure things out, told me where to go and what to do. But now I was a little scared, and a little confused and feeling very unsafe. So I bought the gun.

I slept better after that.

52 NOW: TRINITY

*W*hen the detective was gone, I remained for a while in the room that was half sky blue, half burnt orange. I wanted to pry open the can of blue paint, pour it into a tray, and paint over the walls that had been transformed back into that hideous color. Instead, I shut the door, leaned my back against it, and closed my eyes.

I whispered my sister's name. I don't know why I did. A habit, mostly. I'd come to see that I whispered her name at the times when I realized all over again that she was gone, at the times when I would have sent her a text or called. As if I could send a text through the ether and she would respond, or still, somehow, miraculously, know what I was thinking. Just like when she often seemed to know when she was alive.

There were so many times throughout our lives when we knew what the other was thinking. We would glance at each other across a room, at a holiday meal or family wedding, and we would immediately know what was on the other's mind. We wouldn't have to smile or nod or change our expressions in any way. The meeting of our eyes did it all. Our thoughts joined each other and carried on a silent conversation. Nothing more was required.

Now, I was alone.

My husband believed I'd cheated on him. My best friend had told him she saw me with my body wrapped around a man as if he were my lover, and a neighbor who barely knew me had told the police I was enveloped in that man's arms in the darkest hours of the night.

I whispered Jennifer's name again. Not out loud. If anyone heard me, it would confirm their belief that I was losing my grip on reality.

The door rattled as someone tried opening it, shoving it into my back.

"Trinity." David's voice was loud, reverberating through the door into my ear. "What are you doing?"

"Nothing."

"I need to talk to you. Why are you blocking the door?"

"I'm trying to think."

"Let me in."

He jiggled the door again, jarring my shoulder blades. I moved away, and the door opened.

David stepped into the room. "What did he want?"

I shrugged. I didn't want to tell him. Whatever Danielle, or a stranger, maybe it had been a neighbor I hadn't met yet, claimed to have seen, it was a lie. No one had seen me in my backyard because I hadn't been there! I wasn't going to make it real, I wasn't going to make this person a legitimate *witness* by repeating the story. It was possible it would get passed all around the neighborhood. It might already be on its way. Between Danielle and Tom, and the detective himself, the lie was running up and down our street, circling around to everyone who had known Brian, as I stood here staring at my husband, looking at the distrust bleeding out of his eyes.

"What did he ask you?"

"I don't want to talk about it."

"You have to. We need to stick together."

"It has nothing to do with you. All of this happened when you weren't here, so I don't see what sticking together has to do with anything."

"I'm ..." He took a step away from me. "It has everything to do with it. What did he say?"

I crossed my arms.

"Why are you doing this? If he has ... tell me what he said."

"Why?"

He glared at me. "Because I'm your husband. Because if you're in trouble, I should know. How else can I—"

"How else can you, what? Help me? Support me? All it took was one misinterpreted gesture, and you think I cheated on you?"

"Yeah. About that ... I'm really sorry." He stepped around me and closed the door. He lowered his head slightly. "I know I'm just making excuses, and there's no excuse. But I'm just exhausted. I didn't sleep, I'm still on London time—"

"So you keep saying."

"Okay. I need to stop making excuses. I totally overreacted. Totally. I was a jerk. I realize that. I don't even know why I thought that for even half a minute. You wouldn't do that." He laughed.

"You think it's funny?"

"No, no." He came toward me and put his arms around me. "I'm so sorry." He put his hand on the back of my head and pulled it toward his chest, cradling it, holding it as if he could soothe my thoughts with the warmth and strength of his fingers massaging my scalp. "I'm so, so sorry," he whispered.

"Why did you laugh?"

"I laughed because I'm such a moron. You would never ... And I don't know why ... I overreacted big time. Can we forget it?"

I sighed. But I didn't nod my head and I didn't say anything. How could I forget it when the detective claimed he had a witness saying that was exactly what I'd done? "Mia said she didn't tell you I cheated on you."

"I know, I know. She just said she was worried about what this guy was after. She didn't trust him. I took it and ran with it. I'll stop making excuses why I did that. Let's just … I'm here now. And I'm sorry, *now*. Okay?"

I let him hold me, but it didn't stop me feeling as if my life was spinning out of control. I had no idea how to stop it.

"What did he ask you?" David said.

Without considering my motive, I decided to tell a lie of my own. "He asked if there was anything I hadn't wanted to tell him when Mia was there."

"Why?"

"He was being thorough. He thought he'd picked up on some hesitation from me."

"That's strange." He released his grip on me.

I wasn't sure why I'd lied. He would find out eventually and lying would make him wonder again about Brian, but for now, it seemed easier.

53 NOW: TRINITY

*I*t took me a long time to fall asleep that night. David was out immediately, before I'd even finished brushing my teeth, because when I slid under the covers, he was snoring softly. I gently pushed him onto his side. Then, I lay on my back, as fully awake as if it were already morning. I stared into the darkness, reliving the day, recalling the endless array of emotions since David had returned.

I felt mildly anxious that the next time Detective Robbins appeared unannounced at our front door, he would be dangling handcuffs in front of him. Did they still use handcuffs? On many of the TV shows I'd seen, they used zip ties, which looked painful and even more confining. Wrapping you up like you were a sack of garbage.

Could he arrest me without any actual evidence? Was a fabricated story considered an eyewitness account until it was somehow disproven? How did I go about disproving something like that? It seemed impossible. I couldn't find evidence to show that I wasn't outside. I hadn't had the security camera that would offer dated images to show an empty backyard, to show the details of whatever *had* had happened that night. To show that no one came out of my house until daylight.

I turned onto my side and adjusted the pillow, trying to relax the rigid muscles in my neck so I could escape into sleep. I curled my knees up.

I envied my husband, peacefully unconscious beside me. He was no longer snoring. It was possible he would be awake when the clock struck six a.m. in London, but for now, he was resting with soft, contented sighs.

Maybe I should try talking to Danielle. Would that make things worse? When I thought about how the detective had treated me so far, I could imagine him accusing me of tampering with a witness or some nonsense like that.

I flipped onto my other side and adjusted my pillow again.

Why couldn't I make my thoughts stop? I wanted my life back!

I wanted to get the rooms painted and the floors refinished. We were running out of time. Ryan needed me. My brother and sister-in-law were anxious to get ready for their own child.

Tears started pushing their way forward. A few trickled onto my cheeks. How could everything have gotten so messed up? I put my hand on David's shoulder. He moved slightly. My hand slid off and fell onto the mattress. I turned over again.

Maybe a hot cup of tea would help relax me and then I could sleep, but it also seemed as if the time it would take to prepare and drink a cup of tea would keep me awake longer. Surely sleep was close by. I took a long, deep breath and felt calmer.

* * *

The air around me was cool and smelled of damp earth. The nighttime dew was settling on the exposed patches of dirt between the uncared for patches of grass. Small rocks made the ground uneven and difficult to walk on. My feet were bare and I couldn't understand why I'd come outside at night without shoes.

Walking was painful and slow, yet I was inexplicably moving quickly. I was angry and upset, although I had no idea why. I just knew that something was boiling inside me. It had started in my heart, swelling, then spilling over until it filled my entire body.

Now, I needed to get it out of me. So much anger, it had blossomed into a need for violence. I'd never experienced anything like it. I needed to use my fists. I needed to kick and scream and let loose everything I had on the body of another human being. Where was it coming from? I didn't understand. I wasn't violent. I'd never hurt another person.

As I continued stumbling over the rough ground, rocks stabbing the soles of my feet, I saw someone standing by the open well. A man. I couldn't see who he was. It was too dark, but it was someone who meant to hurt me. I knew that without question. He glared at me in the darkness.

This also confused me. How could I know he was glaring at me? I could hardly see. I couldn't even see clearly enough to be certain it was a man. The figure was larger than me, so it had to be male, didn't it?

Now, I was running, rushing toward him, running faster than I knew was possible, no longer feeling the discomfort on my feet, not caring that I couldn't see where I was going. I was charging at him, knowing that when we made contact, I would crash into him with a force that might break me.

It felt as if I'd been running forever.

And now I was upon him. I was raising my arms, my hands in front of me, palms flat. I shoved him with a force that seemed to come from somewhere outside my body. He fell back.

In the time it took for me to inhale and catch my breath, he vanished.

I was surrounded by absolute silence. He didn't scream as he fell. The only sound as he hit the bottom of the well was a soft, faraway thud. I'd expected to hear bones snap, or the splash of water. I'd expected him to howl in pain, a cry of rage and terror. Now, all I heard was the sound of the breeze moving softly through the night air.

A moment later, my breathing calmed. My heartbeat slowed. I could no longer hear the sounds of my body crying for action. The burning I'd felt had evaporated the moment the man disappeared from sight.

The man was Brian Price. I'd pushed him to his death. I didn't even know why.

As I turned away, tears began falling down my face.

* * *

When I woke, it was still dark. I touched my cheeks. They were dry.

I sat up, grabbing my pillow and hugging it close. It had felt so real. I wanted to get out of bed and rush down to the backyard, peer into the well. Had it …

I leaned over and picked up my phone off the floor. Twelve seventeen.

I laid it down again and got out of bed. I went to the window, slightly embarrassed that I doubted I'd had a frightening dream, that I feared it was real. The backyard appeared empty, but it was hard to tell. There was only a thin sliver of a moon. It was close to the horizon already, making it impossible to see anything but the indistinct outline of the garage at the end of the driveway that extended past the side of our house into the backyard.

The dream was so real, but if it had been real, what did I expect to see? Looking out into that empty space now, imagining that hole deep in the earth, I shivered. I turned and climbed back into bed, pulling the covers over my head, hugging my knees to my chest.

It was a dream. Of course, it was a dream. I would *never* kill someone. Never. Even the things I'd experienced as I'd rushed at him were feelings that didn't belong to me. It wasn't *me*. Brian was a good man. He'd been kind to me.

Other people had put this into my mind. Their whispers and doubts had caused it to fester into something ugly there. It wasn't me.

54 NOW: TRINITY

*D*espite curling up, holding my legs, with the blankets over my head, I was still cold. The dream repeated itself behind my closed eyes, making itself more real as I tried to soothe myself back to sleep. The more I tried to calm my thoughts, the more wild they became and the more wide awake I was.

I felt like crying. I folded my lower lip over my teeth and lightly bit down. I would not give in to this. There had to be a way out of this nightmare. I knew the one I'd just experienced would fade once daylight arrived, but the nightmare I was living since moving into our summer home, getting worse with each day, was poised to deliver endless torment.

I wanted the detective to recognize that the murders in my backyard had absolutely nothing to do with me, to leave me alone and go looking for solutions elsewhere.

Finally, I had what I needed to make progress on the house. David had given me the necessary details from the inspection report. The main beam in the living room ceiling needed replacing. That was the only major structural issue. The rest were minor issues. I'd made a list that afternoon of what needed to be done and all I wanted was to interview contractors, hire someone, get the repairs for the living room and laundry room scheduled, and work started. I wanted to finish my own projects and bring Ryan here so he could begin healing from his loss. I wanted him to play in the yard and help me plant a garden. I wanted to read stories and take him for walks, pulling his wagon.

Feeling alienated from my husband, distrusting my best friend, fearing the neighbors, and worrying about being accused of murder was not the way it was supposed to be. I pounded my fist into my pillow. I thought the force of it might wake David, but he didn't move.

Instead, I heard the distinct sound of a door closing downstairs. I sat up and shoved the blankets off me. I would not sit here and debate with myself whether the sound had been real. Not again.

Before I could think, I was out of bed, grabbing my phone, and headed out of the room. When I reached the landing halfway down the stairs, I heard a gentle thump, like an open door that was knocked against the wall behind it. I should have woken David, but I didn't want to wait. I wanted to catch whomever it was before it was too late. This time, I would get there in time.

I scrambled down the last set of stairs and into the hallway.

A cold draft hit me. The front door stood open, light from the porch spilling into the hallway. I froze, suddenly unsure what to do. My first instinct was to rush to the porch to see if someone was out there, already headed down the driveway. But another part of me trembled, wondering if someone was in the house, in any of the dark rooms surrounding me.

Screaming for David and Mia would alert the intruder that I was awake. I moved up two steps and texted David, wondering if the vibrating of his phone on the floor by our bed would be enough to wake him. Probably not. I texted Mia, my mind racing.

Should I creep through the house to see whether someone was already leaving through the back door? Indecision now had me glued to the stairs, sending ridiculous text messages that would to be enough to wake my husband or my friend. But neither could I head in both directions at once, and as long as I kept quiet, whomever it was might stay in the house where I could catch him. Or her.

For the first time, a thought lurched into my mind. Could this be Danielle? It made sense that she would be almost as likely a candidate as Brian to know about a window lock that was easy to wiggle loose, or some other access to the house that I wasn't aware of, although so far, I'd been unable to discover any such thing.

I tapped David's number to call him. It rang four times and went to voicemail. Mia's phone did the same.

Clutching my phone, I stepped down into the hallway and silently walked to the front door. I looked out across our empty driveway and yard. The street and our neighbors' yards were also quiet. I closed the door, turning the knob slowly to avoid a click.

First, I checked the playroom and guest room. Both were empty. It was easy to walk quietly in bare feet down the hallway, pausing to check the laundry room and Sara's former studio, also empty and silent. I moved more slowly as I approached the living room.

Just as I was about to move toward the arched opening into the kitchen, one of the curtain panels on the living room window moved slightly. I screamed, a sound so loud and terrifying it scared me, sounding as if it came from someone else. If anyone had been standing by the curtain, surely they would have shown themselves at the shocking, sudden scream filling the room. But there was nothing. The curtain stood completely still.

I turned on the light as David and Mia barreled into the room, both nearly crashing into me from behind.

David grabbed my upper arms, pulling me toward him. "Are you okay?"

"What happened?" Mia's voice was shrill, despite being rough with sleep.

"I heard something and came down. The front door was open. When I came in here, the curtain moved."

Mia shrank behind us. David let go of my arms and strode across the room. He tugged the cord and opened the drapes. The darkness pressed against the glass. The curtains swung wildly at the abrupt movement. He pulled one side of the drapes away from the wall, then moved to the other side of the window and did the same. "No one's here."

"I know," I said.

"Then why ...?"

"I knew when I screamed that if anyone was there, they would have reacted. I don't understand." My voice shook. "I don't understand."

"Are you sure?" Mia asked.

I turned. "Don't."

"Sorry."

David closed the drapes. "Let's go to bed."

"But ..." I couldn't. Not after that dream. Not after this. I wanted it all to stop. I wanted an explanation. I'd never felt so utterly helpless. I wasn't used to feeling like this. I'd always taken care of things. When something went wrong, I figured out how to work my way out of a problem. I made decisions. I talked my way through conflicts.

"You need to get some sleep," David said. "I need sleep." He took my hand, but I resisted, forcing him to tug me toward the stairs. For a moment, I thought he might take me in his arms and carry me to bed like a child. Instead, he let go of my hand and started up.

I followed obediently, like a child after all, each step up admitting defeat.

55 NOW: TRINITY

I woke at six and found the bed empty beside me. I ran my hand over the sheets. They were cool.

In the kitchen, I found David and Mia, both showered and dressed, seated at the table drinking coffee. I felt as if I'd overslept by hours and had missed an important meeting.

"Hey," Mia said.

I filled a mug with coffee and rested my hip against the counter, waiting for one of them to say more.

"How did you sleep?" David asked.

"After finding the front door open and seeing someone in the living room?" I asked.

"Oh," Mia said. "She does remember."

"Oh," I said, my voice cool with sarcasm, "You've been talking about me."

"We're worried," David said.

How long had they been sitting here? And what had they been saying? As if I were a mental health patient whose condition needed to be discussed when I was out of earshot. "Worried about who was in the house? And how they got in? That's what you should be worried about."

"The front door was closed when we came downstairs," David said.

"Because I closed it." I took a sip of coffee.

He nodded very carefully, as if moving his head too vigorously might upset me. "Mia reminded me …" He looked at me, his eyes gentle, or maybe worried, maybe trying to assess my mood. "How you walked in your sleep a few times when you were a—"

"I wasn't sleepwalking. And Mia and I have already been through that. I don't want to hear it again." I pulled out a chair and sat at the table. "Why don't you make one of your fabulous omelets, Mia? I'm starving."

"Sure." She jumped up, not eager to feed me as she'd been for the past week or two, but eager not to upset me, I was sure of it. Unless I was imagining.

As she opened the fridge, I took another sip of coffee. I watched my husband watching me.

"Why are you looking at me like that?" he asked.

I put down my mug. I had no idea what he saw in my expression and I wasn't even clear what my thoughts were at that moment. I just knew I was tired of the sleepwalking story and tired of not knowing what was happening in my house, tired of feeling like I was floating in a jar of thick liquid like a specimen set on a shelf. "Never mind about the omelette."

"No, it's fine. We're all hungry. We need a solid breakfast." Mia cracked an egg on the edge of a glass bowl.

"I want to search the house," I said.

"For what?" David asked. "Even if someone was inside, they're long gone now."

"Please stop."

"Stop what?"

"Doubting my experiences. You said *if* someone was inside. I came downstairs and the front door was open. I saw the living room drapes move. Can't you at least give me the respect of trusting I know what I saw?"

"Okay. But I looked at the security camera recording. It didn't show anything."

I felt defeated, but I would not let go of what my senses, alert and awake, told me I'd seen. "I can't explain it. I'm not going to try. But I *know* what I saw, and I just want to see if there's anything that looks out of place."

"There's hardly anything here. How can it look out of place?" David asked.

"I don't know! I just want to look. I'm taking a quick shower. You can help me or not."

We went through every room, checking closets for possible access to the outside of the house, testing window locks to see if they were loose or could be manipulated from outside with a screwdriver. The three of us returned to the basement. It had a faint aroma of beer that I didn't recall from the previous time we'd been down there, but there were no empty beer cans, and no sign that anyone had been inside. There was no evidence of wild animals. And once again, looking at the narrow windows just a few inches above ground level, it was clear that not even a child could crawl inside through an opening designed only for ventilation.

When we returned to the main floor, I went into the sunroom. Feeling mildly guilty, I wondered if Brian had done something when he'd installed the screen door to allow someone access, but we found nothing. I'd used that door multiple times since Brian had installed it, and he'd handed over both sets of keys the day he'd done it. Besides, the locking of the screen hardly mattered, since there was a solid wood door behind it.

I could tell from the theatrical way that David and Mia went about searching closets and checking window and door locks, they were simply humoring me. They still believed I'd been sleepwalking or had had a vivid dream. Worse, they thought I'd imagined the entire thing, believing I was experiencing supernatural phenomenon, possibly tied to my sister's death and the awareness of Sara's death, followed by two murders.

When I'd tried to talk to David about Jen's death, hinting around about the whispered conversations I had with her in my mind, he'd shut me down. Fast. Even when I'd erupted in a flood of explanation that it wasn't what it sounded like, that he was taking it the wrong way, that it was a feeling of her presence, the memory of her face and her voice, the memory of her opinions and feelings, knowing what she would say in so many situations, laughing out loud as I imagined her teasing me in ways she'd done over the years, he'd lectured me about not *going off the deep end* and *losing my bearings*.

"I don't think she's actually there. But it's comforting to imagine she can hear—"

"This is how people let grief consume them," David had said. "If you need to talk to a therapist, we can certainly afford the best there is. Please don't let your mind veer out of control."

So that's where David stood.

Mia was so slippery, it was hard to say what her views were sometimes.

Why David gave her an amused pass on getting advice from a deck of mysterious and randomly interpreted, sometimes down-right creepy-looking cards, was beyond me.

Now, I stood in the foyer, my back to the front door. I heard Mia and David talking, but I couldn't determine where their voices were coming from. It sounded as if they were deliberately keeping them low. Discussing me, again. Maybe they were talking about approaching my brother and sister-in-law and telling them I wasn't equipped to care for Ryan. Was that where this was headed? Neither one of them seemed inclined to talk much about Ryan. In fact, I couldn't recall Mia mentioning him more than once or twice. She acted as if he didn't exist. She hadn't asked to see pictures or asked how he was doing.

David had been the same. He'd known about that beam in the living room that needed replacing. That was a critical safety issue, and he'd said nothing. I should have been on the phone looking for contractor bids the day I arrived. In fact, *he* should have been lining up a contractor the day the house closed escrow!

I moved quietly toward the back of the house, wondering where they were, hoping I could get close enough to hear what they were saying, desperate to know what they didn't want me to hear. I didn't understand why they didn't believe anything I told them.

All my life I'd been a truthful person. I'd never experienced people treating me like this and I didn't know how to handle it. What was I supposed to say? How did you prove you were being truthful? It was an impossible task. Maybe they thought I shouldn't be responsible for my sister's child because they believed I'd murdered Brian. Possibly Charlotte.

From my perspective, it seemed as if they were the ones who had lost their own minds. How could they look at two random deaths and assume it was someone they'd known in the closest possible way? *Was* that what they thought? I wasn't even sure.

I moved quietly down the hallway. Their voices grew louder, but the words were still indistinct. I tried to step lightly to avoid making the floorboards creak under my weight, pressing myself close to the wall as I neared the kitchen where their voices, breathy whispers now, were coming from.

Something clinked on the table. As I stepped away from the wall, still standing back from the entry, out of their line of sight, Mia swept the object off the table. She shoved something into her pocket and they both started toward the doorway.

Turning quickly, I scurried down the hallway like a rat, turned again, and ran up the stairs two at a time. What had Mia shown to David? Did she have evidence after all that someone had been in the house? Were they lying to me, trying to *make* me feel as if I were losing my mind?

56 THEN: PETER

$\mathcal{M}$ ost men probably would have felt like a ping-pong ball. They would have felt used or possibly manipulated. I wasn't sure if any of those applied, but I didn't care.

Sara had grown tired of Brian's steady, quiet presence. She told me this when she called me at two in the morning. She was in her studio, shaping clay into the form of a woman leaping as if she were about to take flight. Her sculpture had grown more fanciful since she'd been sick. All her figures seemed to be climbing, jumping, dancing their way up to the sky. Their bodies were leaner, their arms and legs almost like wild grass, blowing in the wind, as if she saw herself in them, and she saw parts of herself fading back into the earth, her spirit absorbed by the sky.

"I'm working on a series of dancers that will be sold in the new gift shop at the performing arts center," she whispered.

"Why are you whispering?"

"Brian is sleeping."

"You're in the studio. Isn't he upstairs?"

"He's a light sleeper. I don't want him to know I'm talking to you. He'll take it the wrong way."

I didn't want to ask how he would take it. I was sure I knew. He would feel as if history were repeating itself. Even though they hadn't gotten remarried. Even though it was still a little unclear whether they were even a couple again, she didn't want him to feel she was cheating on him. Again. But she was, I suppose. Or, had she been cheating on me? That's how I felt, but I couldn't say that. We'd broken up, so it wasn't cheating. That would be her view.

All I cared about was hearing her voice, knowing that I was the one she wanted to talk to. That when she couldn't sleep at two in the morning, mine was the voice she needed to hear. She didn't wake Brian, longing to share her thoughts. I squashed the niggling voice that whispered, mine was the only pair of ears, the only voice willingly available at that hour.

When I moved back in two weeks after that, there was no trace of Brian in the house.

"Brian will still be taking me to chemo," Sara said.

"Oh. Well I could—"

"He offered. And he really wants to. It's important to him."

"What's important is your comfort and how you feel," I said.

"It doesn't matter. It's so sweet that he wants to help."

She put her arms around me and rested her head on my chest. I held her close, feeling as if we'd never been apart, trying not to let my hands notice the sharpness of her bones beneath her skin, the way her pulse seemed to feel more prominent.

So Brian came by every Thursday and picked her up. He drove her to her appointment. He sat with her while the drugs dripped into her veins. He brought her home and together, he and I helped her into the sunroom where we'd moved our bed so she didn't have to climb the stairs.

He and I were civil, even friendly sometimes.

I'm not a petty man. But it was a satisfying moment when I told Charlotte she didn't need to deliver any more casseroles for Sara. I would be taking over the cooking.

The look on Charlotte's face was one I would have liked to photograph.

It felt good to be together in the house I'd now come to think of as ours. Every room had memories. The entire property felt as if it echoed with our laughter and my music, our conversation and the pleasant sounds of our quiet lovemaking, when Sara had the strength.

This was *our* home. Our entire lives played out between its walls as Sara became less able to go out.

I still performed with my band, but the moment the final note was played, my guitar was in its case.

Sara never asked why I couldn't have done that before, and I never explained the difference. We were happy, and we lived as if we were alone in a universe of our own creation.

57 NOW: TRINITY

*a*s soon as I reached the top of the stairs, I regretted scurrying away from my spot in the hallway, where I'd tried eavesdropping on David and Mia. Why hadn't I just stepped into the kitchen and asked Mia what she had in her hand? Why hadn't I asked them what they were talking about? I was making myself look more foolish and paranoid by creeping around in my own house, trying to eavesdrop, hiding as if I had no right to know what they'd found and what they were saying about me.

I turned around and walked down the stairs.

Mia was sitting in the living room, gazing at nothing. She smiled when she saw me. She gave a little wave. Through the doorway, I saw David in the sunroom, talking on the phone.

"What were you showing David in the kitchen a few minutes ago?"

She tilted her head and tucked her hair behind her ear. "Hmm. Were you ... where were you?"

"In the hallway, I saw you, but I ..."

She frowned. "Were you spying on us?"

I laughed. "Why would I need to spy on my husband? Or my best friend?"

"It's so strange that I didn't see you."

"That's not important. What were you showing him?"

The sunroom door opened and David stepped into the living room, sliding his phone into his back pocket. He came toward me and gave me a light kiss on my forehead. "Just had to put out a fire, but it's all taken care of. I'm still here until Thursday, as planned."

I'd thought he was staying longer. "Did you find something that proved someone was in the house last night?"

David glanced at Mia, then back at me.

"She heard us talking about the keys," Mia said.

"What keys?" I asked.

David dug in his pocket and pulled out my keys. He handed them to me.

"What do my keys have to do with anything?"

"Mia found them in the basement," David said.

"How did they get down there?"

"That's what we were talking about," Mia said.

"Whispering," I said.

"Were you listening?" David asked.

"I don't appreciate you talking behind my back."

David slipped his arm around my waist. I tried to pull away, but he held me tightly, pressing the side of his head against the top of mine. "Shh, shh," he whispered, as if soothing an infant.

"We think if the front door was open, you must have done it yourself. You must have—"

"I'm tired of this." I wriggled free of David's vice-like lock on my waist. "Why are you trying to make me look like I'm crazy?"

"We're not trying to make you look like anything at all," Mia said.

"At the same time, you're acting as if you believe this place is haunted." David looked worried. He tried to touch my cheek, but I moved beyond his reach.

"Everyone is treating me like I've either lost my mind or I'm a killer. Or both."

"You're just …" Mia put her hands over her mouth, pressing her knuckles into her lips.

"So you agree? That's how you're treating me?"

"We're *worried* about you," Mia said. "You've been through so much and it's perfectly okay if it's getting to you. Everyone understands."

"Stop patronizing me! I'm *fine*."

"I don't think you are," Mia said. "You're upset all the time. And so confused."

"I am. Upset and confused. There's clearly been someone in this house and you know it because you were really freaked out, too."

"Yes, but I don't think it's a ghost!"

"Neither do I."

"Then what do you think?"

What I worried about was that I was genuinely starting to lose my grasp on reality. That's how I felt, but I definitely wouldn't say that.

58 NOW: TRINITY

*J*couldn't breathe. Standing in my own house, looking at my husband and my best friend, their faces full of concern, I felt as if they were smothering me with their only partially spoken beliefs. Their thoughts lurked behind their eyes, like bona fide ghosts I couldn't see or touch, imagining things about me they wouldn't speak clearly.

At the same time, it seemed as if some of the things I'd said, my behavior, might be proving them right.

This was my husband! The man with whom I shared my life, my body, most of the thoughts that passed through my head. My future, my dreams. He did the same. Didn't he? How had I fallen into such a deep pit that I imagined he was thinking these things about me? But he'd said them. Hadn't he?

And my best friend. In some ways, she knew me better than I knew myself. I was certain she would say the same about me. She'd always wanted the best for me. She'd been beside me through the most thrilling and the most awful times of my life. She was almost part of me—a twin. A friendship that she and I had known from the beginning would last a lifetime. I still believed that.

My head was filled with a white noise that was growing louder.

The concern on their faces was increasing. Any moment, I expected them to lunge toward me, each grabbing an arm, tying me down before I did something to hurt myself, or them.

I turned and ran from the room, down the hall, and out the front door. I raced across the lawn that flowed seamlessly from our house to our neighbors'. I wasn't sure why I'd imagined I would find a sanctuary there, but it was the only place I had to go.

Stepping onto their front patio, I swept my fingers through my hair to calm it. I took a deep, slow breath. Now that I was here, their front door a reality, rather than just my only escape, I had no idea what I planned to say to them. Confronting Danielle about her report to the detective wasn't an option. If she answered the door, it was likely to shut in my face. In fact, if she looked out the window, the door might remain closed.

It felt as if I were facing a door that hid my future. I laughed. Even though I recognized how foolishly dramatic I was being, the feeling persisted. My husband had found it easy to believe I would cheat on him. He was convinced I believed in ghosts. Did I? My friend had toyed with the idea that I might have killed a man while sleepwalking. Had I? Did she still assume that was the most likely explanation for Brian's death? Behind this door, I faced a fifty-fifty chance of facing a woman who had told the police I was akin to a black widow, loving a man, then shoving him into a deep, dark pit with no chance of survival. Or a man who vaguely believed I was an innocuous and pleasant enough neighbor, a man who might also be concerned about a serial intruder.

I rang the bell.

It seemed an eternity before the door opened.

Tom looked down at me. "Everything okay?" He glanced over my head, then leaned out slightly to check the area between our homes.

"Yes ... well, no, not really. Someone was in our house last night and—"

"Who?"

"I woke and found our front door open."

"I thought you'd installed a security camera?"

"We did. It didn't capture anything, but—"

"How would anyone open the front door without being seen? Was it locked?"

"If they got in another way. Maybe they opened it and saw the camera, so they didn't leave that way. There's a side door from the laundry room. We don't have a camera there."

He nodded.

"Broken windows? Unlocked—"

"We checked everything. I can't explain it. I just wondered if you'd seen or heard anything. Do you mind checking your cameras to see if they picked up anything?"

"I can do that, sure."

"Thanks."

He stepped outside and closed the door. "I will check, but the houses are so far apart ..."

"It's not the first time. And I ... I really don't understand. I can't explain it."

"What does your husband think?"

I shrugged.

He glanced over my head again, studying my house, as if he thought he might figure it out simply by observing all the windows visible from his front patio.

"I'll check our cameras, but it's unlikely, as I said."

"Have you spoken to the police recently?" I asked.

"Yes."

"What did they ask?"

"Probably not as much as they asked you." He laughed.

I didn't find it funny, but tried to offer him a limp smile because I saw he was trying. From his perspective, maybe some dark humor was called for. "I'm sure not," I said.

"Just the basics," he said. "Seen anything, heard anything. Know anything about bad blood between the victims and anyone you know? Any bad blood between us and the victims?"

"What did you say?" I hated asking. It made me feel desperate. But it occurred to me after his not very funny joke that he might not have any idea what Danielle had said to the detective.

"I wasn't here, actually. Danielle spoke to them."

"I guess you don't really know the details of what they asked. That's too bad."

"I can get Danielle."

"It's not important."

"She gave me a rundown. I think that was about it."

It sounded as if Danielle had gone out of her way to reshape the conversation for her husband. Was I going to draw out more of her hatred? Once I told him what she'd done, if he didn't already know, which it sounded as if he didn't, could she do more damage? "They told me someone had seen me with Brian the night he died. Kissing him," I said.

"Were you?"

"No!"

"Just asking. Don't—"

"I didn't do anything with him," I said. "And I wasn't outside that night. At all."

"Got it."

"But the detective is taking this person seriously. Even though it was dark. And I said I wasn't there, I guess someone able to see a fairly long distance in the dark is absolutely credible."

He shrugged.

He didn't seem to have made the connection it might be his wife. Or, he had an excellent poker face.

"You shouldn't let them intimidate you. They need more evidence than that."

"I've never experienced anything even close to this before. I do not know what they need in order to charge me with killing some-one. I really don't." I laughed, my voice tinged with tears. "It feels so ridiculous. All I know about the police or investigations is what I've seen on TV." I laughed again, the tears gone, but I still felt as if everything inside me was shaking, coming loose and floating around beneath my skin.

"I'm a retired attorney," Tom said. "Probate, so this is not my area. Way out of my area, obviously. But if you want someone to sit with you the next time the detective shows up, just to make sure your rights are respected, I'm happy to do that. It would look ... odd, I think, to hire an attorney when he hasn't accused you of anything, and he doesn't seem to have any physical evidence. But if you want, I'm available."

"That's really nice of you." I felt my entire body relax, as if I'd been hanging onto the edge of a cliff and only now realized the ground was just inches below my feet rather than a two-hundred-foot drop.

I was pretty sure it wasn't the offer to watch over my rights. It was simply knowing that someone believed me.

59 NOW: PETER

I saw the woman cross between the houses. She was almost running, as if she were being chased across the lawn onto the Vargas's patio. Instead of immediately knocking, she stood several feet from the door for a moment or two. She looked around, then took a step back. Finally, she flung herself at the door, stabbing the bell with her finger.

Tom answered. They spoke for a few minutes, then Tom came out onto the patio, closed the door behind him, and they talked for a while longer.

When she left, she walked down their front path and along the street, taking her time to return to Sara's house. She climbed the front steps and sat on the top one, staring up at the sky.

I waited until she went inside before I knocked on Tom and Danielle's door. I'd already sent a text to let them know I was coming. It was our habit.

Tom answered, holding two mugs of coffee. "I thought you might like a second cup on a sunny Saturday."

We settled on the patio chairs, coffee mugs in hand. Anyone passing by might have thought we were neighbors talking about lawn care, local news, or sports.

"I noticed the new owner of Sara's house was over here." I wished it had been Danielle. Tom was not going to be receptive to this topic of conversation.

"You really need to stop calling it Sara's house," Tom said.

"That's what it is, to me."

"It's not a good look."

"Who's looking?" I laughed, watching his expression turn to one of irritation, filled with pity for me. "I know it's not her house. What was she upset about?"

"The detective is asking her a lot of questions about Brian's murder."

"Just Brian's?"

"It sounds like it. They think she was involved, and she's scared."

"What's she scared of?"

"I probably shouldn't talk about it," Tom said.

Now I really wished it had been Danielle. She would have talked about it for hours. She would have told me every word the woman who had begun to capture my attention had spoken. She would have known every question the detective asked. The woman who at first reminded me of Sara in some indefinable way had moved in with such hope on her face. Now, she looked so terribly frightened. Danielle would have dissected every detail. She would have given me more information to brood about.

But maybe I didn't need that.

It was possible Tom was right. Not only was it not a good look, it really wasn't a great feeling.

I picked up my mug and took a few sips of coffee. Danielle made great coffee. "Maybe the detective is asking the wrong questions," I said.

"How do you know? You didn't hear what he asked."

"I'm pretty sure he didn't ask this." I was setting him up, but it was fun. The guy was always so cool and calm, never seemed to feel anything that might make him sweat even a little, that might make his skin flush.

"Ask what?"

"Maybe Brian ended up in the bottom of the well because Sara didn't want him in her house."

"It's not *her* house anymore." Tom's voice was tight. He was losing patience.

He'd made his point. He didn't need to keep reminding me. "She wanted me to have it."

"If she had, she would have made arrangements in her trust."

"That's not what I meant."

"Why don't we discuss something less speculative," Tom said.

"Because I'm trying to make a point."

"Have at it, then." He stared across the yard.

I didn't care whether he was fed up with me. I wanted him to hear this. Or maybe, I just needed to hear it spoken out loud, because I wanted to hear it, even though it was speculative. I just needed it out of my gut. Purged.

"Maybe Brian's dead because Sara didn't want him in her house. Maybe that's why both of them are dead. Charlotte shoved Brian down the new owner's throat as the only guy who could help her with repairs. Before she could blink, the people who threw me out were creeping all over the place like roaches."

"Get a grip, buddy," Tom said. "Get a fucking grip." He stood and moved toward the front door.

As I turned to watch him go, wondering if my welcome there and all those terrific dinners had just come to a sudden end, I saw Danielle standing in the doorway.

"You might be right," Danielle said.

Tom groaned and disappeared inside the house. Danielle followed him.

I desperately wished I could be inside their house. I would have enjoyed hearing that conversation.

60 NOW: DAVID

Trinity was so unlike herself, I wasn't sure what to make of it. Every time I spoke to her, it seemed as if I was talking to a different woman. I felt as if we were headed toward more trouble than I'd anticipated.

Being in the house with a minimal amount of furniture wasn't helping the surreal nature of the situation. There was no place I could go to get some work done, to have any time to myself, to think things through and get my head on straight after weeks of non-stop meetings and detailed planning that had beaten me to a pulp. Literally.

I'd carried a kitchen chair into the sunroom, which was the only place I could get some privacy, unless I was going to sit on our bed and respond to email and conduct business calls. I knew Trinity didn't want me working, but a few things had to be taken care of. I couldn't just walk away from my job to devote myself to her house projects.

I was well aware a small part of her constantly wondered why I worked at all, which I found demeaning. What man wants to live off his wife's windfall? If the windfall belongs to him, sure. But not when she's *generously sharing* it with him, assuring him it belongs to both of them *equally*, that she has *no problem* with him spending it however he chooses. There was a subtle tone of ownership.

Bottom line, the money was hers. Therefore, I wanted a career that was mine.

Trinity liked to tell me she didn't see the money as belonging to her. She was simply born under a lucky star. She didn't realize that kind of thinking didn't sit well with me. How could she? I'd never talked much about my dad. He wasn't a guy worth talking about. My dad went on and on and *on* about people born under lucky stars. It ate away at him.

My dad made some bad investments, one very big, very bad investment in particular. He'd been seduced by his buddies, but his buddies were born under *lucky stars*, so they all came out great. They got in early, thanks to being born under those lucky stars. And there went my college fund. And with it, my chance for a leg up, my chance to get ahead of the game. It set the course for my whole life.

I'd recovered okay, and I was doing well for myself, but I wasn't in the top tier, so to speak. Not that Trinity noticed. She complained I worked too much, traveled too much. I did. It was impossible to argue with that, but I also liked my work, and loved the thrill of success.

Through the sunroom door, I heard her talking to Mia. I couldn't make out their words, but it sounded as if she was a lot calmer than when she'd bolted out of the house full of hurt feelings, furious that we were talking behind her back, that we didn't believe her, that we thought she was capable of murder. I'd never seen her look like she had. The rage in her eyes and the knot in her jaw, as if it had been locked into place, made me wonder if she *was* capable of killing someone. For a moment, I'd thought she might punch one of us in the face. And then she was gone.

I placed my phone on the floor beside my laptop, stood, and stretched out the kinks from sitting in the straight-backed chair. I opened the door into the living room.

Mia looked at me, then stood and left the room. What did that mean? Had they argued? Did she think Trinity and I needed privacy to talk? It wasn't a room that offered privacy. If Mia was inclined to listen, she could easily do so from the hallway or the stairwell.

I walked cautiously toward Trinity, unsure what kind of reception I would get. I put my hand on her shoulder and squeezed it gently. She looked tired.

"What's going on? Did you and Mia have a fight?"

"No. I was telling her about Tom."

"Tom?"

"Our neighbor. He used to be an attorney."

"What does that—"

"He offered to sit with me if Detective Robbins has any more questions. Or accusations."

"You haven't even told me what he said the last time."

"He claims someone saw me with Brian the night he died."

"Who?"

She shrugged. "He won't say."

"That doesn't seem right."

"I know. But he wouldn't budge. Tom said he'd be happy to be there to make sure I know what my rights are."

"Is he a defense attorney?"

"He's retired. But no, he was a probate lawyer."

I laughed. "How will that help?"

"He knows the law."

"You need a criminal lawyer. Not a retired guy who used to write trusts."

"I don't need a criminal lawyer! I didn't *do* anything! I just need someone to make sure that detective doesn't harass me."

"Is he harassing you? Or asking questions?"

"Whose side are you on?" She wrenched away from my hand that had been gently massaging her shoulder, trying to keep her steady.

"It's not about taking sides."

"Yes, it is. You're acting like you think I killed him!"

"I'm definitely not doing that. Calm down."

"Don't tell me to calm down. One minute you treat me like I'm crazy—walking in my sleep, seeing ghosts, and then you accuse me of committing murder."

"I did not accuse you of committing murder."

"It sure sounded like it to me."

"That's because you're not being rational."

"Why are you doing this? You don't believe anything I say. I feel like you … I don't even know. You don't want to help with the house. You haven't said a word about Ryan."

"What does Ryan have to do with it?"

"Everything!"

She was screaming at me now. I couldn't follow her train of thought. It looked like she was going to start hitting me. If there'd been anything in the room besides a couch and chair, she would have picked it up and thrown it at me. Instead, she bolted out of the room. It was her new go-to reaction to every situation she didn't like.

61 THEN: PETER

When Sara took her last breath, we'd all known it was coming. She'd started hospice care. She was sleeping in a hospital bed, set up in the sunroom where she could look out at her peaceful backyard.

All three of us were there—Charlotte. Brian. Me.

"My team," Sara said.

We all gave her tender smiles, even if our hearts felt something distinctly different.

"My two men," she said.

I hoped it was delirium. I hoped we hadn't become equal in her mind. I didn't think it was that way, but Brian certainly thought that, and Charlotte had a beaming glow about her that suggested she'd won a victory of sorts.

Even when you know it's coming, death is a punch to the gut that feels like your own breath has been taken away. It feels as if your skin is ripped off, your heart squeezed until the only feeling left inside you is pain. Unrelenting pain.

But apparently I was alone in feeling that way.

Because the moment her eyelids closed for the last time and Sara was gone, only the shell of her body resting on the bed, Charlotte had a few words to say.

"You'll have two weeks in the house, Peter. That will give you some time to grieve and pack your things."

"I—"

She stood and moved toward the doorway. "It's important that her estate is dealt with in a timely manner. And I know you have a tendency to wallow. You take a long time to get things done. That's not respectful to Sara."

"That's not fair. Our whole lives were here. I need time to—"

"Man up," Brian said. "We all suffered a terrible loss here, but we knew it was coming. We've known for months."

"Of course I knew."

"Sara knew. Surely you've talked," Brian said.

"Yeah, fucker. We talked. A lot. More than you'll ever know."

Brian shrugged.

"So ... the house," Charlotte said. "Two weeks. I need you to agree."

"She just died! I'm not agreeing to anything. I'm going to go lie down." I started toward the hallway.

"I didn't mean I need you to negotiate an agreement," Charlotte said. "I need you to verbally assent to what I've said. I'm the executor of the estate and I need—"

"I'm aware, Charlotte. And I don't give a fuck what you need."

"You have two weeks." Her voice was steady. "Can I hear you acknowledge that?"

"No. You can't." I was on the opposite side of the living room now, almost out of their sight. Soon, the mortuary would be there to take her body. And this was what Charlotte and Brian wanted to do? While Sara was still in the house? Our house? What a bunch of sick, disgusting vultures.

Could Sara hear this?

I felt physically ill. I wondered if I was going to make it up to the bedroom.

"You have two weeks, Peter. After that, I'm changing the locks."

And that was how it ended. I spent eight days reliving my time with Sara. I shoved away the memories of those months—nearly a year—when I'd stupidly chosen to hang out with my fans every night instead of coming home to her. What an absolute, utter fool I'd been. The fans were still there. They would always be there. The crowds hadn't diminished at all on those nights I came home right after a set when Sara was first diagnosed and dealing with chemo. Not by a single person.

I would live with that forever.

Finally, I packed up my things and moved out. I tried not to think about how much I wanted to be in that place where I still felt her presence and heard her voice. Where I smelled her scent and sometimes, I swear, felt her fingers touch my skin and sensed the warmth of her breath in every single room.

62 NOW: TRINITY

*U*pstairs, I went into the empty bedroom between Mia's and ours. It was a larger room with its own bathroom, but Mia had wanted to take the room at the front of the house, facing the street. She liked looking out at the towering eucalyptus trees rather than over the neighbors' roof, she'd said that first day.

Now, I stood at the window and looked into their yard. I had a clear view of their entire property. If their house was two stories like ours, I might have believed it was possible for Danielle to have seen our backyard when Brian fell, or was pushed, into the well. As far as I could see, the detective hadn't yet proven he was pushed.

Wasn't it possible he'd removed the cover himself? I couldn't explain why he would have done that in the middle of the night, or why he would have done it at all, but it was possible.

As I stood at the window, wondering if any of my questions would ever be answered, wondering if my relationship with my husband was breaking apart in a way that couldn't be repaired, the black mid-sized sedan driven by Detective Robbins came into view. It slowed and turned into the driveway next door.

The detective got out and approached the house. Once he disappeared under the patio roof, I considered going downstairs to the front bedroom for a better look, but I felt an inexplicable need to see how long he stayed without anyone being aware I was watching.

A few minutes later, he returned to the car and backed slowly down the drive into the street, then drove away.

I hurried down the stairs and across the lawn to the house next door. I rang the bell, hoping again for Tom. Danielle opened the door just as my finger touched the bell for the second time.

"Is Tom available?"

"Why?'

"I have a quick question."

"About what?"

I regretted my choice. I should have asked her directly. Instead, I'd roused her suspicion. She wasn't going to grant me access unless I told her. Lying could land me in a trap I might not escape, and might also pour fuel on the lie simmering in her mind, increasing her desire to embellish what she'd already told Detective Robbins about me. Telling the truth might get the door slammed in my face.

She glared at me, waiting.

"I wondered why the detective was here."

"Why do you assume Tom can answer that nosey question and I can't?"

"I don't think it's nosey, considering everything that's happened around here."

"Around here? Do you mean in your backyard? Nothing *happened around here* until you moved in."

"It has nothing to do with me. Please believe that. I just want to say, I feel like things started out badly between you and me, and I'd really like to—"

"Why do you need to speak to Tom about the detective?"

It seemed as though things had started out badly because she'd wanted them to. I was the intruder. The unwelcome occupant destroying the legacy of her friend.

"I didn't know if he had new evidence or …"

She smirked, moving to the side as if she could make her small body fill the entire doorframe, pulling the door closed as she did.

She wasn't going to get her husband. Maybe I could achieve that myself. I shifted my position, so I was facing the opening directly. I raised my voice to a semi-hysterical pitch. "It's so awful. You have no idea. I came here to plant a garden and fill the pond, and make the playroom and bedroom ready for my sweet, orphaned nephew!" I let out a painful cry. "And now, everything is turning so ugly!"

Tom appeared in the doorway behind her.

"What's wrong?"

Danielle pulled the door closed until there was only room enough for her face, blocking my view of Tom. "I shouldn't be talking to you. I'm ... well, I don't have to explain. Thanks for stopping by."

Tom's hand appeared on the edge of the door above her head. The door opened several inches. Danielle gasped as it slipped out of her hands.

"Is everything okay?" he asked.

"I was upset seeing the police here. I just wondered ..." My lower lip trembled, and it wasn't put on for the sake of my story about Ryan, which was designed to project my voice through their house. My heart hurt for Ryan more deeply every day. I felt as if I could see his future happiness evaporating before my eyes.

Tom stepped around Danielle and took my elbow. "Are you sure you're okay?"

I nodded. "Why was Detective Robbins here?"

"Yes, Tom. Why was he here?" Danielle's voice was sharp. "Because you betrayed our friend. A man who needed us. You might as well have stabbed Sara right through the heart. You're no better than Charlotte."

I felt the air freeze in my throat.

Tom looked older than he'd appeared the other times I'd spoken to him. He looked as if he wasn't as sure of himself, as if his thoughts might be as tangled as mine.

"Danielle. He ... Robbins directly asked me if I knew anyone who—"

"And you don't," Danielle said.

"But Peter said he thought—"

"He's grieving, Tom! Don't you understand that? What's wrong with you? He says things. They treated him so badly. He was hurt more than you can begin to comprehend. When people are grieving, they say things they don't mean, they say things that don't make sense, they—"

"That's enough," Tom said. "Why don't you—"

"Are you going to tell her? She's just being nosey. She said so herself."

"She has a right to know. It's not a secret."

"You're ... you're ..." A sob caught in her throat. A moment later, she was gone.

Tom stepped outside and closed the door. His face haggard and guilty, he said, "They were looking for Peter Jordan. One of the former occupants of the house. Sara's partner—after she split with Brian."

"Why are they looking for him?"

He gestured toward the wicker chairs on the patio and we sat down. He told me about Sara and her husband, and Peter. About the break-ups and the reconciliations. There'd been several, with both men.

"In the end, they were both there when she died, and for her sake, they were amicable."

"It sounds difficult."

He shrugged. "Charlotte didn't treat Peter very well. She was the executor of the estate, as well as the real estate agent. She kicked him out of the house, at least verbally, the day Sara died. Told him she would be changing the locks.

"Peter hasn't been able to let go of it. I don't think he believed he should inherit the house, or anything like that, although who knows? But he's made some comments about not being surprised that she was murdered because of how she treated people. And as far as I know, he's the only one she treated like that. But the thing that made me call Robbins was he said that Sara didn't want Brian in her house, making repairs for you. And maybe that's why he died. He laughed about it. A somewhat disturbing laugh. It bothered me."

"Oh." I felt relief wash over me. Relief tinged with fear. Maybe the detective would turn away from Danielle's ridiculous *eyewitness* story. Even if he still believed it, couldn't two men struggling with each other, in the dead of night, look similar to a couple with their arms wrapped around each other, holding one another close?

This Peter sounded like a madman. I didn't recall seeing an unfamiliar man anywhere around ... but the open door, the carefully arranged Tarot cards ...

"I didn't feel right, not telling the detective about it. Peter is a good guy, a really sensitive, generous guy. But I couldn't let that just sit there."

"No," I said. "Thanks for letting me know."

I returned home wondering how much I should say to David. Whether I should try to explain to Mia, or let things unfold without my involvement.

63 NOW: TRINITY

Keeping what I knew about Peter to myself turned out to be the right choice. Maybe we were all simply exhausted from nights of interrupted sleep and the trauma of violent death.

Now that my mind was partially eased that perhaps the detective would turn his suspicions somewhere else, somewhere that made a lot more sense, I wondered if I *had* been acting strangely. Maybe David was truly concerned about my state of mind after the loss of my sister and everything that had happened here, as well as my burning desire to provide the absolute best life for Ryan. Maybe Mia cared about me more than I'd ever realized, and they were simply trying to help me see how distraught I was.

She'd told me repeatedly that I'd been through a lot. I hadn't listened.

We're not always the best judge of our own behavior. Maybe I didn't have a clue how I was coming across to them. Maybe I was terrifying, giving the impression I thought ghosts were drifting down the stairs and through the rooms of my house. That the spirits of the dead were moving cards and painting rooms.

For whatever reason, we chose to ignore what had happened

over the past twenty-four hours. Maybe we all felt the need for a re-set.

I busied myself re-painting the playroom. David helped Mia move the bookcases, and they got to work scraping the streaks of paint off the dining room walls, prepping it for fresh paint. David filled out two online forms at contractor websites, requesting quotes for the beam in the living room ceiling and a modest kitchen remodel.

I had a video chat with Ryan, followed by a longer conversation with my brother, assuring him we would pick up Ryan well before their baby was due.

We returned to the Mexican restaurant where Mia and I had eaten. We ordered an entire pitcher of margaritas, which honestly, but sadly, made us all feel like friends again.

At home, giggly and misreading my mood, Mia offered to do a Tarot reading. I declined. She offered one to David. He grinned and said he didn't want to spoil the present moment with information about the future.

He got out his large tablet, and we watched a movie, huddled together on the couch, nibbling popcorn. It felt cozy. I didn't feel they were looking at me strangely. It seemed now as if everything that had been bothering me had truly been in my mind—all of it mushrooming into dark clouds of fear, born from the detective's insistence that someone had seen me with Brian moments before he died.

Why did everything feel better, somehow? Was it, truly, better?

A dull ache began to grow behind my eyes and I wasn't sure if it was caused by our slightly false behavior or the margaritas, drunk too fast, the alcohol buzz now wearing thin.

As soon as the movie ended, I stood and picked up the bowl with the un-popped kernels. "I'm really tired."

"I'm up for another movie," Mia said. "Maybe a glass of wine? We've been going to bed so early!"

"Painting wore me out," I said.

"You only did two walls," she said.

I yawned. "You can watch another. I need sleep."

David stood. "Red or white?"

"Red." Mia shifted her position, sitting cross-legged, now that I'd left more room on the couch. "Night-night."

"Night." I took the bowl into the kitchen. David followed me. We kissed, and it felt gentle and nice, as if everything was indeed okay. I wasn't sure it was, but I also didn't want to fight it. I wanted the detective to arrest that guy, I wanted all of it to be over. Then, maybe we could sort things out.

"Sleep good," David said.

Two hours later, I woke suddenly. I felt the weight and warmth of David beside me. I pulled the pillow closer to my neck, frustrated that once again my sleep had been disrupted, and I didn't know why. David wasn't snoring. The blankets hadn't come off. I was perfectly comfortable.

I turned onto my back. I stared at the ceiling, trying to make out the shape of the overhead light, thinking about all the things that had happened the previous day. It was too much. Every day, there was too much. I only had a few weeks before I needed to pick up Ryan.

My house was in absolute disarray. At least I knew the furnishings for Ryan's bedroom and playroom didn't have to be taken care of. We would be moving all his familiar things here. Once summer was over, I would have to decide what to leave here, what to take home with us, and what to purchase new. But that seemed years away right now. Even the idea of having Ryan with me twenty-four hours a day, tucking him into bed every night, making his meals, and keeping him entertained and nurtured throughout the day, seemed far away, not quite real. A mirage.

Something tickled at my brain as I lay there.

I shifted my position slightly. I rested my hand on David's hip and felt his breathing change, but he didn't move. What was it? A distant sound that I couldn't identify. Something that made my head feel as if it were bleeding with the strain of trying to pick it out of the silence around me.

I heard a noise, but it wasn't one of footsteps or a door opening.

I sat up. The silence felt heavier, but there was still a soft … something. Like a far-away ringing in my ear that was hardly noticeable.

I got out of bed and grabbed my hoodie, stuffing my phone into the pocket. I went downstairs, wondering if the sound might be coming from next door. I went to the front of the house, into the future guest room, and looked out the side window. The house next door was completely dark except for the solar lamps lining the path from the driveway to the patio.

Returning to the hallway, I stopped and strained to listen. The sound was slightly more distinct now. Music. It was the soft strum of a guitar, maybe.

My first thought, one that I tried to shove out of my head as quickly as it had come, was that maybe all the strange things happening had been signs of a supernatural presence after all. Hearing music was something I couldn't explain. There was nothing inside my house, aside from someone's phone or tablet, that would play music. Had I missed it, coming down the stairs? Had Mia set an alert that hadn't woken her and was now playing repeatedly?

I went to the bottom of the stairs, but the faint notes weren't coming from there. I turned and walked down the hall and into the kitchen.

It was now definitely and distinctly music. The plucked strings and intermittent strumming of a guitar. It was coming from the basement.

64 NOW: PETER

*M*usic was the way I worked things out of my head, through my gut, and into the world. Most of the time, my work, my art, resonated with other people, resulting in a connection. Other times, it was just for me.

I hadn't written a song or played fresh notes since the morning Sara died. So everything had stayed in my head, knotted in my belly like undigested food, weighing me down.

Charlotte was not going to take that house from me. I decided that the day after Sara left me behind. She'd left unfinished sculptures and her unfinished life. She'd vanished from the earth and the house was all I had left of her. I'd been stupid enough to walk out of there and abandon her before, I wasn't about to do it again.

Locks were not going to keep me out.

I had two weeks to get things organized. I packed what I needed into moving boxes and stored them neatly under the workbench in the basement—clothing and some snack food, bottled water, a sleeping bag and pillow, my guitar. Even though my guitar had been silent, I had a sliver of hope whispering it wouldn't be that way forever.

Then, I spent time working in the basement closet. I cut a hole that went up into the space under the steps that provided outdoor access to the laundry room. I created a panel of wood that could be removed to allow me easy access in and out, dropping with the help of a rope into that closet, using the same rope to hoist myself back out when I wanted to leave.

I ate my meals in restaurants and, more often than I'd dared to hope, with Danielle and Tom. I parked my car a few blocks away. I returned to my house for showers and occasional meals, although I preferred eating out. I didn't want to be in my own house at all. It reminded me too much of those months when I'd chosen to go home long after midnight, sleeping alone, still high from talking to fans, instead of leaving our performances early to be with her.

When the inspector came after the Felds made their offer on the house, I thought my time living with my memories was over. No more nights spent climbing the basement stairs, placing a large pillow on the living room floor, sipping a beer while I closed my eyes and imagined Sara beside me. No more carrying my sleeping bag up to our bedroom to spend the night dreaming of holding her in my arms, waking to the light and its brutal reminder she was gone.

But the inspector didn't notice. Once he found that compromised beam in the living room, he was focused on major, and potentially dangerous structural issues. He didn't spend a lot of time in the basement. He didn't check under the stairs leading to the laundry room door.

It seemed possible that I might be able to live there for years. Unless the basement was used for something on a regular basis, how would anyone ever know? I reveled in my freedom, in my chance to stay with her indefinitely.

And then Charlotte saw me. At least, I think she did. I wasn't sure.

I'd just finished replacing the panel behind the stairs. I'd checked and hadn't seen any cars in the driveway. The house had sold, but I knew from Danielle it was being turned into a vacation home. I think Danielle wondered why I couldn't stop smiling that evening. A vacation home meant I would have it to myself for most of the year. Danielle had also mentioned the new occupants wouldn't be there until June.

Then, as I started around toward the front of the house, there was Charlotte—bold and bright as day. I ducked back around the side, but I know she saw me. She didn't come after me. She did nothing. The next day, I found some of my boxes had been repositioned.

If she knew I was hunkered down in the basement, why hadn't she said anything? It was so strange. Maybe she'd decided to concede the final battle to me. Maybe she just wanted to be done with it all. I suppose she'd finished all her paperwork, made her disclosures, and she didn't want the headache of confronting me. Maybe she figured she would hand the problem over to the new occupants.

The screams coming from Trinity the morning she found Charlotte's body woke me from the best sleep I'd had in weeks. I looked out through one of the narrow windows that gave a panoramic view of the backyard from a gopher's perspective. I couldn't see what she was screaming about. But once the police showed up, I was trapped. I ended up having to piss into an empty beer bottle. By the time they left, I'd eaten all my energy bars.

Brian was a different story. For several days now, I'd been tormented by the circumstances of his death.

I wasn't sure what made me look out the window that night. I'm almost certain I didn't hear a sound, so it wasn't that. But I looked. I saw a man punch Brian hard in the gut, then shove him into the well without a moment's hesitation. I didn't get why the guy didn't cover the well. If you want to be rid of someone, that would have been the smart move.

The man was tall, but I knew it wasn't Tom because that white hair of his would have reflected the moonlight like a mirror.

Besides, this guy was thinner. Tom was beefy, he dwarfed everyone around him.

I'd never seen this guy before, so when Danielle told me the detective thought it defied the law of averages that two people were murdered in Trinity's backyard and she claimed to know nothing about it, I still didn't think I needed to get involved. Telling them what I'd seen would put an immediate end to my stay in Sara's basement. I didn't know the guy. Of course, I knew it wasn't Trinity who killed him, but I didn't think they'd actually start believing she'd murdered two people she barely knew. They would find evidence, they would get answers.

Then, I saw the guy who drove the white rental car. The guy who was now sleeping two floors above me. I realized who had pushed Brian into the well and now, I couldn't sleep.

For the first time since Sara had left me, I picked up my guitar because I wanted to. Not because I was performing. Not because it was my livelihood. Not to pluck and strum and sing the music I'd performed a thousand times before. But to create something new.

Letting my fingers drift gently across the strings, closing my eyes, I began singing a song to Sara. I told her goodbye. The experience stunned me, because the music made me feel good. As I sang, I realized my eyes were clear and completely dry.

In the next verse, I asked her what I should do.

65 NOW: TRINITY

I turned the knob as slowly as I could. It was original to the house, and it squeaked when it turned, so I pressed down slightly, hoping to keep metal from scraping metal, thus minimizing the noise. As the door opened, the music grew louder. When I'd first come close to the door, I'd heard words, but now all I heard was the strumming of the guitar.

A dim light splashed up the stairs.

I walked down.

A man sat on a sleeping bag with a foam mat underneath and several pillows nearby. He was strumming the guitar and humming quietly, his eyes closed. A beer bottle stood on the floor in front of him. The boxes under the workbench were open and two small electric lights sat on top of the workbench.

"Who are you?"

He startled violently, hitting a discordant note on the guitar, nearly dropping the instrument.

I tapped my phone, poised to call 911. "How did you get in here? What are you—?"

"Don't call the cops. Please. I won't hurt you. I'm just ..." He placed the guitar beside him and uncrossed his legs.

I realized I hadn't felt fear, hadn't expected him to hurt me. Not from the moment I followed the music down the stairs. I was curious, not afraid. Shocked, but also flooded with a sense of calm, that I was looking at the source of all the inexplicable things that had happened inside my house—the repainted walls, the open door, the bookcases, the Tarot cards. All of it making me feel I was losing my grip on reality.

"I'm not a killer. I didn't kill them."

"How do I know that?"

"I guess you don't."

"No." I didn't know that. Yet, I still didn't feel a prick of fear, any sense that I needed to race up the stairs and barricade the door behind me, trapping him like a rat in the small space. But how had he gotten in? And why wasn't I afraid? There was a man who appeared to be *living* in our basement! I should be terrified. More so than when I'd seen a curtain move in my living room or found the front door standing open. Maybe it was the music. Maybe it was the slightly frightened look in his own eyes.

"I probably had a good reason to kill both of them," he said softly. "More than most, but I didn't."

"You ... who are you?"

"I used to live here. With Sara." He pushed himself to his feet. "I'm Peter." He extended his hand, then let it fall slowly to his side when I didn't do the same. He laughed briefly, letting it fade quickly. "I guess you don't shake hands with the creep squatting in your basement."

"The police are looking for you. Is that why you're here?"

"No. I just ... I'm here because I missed her so much. I ... I couldn't leave. It felt like this was the only way I could stay close to her."

"How long ...?"

"Since they locked me out."

"They?"

"Charlotte, mostly."

I nodded.

"It's a long, complicated story."

"Do you want to come upstairs? I can make tea."

When we were seated at the kitchen table, he told me in a sooth-ing, melodic voice, the same tones I'd heard accompanying the guitar, about his life with Sara.

Some of the things he said brought tears to my eyes. His words also confused me as I thought of Brian and how kind he'd been to me. I felt as if I might be living for a few moments inside Sara's skin, recognizing her affection for both men. But love? Had she been in love with both of them? At the same time? Who would ever know?

When he was finished, he sipped his cooling tea.

"And you were inside my house? You laid out the Tarot cards? And repainted the front room?"

He nodded.

"You disconnected the hose and moved the bookcases?"

"The bookcases, yes. Not the hose."

It seemed odd he would deny one thing. "Why?"

"I don't know. I was ... maybe out of my mind. I've been out of my mind, wanting to talk to her again, wanting ..."

"I know," I whispered.

"I can't explain the cards. I guess I thought I could scare you away. Sometimes, I thought you were Sara." He laughed. His cheeks flushed, and he turned his face away from me for a moment. "I realize that wouldn't have accomplished anything. The paint ... I just. She loved the color of that room and seeing it painted over just sent me ..." He put his elbows on the table and rested his head in his hands. "I haven't been ..." A sob rose out of him like a cry of pain. "I left her before she left me. I'll never—"

"What the hell is this?" David's voice roared into the room. Peter and I jerked away from the table. David stood in the entryway, his arms folded, his legs spread.

66 NOW: DAVID

I could not believe what I was looking at.

My wife was leaning over her mug of tea, her hoodie falling open, as she smiled and chatted with a scruffy but very good-looking guy seated across the table from her. It was two o'clock in the morning. What the hell was going on? I'd asked the realtor about this guy. She brushed me off, said not to worry about him. I pushed the issue, demanding to know who he was.

Charlotte had gone on the defensive fast. She was very upset and obviously did not want to talk about it. "He was Sara's partner."

"Why is he here? He's trespassing."

She sighed. "I know. But while the house is for sale, it's not really tress—"

"We've made an offer. We're in the middle of inspections. This isn't an open house," I said.

"I understand. I'll speak to him."

"A call to the police might be more effective, if this is an ongoing problem."

She'd laughed, but she sounded nervous. Very nervous. Were the cops afraid of this guy? Or was she? I couldn't get a read. I thought about pushing it, but decided since we hadn't closed escrow and I wasn't yet liable, I wouldn't make an issue of it.

Now, here he was. And Trinity was acting as if they were old friends. Did she know him? Had she been friendly with him before I'd arrived? I couldn't figure out what I was looking at. When they both startled at the sound of my voice, which was admittedly loud and intimidating, deliberately so, I still wasn't sure what I'd walked into.

"This is Peter," Trinity said.

The guy started to push out his chair.

"What's he doing in our kitchen?"

"It's hard to explain," Trinity said.

"Why?"

"He …" she laughed softly. "I guess all the strange things I've experienced have an explanation."

"Is that right?" I'd never doubted that. Unlike my wife, I'd known the place wasn't haunted. Given this guy's propensity for lurking, given the other guy's attachment to the house, I had no doubt these men who appeared to be as haunted by their loss and regret as Heathcliff, were the cause of the things that were making Trinity so unstable.

She'd already been on the precipice when we bought the house, already blurring the lines between life and death, reality and fantasy. She thought Mia was the one living in a fantasy world with her card readings, but Mia was fully grounded in practical matters. Sure, Mia thought the cards spoke to her, but out of that, she lived a reality-based, aspirational life.

"You've been breaking and entering? You somehow got your hands on a key? I guess we need to put in a call to the police. Although entertaining him with a cup of tea will make it difficult to present our concerns." I gave Trinity a stern look.

She smiled at me as if she were pleading with me to consider buying a puppy or to allow her to feed a stray cat, guaranteeing it would become ours. Maybe that's what this guy was to her—a good-looking, if bedraggled, stray. Someone she wanted to feed and care for. It seemed to be her nature.

"I don't understand you," I said. "You've been scared out of your mind, and now you're serving tea?" My voice was too loud. I needed to stay calm, but I was finding it difficult.

"What's going on?"

I turned. Mia stood behind me. She wore a long T-shirt. Her legs and feet were bare. She wrapped her arms around herself and looked at Peter, staring at him as if she wanted to memorize his expression.

"Peter was Sara's partner," Trinity said.

It didn't seem necessary to mention I already knew this. What I wanted to know was why the hell he was sitting at our table in the middle of the night. No one had explained that. "How did you get in? But more importantly, time to go." I gestured for him to stand.

"Don't get upset," Trinity said.

"I'm not upset."

"You sound angry."

"It's outside my normal experience to see a strange man sitting in my kitchen at this hour of the night. With my wife."

She gave me another pleading look.

"Don't get upset about—"

"About what?"

"He was—"

"I've been living in the basement." Peter pushed his chair out and stood.

"Oh, my God!" Mia said.

Peter ignored her. "I was kicked out of the house before I was ready to go. And, as I explained to Trinity, I had a hard time letting go. Losing the woman you love is ..." He looked at Trinity and let his voice fade.

I wasn't shocked. I was prepared. I already knew my course of action. I'd known when I walked into the room, even though I hadn't originally expected this to happen. I'd never expected things to turn out the way they were now unfolding, but life has a way of surprising you, of taking what you have in mind and twisting it in an entirely new direction. Often, that twisting works out just fine. Every once in a while, it turns out better than you could have imagined, if you're born under a lucky star.

I had my phone with me. I always did. We all do, except for those strange characters who imagine they can live off the grid, or the ones who think they're going to live in the moment, putting their entire focus on the people they're with. The rest of us can't be cut off. We know there's always something demanding our attention. Mostly work, but sometimes, other people we care about. There are so many things happening all at once, all across the planet. And we need to know, or it feels like we do.

I need to know what's happening. Always. I have a lot of balls in the air, lots of things I'm working on, so I stay connected at all times. For that reason, my phone is as much a part of my body as my right hand.

I tapped 911 on the phone.

"Don't," Trinity said. "Please. We don't need to do that. He didn't hurt anything. He didn't take anything, or do any damage."

"He scared the hell out of you. Have you already forgotten how you've been acting the past few weeks? You've been a nervous wreck."

The call connected, and I reported a trespasser on the premises right now.

After determining that we weren't in immediate danger, that there was no weapon, and no obvious threat to our lives, the dispatcher promised a car would be by as soon as possible. I wondered what that meant in this rural area.

It turned out their response time was impressive—seven minutes until the doorbell rang. Two officers stood on the porch.

I'd already asked Trinity to leave the kitchen. She'd refused, so I'd grabbed the intruder's arm and escorted him firmly into the room she was painting for her nephew's playroom. He didn't resist, which surprised me. I suppose he realized I outweighed him and had a good two inches on him.

We stood there, surrounded by silence. Mia and Trinity were in the hallway, standing close together, watching us as if they were waiting for Peter to make a run for it.

The silence grew heavy around us. I had nothing to say. I'd thought he might, but he kept his mouth shut. It surprised me, because when I'd walked in on him and Trinity, he'd been chattering like a squirrel sitting in a tree, watching a dog dig up his winter stash of nuts.

Trinity opened the door for the cops.

When I saw the looks on their faces, I didn't have a good feeling. The first one, a woman with long dark hair in a ponytail, shook our intruder's hand. "Hey. What's going on? Everything okay?"

The second one, a guy who looked like he was on the high school swim team, shot a nervous smile at Peter, then at Trinity who was standing in the hallway behind us, then looked at me as if he didn't understand why I was even there.

"This creep has been living in our basement," I said. "For I don't know how long. He's been coming upstairs, wandering around the house at night, playing pranks. He scared my wife half to death."

"Oh, Peter," the female cop said. "Why? How did you get—"

"That's irrelevant," I said. "He's trespassing. He put my wife in danger. All of us."

The high school swimmer wearing a cop's uniform started to speak. "I don't think Peter would—"

"You're not in danger," the female cop said. "Peter's a musician. He wouldn't hurt a fly."

"He's living in our basement! He's trespassing. I want him arrested. Now."

"You need to leave, Peter," the female cop said.

"My guitar."

The female cop put her hand on his arm. "We'll arrange a time to come back and get it. But right now, you need to come with us."

"To be fingerprinted and held," I said.

"That's not necessary. I don't think we need to escalate it that far. If there was no damage or burglary or—"

"He's been living in my basement for God knows how long!"

"Please calm down, sir," the female cop said. "We're escorting him off your property. I know that's really upsetting, and definitely—"

"You need to arrest him."

"Don't tell me what I need to do, sir. We'll take care of this. In the meantime, please make sure your basement is secured."

"It's not only the trespassing," I said. "He was supposed to be questioned about the—"

"Sir." Her voice was sharp. "It's handled."

They left. Without an apology, without me ever laying eyes on a pair of handcuffs. Without hearing any rights read to this guy.

I shouldn't have let them go. In hindsight, I learned that, but maybe it didn't matter. It would have come back to bite me either way.

67 NOW: TRINITY

*A*fter Peter and the two police officers left, David closed the door and turned to face me. His expression was unreadable. I wondered if mine were the same. We stared at each other. As the silence swelled around us, I found the memory of the notes from Peter's guitar floating through my mind.

Peter had said he'd written the song to ask Sara what he should do. I wondered what he'd meant by that, but I hadn't had a chance to ask. The story about how he'd come to live in our basement had flowed out of his lips so quickly, I hardly had time to murmur my surprise.

I understood why David had called the police. And until my recent experiences with the detective, that would have been my reaction as well. But now, inviting police into my home wasn't something I was inclined toward. I hated their officious presence. I hated the way they took the most insignificant detail and ran with it, leaving me feeling as if I had no voice of my own, no control over my own time, or even my own life. They acted as if my memories and my experiences were open to debate, as if these pieces of me belonged exclusively to them, to pick over and categorize as they chose.

Mia pressed her fists to her mouth. Her hair looked white in the near darkness of the hallway. It was silky, as if she'd brushed it before coming downstairs. Or she'd been awake in her room.

"Is that who … was he watching me do your reading that night?"

I nodded. I was suddenly tired. Now that my mind was eased about all the things that had happened inside our house, all I wanted was sleep. I was confident I would get my first good rest since the night Charlotte had been murdered. But I also knew we were only moments away from either David or Mia accusing Peter of committing both murders. The detective had been looking for him, eager to question him. It sounded as though interoffice communication had broken down at the police department because the two cops who had arrived on our doorstep apparently knew nothing about that.

Was I mistaken to take Peter at his word? Why had I? Was it the guitar and his hypnotic tenor voice? Had they moved me on a visceral level, made me feel affection for him that was overriding my natural instinct for self-preservation? Or was that instinct correct in knowing that I would somehow sense it if a person had the potential to commit murder? Was it possible to know something like that instinctively, or was that wishful thinking?

We all want to believe that we would sense a killer in our midst. But that's probably not true. That's why so many are lured to their deaths by charming psychopaths.

But I had believed him, and I still did. He didn't seem like someone who lost his temper, and he didn't seem like someone who might have held rage inside him all that time. He didn't feel like a man capable of killing another human being. He was drowning in grief. And he'd clung to a lot of resentment, but mostly, he seemed angry with himself.

Mia said it first. "Now they'll stop bothering you." She rushed at me and threw her arms around me. "I think I misinterpreted the cards. I think that last one, the serpent, meant that the one deceiving you was right here. In your midst. The cards were telling us that the serpent was lying in wait in the depths of your house and he—"

"Stop it." I peeled her arms off me. "I don't want to hear about the cards. And he didn't—"

"Are you sure?" David asked. "It makes perfect sense. Who else?"

"That's just as bad as the detective assuming it was me because I was here. You can't assume. Certainly not based on the random appearance of a card."

"He was locked out," David said. "He thought he should have this house."

"Like Brian. They were fighting over it," Mia said.

"You're being ridiculous. I'm going to sleep. Let the detective figure it out."

"The detective is looking for him!" Mia said. "Did you forget that?"

"It looks like the uniform cops didn't get the message," David said.

"Why didn't they arrest him?" Mia said. "What's going on? That guy could have killed us! He was sleeping in the basement all that time! Coming up into the house, prowling around." She gave a violent shudder, wrapping her arms around herself in an effort to stop her shivering. "He was probably looking in our rooms while we slept! It's awful. Why didn't they arrest him if they're looking for him? Do they even talk to each other, the detective and the regular cops?"

"Great question." David moved closer to me. He put his arm around my shoulders. "How the hell was he getting in and out without the cameras capturing him?"

I didn't feel like telling him. I didn't feel like listening to either one of them. For some reason, I wanted to defend Peter. I didn't even know the man, and I was defending him. It made no sense. I couldn't even explain it to myself.

I slipped out from under David's arm.

"What's wrong?" He reached for me again, but I took a step away from him, pressing my back against the wall. It was the feeling of being questioned. All the time. Since David had arrived, maybe even before, I felt that no matter what I said, one of them told me I was wrong. They acted as if I was confused or making a mistake or overreacting.

Maybe the problem was that David and I hadn't had any time alone. We were supposed to be getting ready for Ryan. Fixing up our summer home for a little boy who would effectively become our son. Soon, we'd be a family and instead, Mia was here, turning us into a threesome. It was a threesome in which I felt as if I were on the outside, as if they were managing me. As if they thought I needed caretaking and assistance to be sure I didn't lose my grip on reality.

"I think you should leave in the morning, Mia," I said.

"What?" The look that crossed her face was one of fear.

It wasn't what I'd expected. I felt a small giggle bubbling in my chest, but managed to keep it down—I guess she hadn't seen *this* in her cards. "David and I need some time alone to get ready for Ryan."

"I thought I was helping you paint and get the house ready for the little one?"

"Do you even know his name?"

"What? What are you talking about?"

"David and I need to be alone."

She looked at David. Her face changed slightly. She looked defeated, or maybe it was simply hurt. I was hurting her, but having her here was too much. She was smothering me. For the first time in all the years I'd known her, I felt as if I couldn't breathe, as if she, and maybe her cards, were trying to insinuate their way into my thoughts. Every time I'd tried to think my way clearly through what was happening, she was there with a suggestion, or an opinion, or an offer to tell me what her cards were saying, which of course, was just another opinion that she pretended, or possibly believed, was a voice of authority.

I couldn't take it.

"I'm your best friend, Trinity."

"I know that. But David and I need to get ready for Ryan."

"I know his name."

"We're a family now."

She slid her fingers through her hair, lifting it away from her scalp and letting it fall around her shoulders. "Okay. I get it." She turned and went up the stairs.

When we woke late that morning, she was already gone. A text on my phone told me she was sorry she hadn't said goodbye, but she felt that we'd said everything.

David seemed cool, still upset about how the police had handled Peter living in our basement. He was angry that one minute they'd considered him a suspect in Brian's murder, and the next minute treated him as if the worst he'd done was rudely cut across our front yard, or pick a few apples off our tree without permission. He couldn't let go of it, but I busied myself with painting and asked him to follow up with the contractors. Finally, he left me alone with my thoughts.

68 NOW: PETER

The cops took me to the police station. Detective Robbins wanted to talk to me. That's never something anyone wants to hear, especially when two people with whom you've been known to have bad blood are dead. He'd already talked to me once, but his questions had shown he knew nothing about the bad blood. Nothing about how Charlotte had put me out on the curb like a bag of trash.

Now, we sat in a small room with a tiny black camera pointing at me. No one else had been interrogated in front of a camera yet, as far as I knew. The detective had visited them in their homes, treated them with the respect given to regular citizens. Maybe this was how people living on the street felt. They seemed to be treating me like a guy who had been holed up in the basement because he was down on his luck, with nowhere else to go. I'm sure that's how I looked.

"Tell me about your relationship with Brian Price," Detective Robbins said.

"Before we get into that, there's something I should have told you. But I—"

"Then why didn't you?"

"It's …" How did I explain? It wasn't going to look good.

"Should have told me, when?"

"The first time I talked to you. Or before."

"I'm listening."

"I don't know why I didn't. Well, I mean, I do know why, but I—"

"Get to the point."

"I was staying in the basement."

"I'm aware."

"I saw him." I could feel his impatience. I could also feel how this was going to land. It sounded convenient and out of context. They were well down the road to thinking I pushed Sara's ex into the well. But if I'd done that, I would have covered it. I was almost certain they thought I'd strangled Charlotte, too. And there were a lot of times I would have liked to. Countless times. But that's a figure of speech. An angry, vicious, inappropriate thought. It's not something you *do*.

No matter how I said this, it was going to sound like misdirection, like I was trying to squirm my way out of a bad situation. It was going to sound like finger pointing. "David Feld was there that night. When Brian died. I know he said he was in London or on a plane or whatever, but the guy is distinctively tall and—"

"Ten percent of the male population is over six feet tall."

"This guy, the guy I saw, was over six-two. And not just that. It's the way he walks. It was him. He punched Brian in the stomach, shoved him into the well, and just walked away. It was so fast, it felt like it didn't even happen. At the time, I had no idea who he was. I guess that's why I didn't say anything. I didn't know until he showed up again and I found out he was Trinity's husband. I saw how he does that shoulders back, *I'm-in-charge* thing when he walks. I should have said something. But I didn't want anyone to know I was living in the basement, so…"

As I'd expected, the detective gave me a look that said I was wasting his time, making up stories in a failed attempt to dig myself out of trouble.

"Your memory is convenient," he said.

"I know. I know it sounds like I'm deflecting. Completely unbe-lievable. But that's what I saw."

"They were strangers. Still are."

That was a good sign. He was searching his mind for a motive. I sat up straighter. Maybe I was putting off some of that shoulders-back vibe myself. He wasn't going to blow me off after all.

"Why would a man who just moved here push a stranger into a well? Are you suggesting he also strangled Ms. Hughes? Why would he do that?"

"I don't know. Maybe he thought Brian was after his wife … or … I don't know. I didn't hear what they said. I saw him punch Brian —hard. Really hard. I've never seen anyone throw a punch like that. And then he shoved him in and just walked away. Cool as anything. It was … I almost couldn't believe it. It happened so fast. They were there, and then Brian was doubled over and then he was gone. Like the earth swallowed him whole. It almost felt like I'd imagined it."

"Maybe you did, then."

"No, that's not what I meant. I misspoke."

He gave me a condescending smile.

"I didn't do it. But that's what I saw. I didn't imagine it. I was just shocked, because it was so fast, so smooth. Like he'd planned it."

He asked me questions for another hour and a half. The light on the camera was a solid red dot the entire time. It was hard not to keep looking at it, wondering how I was coming across. I guessed they would pick apart every word I said, every shift in my position interpreted to mean something, when they reviewed the recording.

In the end, he let me go. He told me to provide a written list of my possessions in the basement of the Feld house. An officer would pick them up and deliver them to my home. I was to stay away from the property. He would be in touch if they had more questions.

69 NOW: TRINITY

*W*hen I looked at the security camera and saw Detective Robbins standing on our front porch, I groaned out loud. Why was he so fixated on me? I couldn't understand it.

Was it true after all that detectives picked a theory and then put on blinders and only pursued lines of questioning and looked for evidence to support the story they'd constructed in their minds? He seemed like an intelligent man. It wasn't as if it was easy to become a detective. It wasn't as if crimes were solved by taking that path—guessing at who the perpetrator was and finding evidence to fit. Especially with technology. They had to be right. They needed fingerprints and blood, or DNA that matched the right people. They needed eye witnesses that stood up on repeated questioning and scrutiny. Didn't they?

What story was worming its way through his mind that had him ringing my doorbell every other day? What did he see in me that allowed him to believe the ridiculous story he'd heard from Danielle? Or was he here to get me to implicate Peter?

I walked slowly to the front door, wondering whether I would be better off if David was by my side while I talked to the detective, or it was best to keep it casual. Tom's offer to sit with me drifted through my thoughts, but it was too late. If I texted him now, we would be halfway through before he arrived. Besides, although it had sounded like a reassuring idea at the time, imagining the reality of Tom actually sitting in the room with me, knowing nothing about police work or criminal investigations, now seemed foolish.

As I touched the doorknob, I was flooded with doubt about Tom's motives for offering to sit with me. Had Danielle put him up to that? A probate lawyer knew nothing about the rights of someone who might be accused of a felony. Maybe he was simply curious, or worse. And since I'd felt so isolated from Mia and David, I'd lapped it up like a stray kitten, delighted over a saucer of milk.

I opened the door.

"May I come in?"

I moved back so he could step inside.

"Is Mr. Feld home?"

"Yes."

"I'd like to speak to him."

I wanted to ask why, but it was a question that would go unanswered. I left him standing in the foyer, not caring if it was rude.

David was in the backyard, pulling weeds around the steps leading from the door onto the scrabbly lawn area.

"The detective wants to talk to you." I was aware of how chilly my words sounded. Despite sending Mia away, David and I weren't any more connected. He seemed distracted. He was still incredibly upset that the police hadn't arrested Peter. He was angry at me for having an intimate conversation with Peter instead of calling the police the moment I'd discovered him hiding in our basement.

I don't understand you, were the only words he seemed capable of saying. *You've done nothing but tell me how anxious and afraid you were about someone being in the house. Then, you find someone in the house, and you sit down and make him a cup of tea and listen to his life story. It makes no sense.*

The reason I couldn't explain it to him was that I couldn't really explain it to myself, either.

When I returned with David, the detective asked me to leave. He led David into Ryan's playroom and closed the door. But I'd noticed when I was painting the playroom that I could hear Mia talking on her cell phone through the shared wall with the laundry room. It had bothered me because I didn't want the noise of the washing machine and dryer rumbling through the space when Ryan was playing, and I'd wondered if it could be fixed with insulation. Now, I would take advantage of it.

I went into the laundry room and pressed my ear against the wall. I couldn't hear everything the detective said, but my husband's voice was not only loud, he projected well. He was also irritated, which caused him to raise his voice.

I heard almost the entire conversation.

"We have an eyewitness who saw you punch Mr. Price and shove him into the well."

"Slander. I was in London," David said.

"I'm sure you're aware how easy that is for us to check. Even if you took a flight that you didn't mention to your wife."

David was silent for a very long time. He cleared his throat softly. I could imagine his face. I pressed my hand to my stomach, feeling it lurch, then twist into a knot, his silence answering the question for him.

"Yes, I returned early. But I was nowhere near here."

"Can you prove that?"

David cleared his throat.

I didn't like the constant throat clearing. He did that when he wasn't sure what to say, and David was almost always sure what he wanted to say. He wasn't a person who hesitated before speaking. He wasn't a person who ever doubted what he'd said after the words were spoken. He only paused when he was about to say something that wasn't entirely truthful. Or that he was worried might make me angry.

I pushed my ear harder against the wall until it ached.

"I was with Mia. Mia Theriault. The woman who was staying here."

'Until what time?"

"Two, or two-fifteen. Yes, two-fifteen."

"She'll confirm that? I'd like to speak to her."

"She left."

There were a few seconds of silence. "I believe I have her contact information," the detective said.

"I don't think ..."

"Yes?"

"I don't want ..."

There were a few more minutes, maybe only seconds, of silence.

"My wife ..."

"Are you and Ms. Theriault having an affair?"

"No ... I ... we ..."

"What's your concern?"

"Trinity thought I was in London and she won't like it."

He was right about that. The room was silent again. I tried to picture what they might be doing—having a stare-down? Had one of them left? That didn't seem likely.

"I can call Ms. Theriault right now. Although I'd prefer to talk to her in person. Do you know where she is?"

"At her home, I assume. In Mountain View. She left early this morning."

There was more silence.

"And why were you with Ms. Theriault? *Are* you in a relationship with her?"

"No."

I realized I'd been holding my breath. But David's response came so fast, the air burst out of my lungs, and for a moment, I feared they might have heard me, the exhalation coming with a soft cry of pain. Maybe that had only echoed inside my own head. Had I thought, even for half a second or less, that the answer was going to be different? The thought made my heart feel as if it had been stuffed into a tiny container, the lid pressed on tight.

"Why did you take a secret flight home from London to see Ms. Theriault, and return—"

"It wasn't a *secret* flight."

"If you didn't tell your wife, that's the very definition of secret."

There were several seconds of silence.

"Why did you fly home to see Ms. Theriault?"

"She was concerned about Trinity's mental state."

"Why?"

"She ... Trinity's been imagining things. Someone in the house, furniture moving ..."

He sounded foolish when he said it, and I could tell from the tone of his voice, he felt foolish, as if this failed to explain an emergency international flight to talk to my friend without my knowing.

There was more silence, then Detective Robbins's voice changed. "Ms. Theriault? Detective Robbins here. Mr. Feld tells me he was with you on the night of Tuesday, June 13, until approximately two fifteen in the morning. Is that correct?"

I waited for him to say more, I waited for something that would tell me David was telling the truth. I wasn't even sure what answer I wanted to hear. Because even if they weren't having an affair, or plain old sex without the trappings of a formal affair, what did that mean?

He'd lied to me. She'd lied to me.

Why?

"Yes," Detective Robbins said. "It would be helpful if you would return." He paused. "It's not required, but I want to talk to you in person, so at some point, you will need to return. Now, or later." There was another pause, and then he said, "I'll see you then."

I could feel they might be finished soon. I slipped out of the laundry room, kicked off my sandals, and ran up the stairs barefoot so they wouldn't hear me.

70 NOW: TRINITY

I sat on the front porch waiting for Mia. I wanted to talk to her before she saw David. He had no idea I knew she was returning because I hadn't told him I'd listened to his conversation with the detective.

When David and the detective came out of my nephew's future playroom, I'd been upstairs. I'd waited at the front bedroom window. Although I hadn't been able to hear the detective's parting words from there, I couldn't risk David knowing I'd been eavesdropping.

I watched until I saw the detective emerge from under the porch roof and walk toward his car. Then I'd turned away from the window and started pulling the sheets off the bed where Mia had slept. I tossed them onto the floor. I folded the comforter and blanket at the foot of the bed. I opened the window to let in fresh air.

As I stepped into the bathroom to gather the soiled towels, I heard David come up the stairs.

"Trinity?"

"I'm in here." I stood in the bathroom doorway. "Just cleaning up the room."

He came into the bedroom, greeting me with a blank look.

"What did he want?" I asked.

"That creep who was living in our basement told them he saw me push the ex-husband into the well."

I felt as if someone was choking me. David looked furious. He had none of the fear I'd felt when I'd been accused of the same thing. I thought of the charming, introspective man who'd told me about his grief and how he was just now seeing flickers of light break into the heavy shadows that had swallowed him for the past ten months. "Why? Why would he say that?"

"No idea. Well, actually, yes, I have a very good idea. Either to get himself out of it, most likely. Or, because he lost his chance to live like a rat in our basement. So he decided to have a little fun at my expense."

"Do they believe him? Do you think they'll arrest you?"

"They can't. They need more evidence. It's the same situation that you were in, and possibly still are."

"But that's different. No one has said they saw me push him in!"

He narrowed his eyes. "What's your point?"

"Nothing. Just that it's different."

"It sounds like you think I did it," he said.

"No! Of course not."

He glared at me, waiting for me to say more.

"I don't think that."

"Okay. Well ... so, uh ..."

"I was going to clean the bathroom." I wanted to talk to Mia before he told me what I already knew about his secret flight. I wanted to hear whether her story matched up with the sketchy outline of what he'd told the detective. If one of them was lying, Mia might be easier to catch in a lie because I'd known her longer. Every muscle in her face was familiar to me.

It shouldn't have been that way. My husband should have been the one I knew the best, and it bothered me that I was having these thoughts. It bothered me that I felt closer to my girlfriend, that I felt

I knew her better than I knew him. Maybe I just understood her better. I couldn't explain it.

Now, sitting on the porch steps, I desperately wanted her to arrive before David came outside. I wanted to talk to her alone before it turned into another situation where the two of them lined up against me, telling me I was *confused* and *overreacting*.

As the sun beat down on my hands and wrists, my ankles and feet, all I could think about was the fact that the summer was racing by. I was now four weeks from the day we were supposed to pick up Ryan and bring him to his new summer home. I was concerned he would have dim memories of who I was, worried he wouldn't feel comfortable in the house, worried that the detective would still be dropping by with daily questions about the murders. I had no furniture, the rooms were half finished, and I had no idea how involved the repair of the beam in the living room might be.

How could everything have gone so terribly wrong? I hadn't whispered my thoughts to Jen in days. I felt like my awareness of her presence inside my mind was fading, that she was turning into a memory, less distinct by the day. She was nothing but a large hole inside my chest, and right now, I felt as if David and Mia were about to create enormous holes of their own in the center of my heart.

I rested my head on the hot skin of my forearms. I couldn't start crying. It wasn't the condition I wanted to be in when Mia arrived.

I straightened and took a deep breath. I stretched my arms over my head to regain my composure.

Glancing toward our neighbors' house, I saw Danielle on the patio. She was looking directly at me, as if she'd been waiting for me to look her way, wanting me to see her keeping an eye on me.

When I looked back toward the street, Mia's car was slowing to turn into our driveway. I stood and walked down the steps, ready to meet her as soon as she opened her door.

I didn't even allow her to get out of the car. Opening the door for her, I leaned down, gripping the door and the roof to keep my balance. "Tell me what happened."

"Can I please get out of the car?"

"I need to know why you're keeping secrets from me."

"I'm not. I—"

"You are. Because David said he was with you the night Brian died. And as far as I knew, you were asleep across the hall from me, and David was in London."

She sighed and looked down at her hands.

"Trinity!"

I looked up to see David coming down the front steps.

He laughed with too much enthusiasm. "Let's not keep her trapped in the car. It's hot. Let's go inside and have something to drink. We all need to cool down." He laughed again.

I moved away from the car, and we went into the house. David and I sat beside each other on the couch, and Mia faced us in the armchair. We each held a bottle of sparkling water, all of us sipping anxiously at the liquid inside.

"Look, we probably should have said something sooner," David said, his voice smooth and in control, the voice he used on business calls.

"You think?" I said.

"I was worried about you. So I flew home on the spur of the moment."

"And you didn't bother to tell me? When I was begging you every day to come home?"

"I wanted to get a sense of what was going on. Mia was really worried. She thought that guy was manipulating you."

"He was," Mia said. "He absolutely was."

"Stop saying that. I'm not a child. He wasn't manipulating me. He was friendly and helpful. That's it."

"That's not what I saw," Mia said. "You're in a really vulnerable place right now."

"Stop telling me what I am. I'm a functioning adult. I'm aware of what I think and feel."

Mia rubbed my arm. "Sorry, sweetie. I'm sorry. I know you have a lot on your shoulders."

She did seem to get that, but it didn't excuse her going behind my back, talking to my husband like I needed caretaking.

"Robbins will be here in half an hour," David said.

"You lied to me. Both of you."

"We were worried." Mia squeezed my arm.

Her touch was comforting, even though she'd wildly, and maybe deliberately, misinterpreted my relationship with Brian. She'd caused a lot of trouble by talking to David behind my back.

"You seem so lost without your sister. And the responsibility you're about to take on. It's huge." Her eyes welled with tears. "I felt like you didn't want to hear anything I had to say, and I needed to sort out my thoughts."

"Your cards didn't tell you what to do?"

She gave me a sad look.

It was a bitchy thing to say, and I regretted it, seeing the pain in her eyes, but I didn't apologize.

Nothing was sorted out among us by the time the detective returned. He took Mia into the empty playroom and closed the door. Twenty minutes later, they emerged. The detective looked at me, his eyes full of pity. "I think that's all for now."

I followed him to the door and when it closed, I leaned against it, facing David and Mia. "What did you tell him? I want to know everything."

"It's not important," Mia said. "What matters, is that guy can't claim he saw David murder someone just to get himself off the hook! It's so awful. I can't—"

"I have a right to know what you told the detective. This is about me, too. I'm sick of you lying to me. I want to know why you flew all the way home from London to talk about me!"

"Well," Mia glanced sideways at David. "It's changed now, obviously. Because of that guy hiding out in the basement. But I thought you were hearing things. Seeing things ... you thought the room was repainted while we were sleeping. And—"

"That's not true! You were freaked out by things too! Like the cards being laid out the same way you'd played them."

She nodded carefully. "Yes. At first. But it was so ... outside the realm of believability. I started to wonder if ... maybe ..." She glanced at David again. "I thought maybe you'd done it yourself."

I pressed my fists against the door but said nothing.

"Mia and I talked for a long time," David said. "She was worried. Really worried. She thought Brian was taking advantage of your grief. She thought he was going out of his way to give the impression ... to manipulate your emotions, into believing the house was ..." he laughed, then coughed slightly, "...haunted. You know how vulnerable you've been since Jennifer passed away."

"Don't bring Jen into this."

"It's true. I'm sorry. You're on edge, and honestly overwhelmed. Being Ryan's guardian." He moved his shoulders slightly. "You were already imagining talking to Jennifer. You've been literally drowning in grief. So ..."

I studied the faces of my husband and my best friend. Listening to David had filled me with a sense of calm that washed through me like a cool, crystal clear mountain stream. "I need to think," I said.

They both nodded eagerly.

"Everything is crazy. I promised my sister I would take care of her little boy and give him a loving home. That I would be his mother."

They both nodded again, more subdued this time.

"I want this house to be peaceful and light, filled with love. I haven't had a good night's sleep since I got here. I haven't finished painting a single room. I need some quiet and calm." I paused and took a slow, deep breath, easing it out slowly. "I want both of you to give me your keys. I want you to leave."

"That's a bad idea," Mia said. "You're not in a good place."

"I want your key. And I want you to leave," I said.

David stood and came to my side. "You're upset. You're not thinking clearly at all."

I moved away from him. "This is the first clear thought I've had in days. Please respect my promise to my sister and my need to get things prepared for Ryan."

"But the beam in the living room isn't safe," David said. "You're not safe. That guy from the basement is out there. He could get back inside. We don't even know how he got in there. I need to figure that out and close off access. I guarantee you, he's the one who murdered Charlotte and the ex-husband."

"You don't need to worry about it."

"You can't do this," David said.

"This is what I'm doing. I'll be waiting on the front porch." I walked out of the room, knowing that once they were gone, I could look forward to a peaceful, relaxing evening. I would sleep like a baby.

71 NOW: TRINITY

While I sat on the front porch, my mind spun, wondering if they would do as I'd asked. I thought Mia would. She wasn't going to fight with me. It was my house, and she didn't have any illusion that she had a right to stay here, even though she believed she was uniquely equipped to help me figure out my life. She wasn't going to force herself on me. I knew that about her.

David was an entirely different matter.

Although in a sense it was my house because it had been purchased with my money, it was our joint property. And he was my husband. We were in love. Weren't we? We were a married couple. Very soon, we were due to pick up Ryan together, begin nurturing him together, providing him with two loving parents.

I loved David. And I thought he loved me.

I wasn't sure he would just walk out and hand over his key. Especially handing over his key. He would find it emasculating. He would consider it controlling. And sitting on the steps, waiting for it, I couldn't be sure why I'd asked him to do it, because doing so suggested I didn't trust him.

It wasn't as if I were kicking him out. I wasn't asking him for a divorce, or even a separation, but I desperately needed time alone. I could not think with the two of them constantly telling me *what* to think.

Thirty minutes later, Mia came out and handed her key to me. She walked down a few steps, bent over and gave me a long hug, pressing her head hard against mine, whispering into my ear that she was only a text message or a phone call away. She did not tell me she would do a reading for me. "Take care of yourself, sweetie."

And then, she was getting into her car and driving away.

A few minutes later, David came outside. He sat beside me on the top step. "Are you sure you know what you're doing?"

"Absolutely."

"It feels like you're punishing me for something. I'm not sure what."

I shrugged.

"*Are* you punishing me? I guess, for not telling you I was here?"

"No."

"Then what is it?"

"I told you. I need to think. I need to get the house ready for Ryan. I need—"

"You'll get a lot more done if I'm here to help."

"I don't think so."

"The beam—"

"You don't need to be here. We're hiring a contractor. Please text me the quotes."

"Sure. Okay." He kissed my cheek and stood. "Are we …?" He turned and walked down the steps without finishing his question.

When he was gone, I went inside and locked the door. I moved through the house, locking all the doors and windows. I locked the door to the basement.

I spent the afternoon making a list of what I needed to accomplish. I had a video chat with Ryan and my brother. I washed all the sheets and towels. In the late afternoon, I located the entrance Peter had used to gain access to the basement—a panel behind the outside stairs to the laundry room. It looked like it formed the side of the stairs. If someone took the trouble to inspect it closely, they might see it could be removed, but you would have to be familiar with the layout of the house.

Underneath the stairs was a trapdoor leading to the closet in the basement. When Mia and I had looked into the closet, we'd never thought to look up at the ceiling, never considered there was a strange, awkward side entrance to the basement.

I nailed the panel into place. The following day, I would buy some shrubs to plant around the area, filling it in.

I made pasta for dinner and drank two glasses of white wine. I went to bed early.

Whether I woke because I'd impressed the thought into my subconscious by wondering if I would, or if it had become a habit and my biorhythms had adjusted themselves to sleeping four hours, then waking for an adrenaline-driven walk around the house, that's what happened.

My phone told me in half-inch, pale blue numbers that it was three minutes past two. I got out of bed as if it were critical that I make a security check of my house. It seemed foolish, especially after I checked the app and saw that the only movement picked up by the security cameras in the past six hours had been caused by two cats and a raccoon. Besides, I now knew who had been coming into my house and he no longer had access.

With the phone in my pocket, I stood at the entrance to my bedroom. *Was* it only habit that had woken me, or was there something else? There was no longer a man living in my basement, creeping around, repainting my walls after the moon rose and all the houses around me were dark.

I started down the stairs, straining for any unfamiliar sound.

I paused with my foot on the second step from the top. I heard a faint tap, a sound that wasn't that of my feet on the hardwood of the stairs.

Another tap was followed quickly by a muffled cracking sound and then the tinkle of breaking glass. I shivered and grabbed the railing. The sound came from the laundry room. Someone who had seen, or knew, the cameras were in place, and had approached the house from the side.

Moving carefully down the stairs, I pressed myself against the inside wall, hoping that when I reached the landing, I would be able to see part of the hallway and observe anyone passing by. It was risky because who was to say the intruder wouldn't immediately head for the stairs, with my bedroom the final destination?

I didn't think this was an opportunistic break-in. I imagined David or Mia, returning to save me from myself. If Peter had returned, he would have tried to use the entrance he'd created for himself.

It seemed as if I'd stood there for ten or fifteen minutes before I heard a footstep in the hallway. I hadn't heard a single creak of the laundry room door opening or sensed any movement before that.

There was a whisper of more footsteps in the hallway but before I could move close to the corner of the staircase to catch a glimpse, I saw a thin splash of light from what must have been a small flash-light or a phone just outside the kitchen.

The intruder had moved so quickly, I'd missed my chance.

The lack of fear pounding through my heart, pushing extra oxygen into my lungs, the sense of calm easing its way around my muscles, made me believe that some instinctive awareness was telling me I knew who was inside my house.

My husband wanted a police detective to believe I was so desta-bilized by loss and the fear of lifelong responsibility for another human being that something had broken inside my brain. He'd taken a ten-hour flight to discuss my mental state with Mia, then flown back to London without telling me, all while I'd been texting him, begging him to come home. I hadn't wanted to admit it to myself, but this was the reason I'd asked for his key.

At my core, I didn't trust him. The question I couldn't answer was—had that trust broken when I found out about his secret flight to discuss my mental state with Mia, or was there something else that had bothered me long before that?

I crept to the bottom of the stairs, uncertain about what I planned to do once I encountered whomever was holding the tiny light moving around in my kitchen. Should I have a weapon?

I turned right and went into Ryan's playroom. In the back corner were two cans of paint, slightly damp brushes placed on a small piece of plywood to dry, a tray with a paint roller, and several flat sticks used to stir paint. I picked one up. It was a pathetic weapon, especially if my newest intruder was carrying something serious, but it was better than relying solely on my bare hands with their short, smooth fingernails.

With the softest steps I could manage, I approached the kitchen. I slowed as I entered the living room, watching the small light moving around the kitchen to my right. I heard a soft whisper but couldn't make out the words, couldn't even tell if it was a man or a woman speaking. But it was now clear there were two people because the other murmured two words in response.

The light stopped moving. I felt as if my heart stopped with it.

Maybe I'd misread the situation. Had the feeling in my gut, that sense of calm, been a lie? Maybe it wasn't David and Mia. And here I stood clutching a piece of wood capable of splintering with the slightest impact. It certainly couldn't do any significant damage. It was utterly useless in the face of a knife, or far worse, a gun.

I tightened my grip, unwilling to let go even though I felt foolish and wondered if it might hinder me, or keep me from looking like I'd woken with nothing but innocent curiosity.

I moved into the archway, reached around the wall, and turned on the light.

David and Mia stood in front of the stove.

I let out my breath and inhaled deeply, smelling the sickening fumes of gas.

Mia wore skinny jeans, a baggy sweatshirt that hung past her hips, and white tennies without socks. David was dressed in similar clothes.

"Turn it off," Mia whispered.

"You don't have to whisper," I said.

David twisted the knob, but the odor remained heavy in the air.

72 NOW: DAVID

*B*ringing Mia with me back to the house was a mistake. She was good, but she wasn't that good. I'd brought her because I thought she'd be an asset if Trinity woke unexpectedly. Instead, she'd fucked up from the get-go. She was *absolutely sure* she knew how to get into the house through the basement. Instead, she'd underestimated Trinity, as she always had.

The access point that the ex-husband had jerry-rigged was no longer available. Trinity had taken care of that. We ended up having to break a window and open the side door into the laundry room. Of course, Trinity, jittery about everything, and growing more so every day, had woken.

I'd wanted to sedate her to be sure she didn't wake and smell the gas, but Mia said that was too risky. An autopsy would give us away. But it wouldn't have. My wife had proven herself unstable enough that finding a little Ativan in her bathroom and bloodstream would have been perfectly legit.

After three years of marriage, no one would think I'd married her to get at her money. Most people don't have the patience for a long game, so it doesn't cross their minds that others do. It was unlikely any small town detective who knew nothing about us would dig deep enough to discover that the only reason I'd even started dating Trinity at all had been to get at her money.

The four of us met for drinks because my buddy Jake's cousin said he knew Jake and I would hit it off with Trinity and Mia. He winked, twice, which irritated the hell out of me. He said I would like both of them, but his money was on Mia. Ever after, he couldn't stop going on about how I blew his mind when I chose Trinity.

It really would have blown his mind if he'd known what happened behind the scenes. When you travel all the time like I do, it's easy to juggle two women. Probably more, but I never tried it. I'm a risk-taker, but I'm not crazy.

I asked Trinity out to dinner, I asked Mia out for drinks. Soon, Trinity was falling in love with me as completely as I'd fallen in love with her money. She wanted me as much as I wanted what she had.

One night, when Mia was drunk, I told her what I wanted. It turned out she wanted the same thing. Sort of. Trinity had always gotten *everything*, Mia complained. She was vague about exactly what that meant, but I didn't push her. Mia said she would *love* to see me marry her best friend and get that money. I didn't tell her that murder was the only way to ensure the money would fully belong to me. She would get there, after a while. She didn't need to know everything right away.

Trinity was born under a lucky star. How can an admin land at a startup that gets swept up by one of the biggest names in the tech industry and fall into a pot filled with millions of dollars? It was obscene. The minute she'd told me the name of the company she used to work for, I'd known. She didn't need to give that *oh-lucky-little-me-and-the-great-team-of-incredibly-talented-people-I worked-with* smile, followed by her fake *it-wasn't-about-the-money* giggle.

I called bullshit when I heard that story on our blind double date, and I did the same every minute during our entire marriage, while she controlled every single thing we did with that money.

Oh David, we don't need to splash it around and live in a fancy house. It's off-putting.

I'm not really into luxury vacations, David, it's more fun to travel in a style where you meet interesting people, not privileged people.

Expensive cars just attract unwanted attention, David.

Absolute control. Until she wanted that old house. It was practically a farm. A duck pond? Really? A vegetable garden? If we did end up having kids of our own, they wouldn't want to be dragged away from their friends every summer to feed ducks and pick green beans.

Then she tells me she's going to raise her sister's kid? *We should only do it if you agree one hundred percent,* she'd said. Her lip was quivering, the tears filling her eyes. *But it's not like we can't afford it.*

Jake's cousin was right. Until Trinity started telling the story of her start-up and how fucking *lucky* she was, I wanted Mia. One hundred percent. That girl was hot. Fun and hot. She laughed, and she liked to have a good time. She hung on every word I said. We clicked. I could feel that we wanted the same things.

I'd reached my limit with the *lucky stars*. After a lifetime with my dad, Trinity was one too many. I didn't have to be born under a lucky star, I would grab that star myself. Isn't that what all the songs are about?

* * *

Now, here we were.

Trinity stared at me as if she'd known what I was after all along. But she hadn't.

"I don't understand," she said.

I think she did understand. A little.

Mia looked jumpy. More than I would have guessed. Usually, she was good at adapting, but she didn't seem to be doing so well right now. I needed to get close to her. I needed to put my arm around her to settle her. I wasn't sure how much Trinity understood. She'd certainly guessed we were turning on the gas while she slept. What else was she in the process of working out? It was hard to say.

It wasn't entirely clear to me why Trinity had kicked me out earlier that day, but taking my key told me she was a lot angrier than I'd realized. She'd had a long time to sit in this house and think about things. To think about how I'd hidden the truth from her about the former occupant's death from cancer, to consider why I might want to kill Charlotte Hughes … not because she'd opened her mouth and told Trinity that Sara died in the same way her sister had, but because she was on the verge of telling Trinity there was a man living in the basement.

What a find that had been. I couldn't have asked for a better opportunity to help me carry out what I'd planned for Trinity. When you want to gaslight your wife into believing her summer home is haunted by the ghost of a woman who died from the same disease that took her sister, and the world drops a secret squatter into your lap, you suddenly realize, maybe you were born under a lucky star after all.

For a while, I'd even thought there might be a way to be rid of Trinity without having to kill her. A dead woman in her backyard could have easily removed Trinity from my life. But that turned out to be a short-lived hope. I wasn't sure the money could be fully mine under those circumstances, even with Trinity complaining about unhealthy, fat-riddled prison food for the rest of her life. And I couldn't guarantee it would be the rest of her life. With Ryan in the picture, I wasn't clear on the legal ramifications of what she'd signed us up for. Would I end up the guardian while Trinity gave me parenting instructions from behind bars?

All of this sped through my thoughts at zero to sixty because it had been circling my mind like a formula car on a racetrack since that first night, traveling ever faster toward this moment, which was now entirely fucked up.

I was a man who knew myself. I'd known I couldn't kill my wife with a gun or a knife. Strangling that realtor who wouldn't shut up was bearable only because I didn't know her, but it's a little different with the woman you married, even if you did marry her for the sole purpose of killing her.

I'd considered pushing her into the well, then hesitated, because I wasn't sure I was truly capable of doing even that.

The gas was supposed to be clean. Detached and uninvolved. I would never see her corpse except a quick peek at the morgue. She wouldn't suffer. She would drift to sleep, and that would be it.

While my thoughts tumbled around in disarray, Mia took a few steps away from me. I'd lost my moment to pull her close, my chance to silence her with the press of my fingers into her ribs. She was avoiding my gaze. As I watched her, trying to assess her mood, she took two more steps away from me.

Now, she was backing toward the opposite wall and she'd shoved her arms up inside her sweatshirt. What the hell was she doing?

"It's so cold in here," Mia said. "Are you okay, Trinity?"

Trinity said nothing.

The longer we stood there, the more I felt everything—months of planning, years of patient waiting—starting to slip through my fingers, tearing the skin off my bones. I never should have given up that key. I never should have allowed Mia to come here with me. Simplicity is always the best choice. Surely, I could have convinced Trinity to let me keep that key. Why hadn't I tried? Because Mia told me not to upset her. Mia told me we needed to lull her into a false sense of security. Mia told me she'd figured out how to access the basement.

Mia had all the answers.

But this was *my* plan. The money was supposed to be mine, not Mia's. I was the one who had taken all the risk. I was the one who enticed Charlotte back to the house in the middle of the night to confront her about the creep in the basement before I strangled her. I was the one who shoved that lurking ex-husband into the well before he tore my wife out of my arms. His body was never supposed to be found. Not once the property was mine, and that well was left undisturbed. But hearing someone on the other side of the fence forced me to get the hell out of there before I could drag the cover back into place.

Now, here we were.

And Mia was behaving more strangely by the minute. Her hands were so far up inside her sweatshirt, it looked as if she were groping for a feel of her own tits.

What the hell?

She was holding a gun, pointing it at me. That girl was never one to second-guess herself. Never one to hesitate. I saw her cold blue eyes looking directly into mine, and before I could blink, I heard it fire. I felt something. A warmth ... pain? I couldn't describe it. I was on the floor. Why was I ...? I couldn't catch a breath. It was darker than it had been when we crept toward the side of the house hours ago. Was it hours? Darker than ever. I was tired. I couldn't get a fucking breath.

I thought I saw a flash of light. My lucky star.

73 NOW: TRINITY

*E*verything stopped when Mia fired the gun.

My thoughts stopped. My heart felt as if it had stopped. Mia seemed to stop moving. Worst of all, David stopped—his heart, his breath, his life.

I collapsed onto my knees beside him, touching his face. It was so warm, but there was nothing there. It felt soft. His head was unbearably heavy and yet, almost hollow, somehow, as it fell to the side.

"David! David … don't." Nothing moved. It seemed as if he was something wet and thick and unwanted on the floor, something that didn't belong there.

I fumbled for my phone, my fingers unable to hold on to it properly, too stiff to move across the screen in any way that could get it to function. I recoiled from the blood seeping out of his chest and the vacant look of his slack mouth. I kept my gaze turned slightly away from his partially opened eyes. I placed my hand on his arm, longing to remember the feel of him, then pulled it away.

Whatever he might have told me about what he was trying to do to me, or what had happened in the past few weeks, and in the weeks and months before, was gone. Vanished in a deafening roar, followed by a few gasping, choking sounds that would haunt me for a long time. He would never speak to me again. I would never hear him tell me why he crept into my house, determined to end my life, why he'd murdered a kind, decent man he didn't even know.

I felt a rush of love and hatred, regret, confusion ... so many feelings I couldn't name them. I sat back on my heels. I closed my eyes as sobs poured out of me.

Mia's arms were around me, her head pressing against the back of mine. I let her hang onto me for several minutes as the pain washed through me, the emptiness of my life without David. Finally, I moved, struggling to swipe my fingers across the surface of my phone.

"What will you tell them?" Mia whispered, her arms still locked around my shoulders.

"Tell them?"

"What will you say happened?"

"That he's ..." I couldn't finish.

"But how he died. What will you say?" She released her hold on me and scooted across the floor until she was leaning against one of the table legs. She pressed her hand to her forehead.

"Where did you put it?" I asked.

She pointed to the counter she'd been leaning against earlier.

"Why did you shoot him?" I whispered.

"He was going to kill you."

"Not anymore."

"He wanted your money. I tried to tell you. The cards tried to—"

"I don't want to hear anymore about the cards. Never again."

She gave me a sad, defeated look.

"You were with him. You knew. You knew! Telling me in some secret code wasn't telling me anything!"

"What will you say to the police?" She began whimpering. She sounded nothing like herself. "I don't want to go to prison." Her hands shook as she put them to her mouth like a frightened child. That's what I saw—the frightened child I'd known a long time ago.

"But you shot him."

"Tell them I was here. That he broke in and ... can't you do that for me?"

"But you were with him. I don't understand what's going on. I don't understand why you tried to make me look crazy to the detective, why he ... how do you know he wanted my money?"

"He was trying to turn on the gas!"

"You were right beside him!"

"But I ... that's why I had the gun," she said.

"Because you *planned* to kill him?" I started crying. The man lying dead beside me was a stranger. The woman who had been my closest friend for most of my life looked like someone I'd never known at all.

"You keep asking me questions, and I'm ... I've never shot anyone. I feel so awful and you won't let me tell you what happened."

"I don't want to hear about your cards."

"It's not about that. Please."

"I need to call the police ... the paramedics. Or ..."

"Stop! Just for a minute. Let me tell you."

I nodded.

"I honestly thought Brian was hitting on you. I did. I thought he was trying to manipulate you, that he was taking advantage of how you felt about your sister. I didn't know what he wanted. It just seemed not on the up and up. I texted David, and he said he was coming. I didn't tell him to come, he just came. And he wanted to hear everything that had happened. And ... I'm sorry, I can't tell you this without talking about the cards, so you just have to listen.

"He said he was worried you were unstable since your sister died. That you weren't equipped to take care of Ryan, and that you were making stupid mistakes and you were going to squander the money. I'd done a lot of readings and they kept telling me he wanted your money. And you can choose not to believe that, but he's said things to me, over the years, about how you weren't a key person at that company, so it wasn't really right that you got such a big payout."

"He said that?"

She nodded. Tears spilled over her lower lashes. She wiped them away.

"He was so angry about Brian. Really angry. He just kept saying you would fall for any guy who would listen to you go on about your dead sister."

A sob cracked through my solar plexus, feeling as if it were breaking my bones as it forced its way out of me.

Mia scooted toward me and put her arms around me again. "I'm sorry. I'm so sorry I have to tell you this. I don't want to, but I have to tell you the truth. You have to know what made me shoot him. I was so upset and—"

"Why didn't you *tell* me this?!"

"I *wanted* to, and I … I was scared. He was so angry. It was honestly terrifying."

"Why did you come back with him tonight?"

"He said I had to. Maybe he was going to do something to me and leave me here?" She whimpered again, then started crying.

Did I believe her? I didn't *not* believe her. She'd always hated guns. It wasn't a purchase she'd made lightly. Pulling the trigger must have sickened her. Studying her face now, she looked ill—her skin almost gray, and the whites of her eyes tinged with an unhealthy yellow at the edges, as if something toxic was flowing through her bloodstream.

"Please. Please, can you tell them he came at us? Can you tell them I was here with you? That we heard him break in?"

When I called the police, I wondered what they would think about her mention of the cards telling part of the story. By the time they arrived, I'd had enough time to think about all the difficulties the detective had given me the past week. I thought about how little credibility he'd attributed to me. What was the point in telling him the unvarnished truth, when my best friend's future, and by association my own, and therefore Ryan's future happiness, were at stake?

74 NOW: MIA

Once I convinced Trinity to stick with me, that it would be better for both of us, she called the police.

Detective Robbins walked into the house as if he lived there. He made himself at home and kept us up for the rest of the night. He put Trinity and me in separate rooms. He actually made us sit on her straight-back kitchen chairs like we were being interrogated. I guess there wasn't really any other choice, but still.

Trinity was in the playroom, surrounded by those pale blue walls that she thought were peaceful and I thought were a little institutional, which seemed about right for a woman who had a loose connection to sanity.

This had been David's original plan. At least that was the plan he'd told me—*Make Trinity look crazy with grief*, he'd said. Get her declared incompetent and put in an institution. I didn't sign up for murder. Then he started killing people right and left. Only two people, but when you've never experienced murder, even one dead body feels like your world has changed completely and forever.

First, he told me he had no choice but to kill Charlotte because she couldn't keep her mouth shut. He didn't tell me what she couldn't keep her mouth shut about. Not right away. Later, I found

out David had known all along that Peter was living in the basement. David was in a panic that Charlotte was going to let it slip out
as easily as she'd blurted out that Sara had died of cancer. He'd kept
that to himself, hoping to use his presence in the basement and
Sara's death to make Trinity feel she was being haunted.

Charlotte's body was hardly cold before David declared Brian
an unacceptable threat. I agreed, obviously. I was the one who had
raised the alarm. But was shoving him into a fifty-foot hole in the
ground the only solution? I hardly slept at all after that. Trinity
thought security cameras would keep us safe. But she had no idea
what she was up against. I couldn't very well let her know because I
was caught in the middle. And she wouldn't listen to the cards. I
thought I could hint to her with the cards, but she *would. Not.
Listen.*

So I bought my own security.

The detective asked us to tell our stories. Trinity and I had had
enough time to make sure that if there were one or two tiny threads
coming loose in our individual stories, they were the same threads.
Yet, they weren't so similar that they wove themselves into a pattern
that exposed a fabricated story.

The detective knew I'd been living there, so he had no reason to
believe I wasn't still sleeping in the house when David broke in.
Peter had already said he'd seen a tall man shove Brian into the well.
It would be easy enough to look at David's flights to and from
London and the Felds' bank accounts to see wealth they possessed,
tracing that wealth to its original owner, for Detective Robbins to
stitch together a new story that explained why Charlotte and Brian
had been murdered—a story was very close to the truth. The only
missing pieces were mine.

As I sat alone in the sunroom, thinking back over all the years I'd
known Trinity, there was one thing that formed the solid core of
our friendship—Trinity got everything. She had it all. There was no
denying I was prettier. Everyone said so, even when I was a little
girl. As an adult, other women never hesitated to tell me they were

insanely jealous of how lucky I was with my *perfect* hair and *beautiful* eyes, my body, my smile.

Their words carried a note of cruelty, laughing as if it were funny. *Ha ha. I would never go to a club with you, Mia. All the guys would pick you, and I'd get the leftovers.* Trinity didn't care. She was a good person. Superficiality was not part of who she was. She never made comparisons. There wasn't a jealous bone in her body. For that reason, she failed to recognize jealousy in anyone else. Maybe that was her fatal flaw. Because she wasn't jealous, she assumed I wasn't either.

But those girls had been wrong. It's the superficial guys, men like David, who are drawn to girls like me. At first, I thought he was really something. When our eyes locked during that blind double date, I knew he was into me. He texted me that night. I was thrilled. For the first time, someone picked me, not Trinity. David Feld wanted *me*.

Because for some reason, in every other situation, guys picked her. They just liked her better. She was pretty, too, but she wasn't gorgeous. They were drawn to her. And she got everything. She got a sister who adored her and an amazing brother who would do anything for her. She had a father who hung around to watch her grow up.

She got to go away to college without ever spending a single minute thinking about what it all cost.

And then she gets a stupid job as an administrative assistant because her useless degree, for which her family paid tens of thousands of dollars while she went to parties in between getting to study whatever she felt like, was in world history. And she couldn't quite figure out how to build a career with a degree like that. Then her company invents some technology that everyone in the world considers a must-have. And some mega, cutting edge company buys it and she's a fucking millionaire.

Lucky star.

David was always going on about lucky stars. He was really

bitter about it. He was bitter about the whole college thing too because he was supposed to go to a prestigious school, but he was *robbed*.

That's how people get a leg up, he said. *They make connections. Everything in this world is about who you know. It doesn't matter if you're the smartest guy or the most talented guy or the one who works the hardest. It's about your connections.*

His dad made some bad investment, and *poof*—David's college fund evaporated into thin air. So David figured, in some twisted way that only his brain could make sense of, that Trinity only got that money because of her connections, and now that he was connected to her, it rightfully belonged to him. Or something like that. I couldn't follow his logic.

"Why did you buy the gun?" Detective Robbins asked.

"I was scared! Someone kept breaking into the house. And the realtor was murdered—someone strangled her to death! I was terrified."

He nodded. Then he circled back and asked me again—What woke me? Who came downstairs first? What did I see when I turned on the light? Why did I feel so threatened by a man I knew, someone I was close to?

"Mr. Feld didn't have a weapon," he said.

"It was dark. I heard this clicking, and I didn't know what it was, so I was already holding my gun out. I didn't smell the gas until a few minutes later."

"Why were you on the opposite side of the kitchen from the entrance?"

I sighed. I'd told him this. Did it not make sense? Trinity and I had had only a few minutes to pull the story together. I felt anxious, wondering if she was keeping the pieces straight, if she'd said things in the same way I had. I was glad the room was cold, and I wasn't perspiring. I was good at keeping my feelings off my face, except when I wanted them to show.

I folded my hands and placed them in the center of my lap. I looked down at them, speaking softly. "It's hard to remember. It happened so fast. And it was so scary. I don't think you realize how scary it was. Trinity thought he was trying to make her look like she was losing her mind. And that man in the basement said he saw David shove Brian into the well ..." My voice shook, even without me trying. "Trinity turned on the light, and I wasn't sure if he was trying to do something to the gas that would blow up the house or—"

"That seems unlikely. He would have put his own life at risk."

"I didn't know *what* he was doing! I kept hearing the clicking, and I was scared, so I didn't realize it was the starter on the stove. The smell was awful, and he had this baggy shirt on ... he's so big! You've seen him!"

The detective didn't nod agreeably as I'd hoped he would. He simply waited, staring at me.

"I don't know why I ran across the room. I guess ... I wasn't abandoning her. She's my closest friend—like a sister. I didn't think about what I was doing, but now, I realize I had the feeling he was going to attack her, and if I wasn't right beside her, I could shoot him. If he grabbed both of us, I didn't know what would happen."

He gave a single, barely noticeable nod. *Had* he nodded? Did that mean it made sense? Why did they expect things to make sense? Sometimes, a lot of times, you don't know why you do the things you do. An instinct takes over, your body makes decisions on its own and you follow along. Didn't he get that? Was he a human being or a robot?

Neither of us were arrested. We weren't even taken to the police station for more questions. Now, Trinity has her house and soon, she's going to get her new little baby boy.

So she still has everything. She sold her house in Cupertino. She has an amazing home surrounded by grass and trees and quiet. She's filthy rich.

I got rid of that creepy man who wanted to murder her to get her money. And I think that sweet, good-looking guy who has so much love to give that he spent months living in a basement, is into her. Of course he is. Everyone is.

She'll have a sweet little child and an amazing, comfortable life. She'll make new friends. And soon, it wouldn't surprise me at all, if she has an adoring, devoted man who writes music and sings beautiful songs. A good one, this time.

She's still got me. And she trusts me because that's who she is. She's a trusting, loyal person.

If I'm patient enough, and kind enough, and gentle enough, I can convince her to make me Ryan's guardian. And if something happens to Trinity before she marries someone else, I would have a precious child of my own. A beautiful child, as well as a nice house and all that money.

I'm doing readings every night and the empress card has come up in the third position every single time. The empress, promising the future I want—a future filled with beauty, nurturing, and abundance. I just need to be patient, patient with a sense of urgency. I'll nurture my friendship with Trinity. I'll be available whenever she needs me, as I've always been. I'll develop a bond with Ryan and someday, he'll be mine. The house will be mine. And all that money will belong to me.

75 FOUR WEEKS LATER: PETER

*J*t was surreal to walk into the house through the front door. It was also empowering. That was a word from my therapist. It was a word I preferred not to speak out loud because it sounded a little ... well, disempowering. Especially for a man.

But there was no other word for it. I liked not eyeing the house from Danielle and Tom's living room, gossiping about the occupants and letting Danielle feed my bitterness along with a glass of wine and dinner. Sitting inside their home, peering out the windows and watching the new occupant from a distance, overcome by her physical resemblance to Sara, I'd felt as if I were looking into the past, searching for ghosts.

Every part of me had been wallowing in the past. What I'd done wasn't called grieving, it was obsession.

Hiding in the basement was even worse. I'd descended to the world of the rodents, breathing in damp, dead air. I'd lain in the dark, brooding about everything that had gone wrong. I'd watched what I could through the narrow, ground-level windows. I'd relived the hours spent in the house creaking above me. I'd crept upstairs when I'd thought it was safe, walking through the rooms, trying to reclaim the life I'd lost, trying to retrace my steps.

Now, entering the house through the front door as an invited guest, I was carrying my guitar case because Trinity had asked me.

"And bring your guitar," she'd said.

"I don't know. It's—"

"I've heard your music. And I want to hear more," she said.

"Yeah. That was not the high point of my life." I laughed. I didn't think I needed to tell her I'd been singing a song to my dead lover, asking her whether I should tell the police I'd witnessed a murder. She would think I was a lunatic, after all.

"Not that night," she said. "Not in my basement. I went to the wine bar. I sat in the back, at that little table in the corner. You probably didn't see me."

My fingers tightened on the phone. I thought about what my therapist had said about memory and the human need to connect random events into a meaningful pattern, even when there isn't one. "You're right, I didn't see you."

Stepping across the threshold was easy. The house felt the same, but different. It smelled different. Fresh, as if a spring breeze was blowing through, even though it was the middle of summer. It felt less confining. Instead of filling the rooms with furniture as Sara had done, there were a lot of built-in shelves and cabinets. Most of the lighting was recessed. Gone were the unnecessary tables that Sara had loved to fill with decorative objects she'd collected on her trips. They were all beautiful and treasured, but they'd created a claustrophobic atmosphere at times.

I left my guitar in the living room and she took me on a tour of the house, starting upstairs. When we returned to the first floor, we went out to the sunroom, which was painted yellow and featured white wicker furniture. Prints of beach scenes hung on the walls.

Even though the house was clearly ready for a child, with a play-room, and a high chair in the kitchen, it felt sleek and open. It was a brilliant blend of early twentieth century and early twenty-first century.

"It looks incredible," I said. "It feels so open, so light."

"Thank you."

I appreciated that she didn't feel the need to say what she hadn't liked, criticizing Sara's taste. Or mine, for that matter. And I had to admit, I liked this better.

We looked out at the backyard. "I ran out of time. But I can work out there while Ryan's around, so I'm not too worried about it."

"When does he get here?"

"I'm leaving tomorrow to pick him up. I'll stay three or four nights at my sister's house so Ryan and I can get reacquainted while my brother and sister-in-law are around." She paused for a moment, then took a deep breath. "Then we'll drive ... home. Just him and me."

"You sound nervous."

"I am. I love him so much. So, so much. And I know he trusts me. He was really comfortable around me when I was there taking care of Jen. But it's been weeks now ... over two months. His life has been turned inside out." Her eyes filled with tears. "Caring for him all the time. The responsibility. And I have *no* idea what I'm doing." She laughed, recovering her equilibrium.

"I don't think anyone knows what they're doing when they have kids," I said. "At least that's what I've heard. So you're not alone there."

She laughed. "I guess not."

"Danielle and Tom raised three kids. I'm sure they'll ..."

"Maybe."

"After a while."

She nodded.

She'd made lasagna and salad for dinner. We ate in the dining room with candles on the table, even though it was still light outside. After dinner, I played a few songs for her. We talked and drank tea until nearly eleven.

When I left, I walked across the porch and down the steps. I put my guitar in the back seat of my car and turned to look at the house.

In the moonlight, it had the appearance of a different house entirely. Trinity was standing just outside the front door. She also looked like a different woman entirely, and I wondered how I'd ever mistaken her for Sara. It was possible I hadn't mistaken her. Instead, I'd seen what I'd wanted to see. And now, I was a different man —entirely.

If I got another chance to love someone, I wouldn't make the same mistakes.

76 FOUR WEEKS LATER: TRINITY

I stood in the upstairs front bedroom, looking across the
yard. In less than a week, this space would be filled with
the laughter of a little boy who would grow up in my care. I would
offer him every ounce of love I had to give. Not only because that
had been my promise to my sister, but because I'd grown to love
him in the time I'd spent with him. Looking into his eyes, I'd seen a
magnificent, precious human being, hungry to learn about the
world, eager for life, who might be willing to open his heart to me.

Together, Ryan and I would heal from our loss and build a new
life together.

I closed my eyes and pictured his furniture and toys and books
filling this space. I imagined walking into his room every morning,
greeted by his smiling face and outstretched arms. My heart grew
warm, as I felt ahead to kissing his soft cheek and placing him into
his crib at night.

I walked out of his room and returned to my bedroom. My half-
packed suitcase lay open on the bed. I continued filling it with
comfortable clothes for the days I would be spending playing with
Ryan as we got reacquainted in Southern California. In the bathroom, I packed shampoo and the rest of my toiletries.

Once Ryan and I returned home, I would get started on the vegetable garden. We could still plant pumpkins that should ripen in time for Halloween. Mia had offered to come for a few days to help dig up the garden and fence it in, protecting the plants from squirrels and other hungry creatures that were more prevalent than what I'd been used to in Cupertino.

She couldn't wait to meet Ryan. Her eagerness surprised me. I hadn't realized she was so fond of children. We'd never talked much about them until my sister was diagnosed and I told her I'd been named Ryan's guardian. But lately, I'd begun to realize there were a lot of surprising things about Mia.

I was starting to understand that she'd hidden behind her glossy exterior and lighthearted chatter, that there were deeper crevices in her heart that she'd never exposed. Maybe I hadn't looked closely enough. In some ways, she'd hidden behind her Tarot cards. At the same time, it seemed as if she'd tried to reveal parts of herself through her fanciful interpretations of the cards.

I'd felt as if she was making those cards mean whatever she wanted them to mean. She said it was her intuition, but the meanings seemed to ebb and flow and change shape, depending on her mood. With my radically changed perspective these past few weeks, I still couldn't make up my mind whether or not she'd occasionally used the cards and their supposed meanings to manipulate me.

But she didn't know that I could read those cards just as easily myself. She'd shoved them down my throat and into my psyche for years.

I knew what the serpent meant—the card she'd turned up in the third position—the card she claimed could foretell the future. She'd been frantic about hiding it from me that night. As if the serpent had appeared on its own and she hadn't shuffled them that way. Pretending it was all chance and some kind of divine hand was distributing the cards to their various positions.

The serpent, which was assigned the meaning of seduction, deception, and craving.

Mia had seduced David before he'd ever asked me out after that first blind date.

While assuring me that he was obviously *into me*, she'd already been planning her deception.

She craved everything I had. She craved the man I loved. She craved money I'd been lucky enough to receive through my dedicated work at an innovative company. Now, I was beginning to sense that she craved my sister's precious little boy. She craved my very life.

There was a very good reason I went along with her story to the detective, allowing her to get away with killing David. If I'd told Detective Robbins the truth, I didn't know how it might implicate me. That detective still wasn't sure about me, and it seemed as if things might go better for me if Mia and I stuck together. There was a slim possibility she'd saved me.

I went into the bedroom and placed my toiletries in the suitcase. I opened the dresser drawer and took out several pairs of socks, rolled into neat balls. I turned and tossed them into the suitcase. One of the balls hit the side and bounced onto the floor. I went to the side of the bed. As I bent to pick it up, I saw the edge of a Tarot card under the bed. I pulled it out.

The fox.

It must have fallen off the bed when she'd spread them out that day, looking for answers, or trying to tell me stories to make me feel as if I were losing my mind. I was never sure which.

She was the one who had been there telling me that what I'd seen with my own eyes, and recalled with my perfectly reliable memory, had not happened. She was the one making up stories about Brian and reporting them to David. She was the one sneaking into my house with a gun, watching as David turned on the gas while I slept.

The fox was a card that spoke about trickery and cunning.

Mia wasn't done with me.

But I was done with her. Finally.

I didn't need a deck of cards because I relied on my own intuition. And now, I had a child to protect. She was no match for me.

A NOTE FROM CATHRYN

Thank you so much for choosing to read *The Former Occupant*. I hope you enjoyed reading the book as much as I loved writing it.

Usually, I get ideas for novels which grow and change shape in my mind, becoming entirely different things by the time I begin writing. The story in this book came to me in a rush, almost complete. I remember the moment clearly—I was walking up the hill that leads from the beach near my house to the streets that take me back home. It felt fully formed. Of course, it wasn't complete, but the core was there. In a mad frenzy, I wrote a sketch of it and began plotting from there. The characters of Trinity, Peter, and Brian were alive and speaking from that moment.

As stories often do, several experiences of my life and an unrelated story I'd heard from a friend came together to form something new.

Although I was thrilled with the story in my mind, I was tormented by a question from the moment I began writing the very first page: *Who writes a psychological thriller about cancer?*

But I couldn't stop. I loved the characters and the story too deeply. Like everyone I know, my life has been touched by this horrible disease, starting with my father who was diagnosed with cancer when I was a child. As a young man in his thirties, he was given a twenty percent chance of survival. He turned out to be one of the lucky ones. He went on to live a long, meaningful, enjoyable life after his ordeal, but he suffered tremendous side effects from the treatment that saved his life.

The lives of every single person I know, as well as my own,

continue to be touched by variants of this monster. In just the past two years, I've been occasionally overwhelmed by how it swept through lives, wreaking havoc.

But fiction is a record of how we face the worst things in life and overcome, prevail, find peace and understanding, and ideally, joy in the midst of it all.

Thank you so much for reading this book. You, and the time you spent with my story, mean the world to me.

All the best,

Cathryn

www.cathryngrant.com

ABOUT THE AUTHOR

Cathryn is the author of over thirty psychological suspense novels, including the ALEXANDRA MALLORY series featuring a sociopath you can't help but love. Readers have called the series "addictive".

The things that torment us in real life—obsession and revenge, guilt and envy and longing—are endlessly fascinating in fiction and she never grows tired of writing stories about characters struggling to overcome the worst.

Cathryn also writes ghost stories because who knows what lies beyond our senses—The Haunted Ship Trilogy and the Madison Keith series of novellas.

When she's not writing, she's usually reading, walking on the beach, or playing golf, going way out of her way to avoid hitting her ball in the sand or the water. She lives on the Central California Coast with her husband and her cat, Cleopatra.

You can get in touch with her by email, find her social media links, or sign up for her monthly newsletter at cathryngrant.com/contact. As a thank you for signing up, you'll receive a free short story about Alexandra Mallory.